AF242075

Find Me at the Table

JONATHON ISLAND • SEASON 2

Find Me at the Table

ANDREA CHRISTENSON

SUNRISE PUBLISHING

Find Me at the Table
Jonathon Island | Season 2 | Book 3

Published by Sunrise Media Group LLC
Copyright © 2026 Sunrise Media Group LLC

Print ISBN: 978-1-966463-41-2

This book is a work of fiction. Names, characters, places, and incidents are either products of the author's imagination or used fictitiously. Any similarity to actual people, organizations, and/or events is purely coincidental.

Scripture quotations taken from the New American Standard Bible® (NASB), Copyright © 1960, 1962, 1963, 1968, 1971, 1972, 1973, 1975, 1977, 1995 by The Lockman Foundation Used by permission. www.Lockman.org

For more information about Andrea Christenson please access the author's website at the following address: www.andreachristenson.com.

Published in the United States of America.
Cover Design: Sunrise Media Group LLC

To my mom, who taught me to always see the best in people. Mom, you're my favorite role model.

O taste and see that the LORD is good;
How blessed is the man
who takes refuge in Him!

Psalm 34:8 NASB

Jonathon Island

SEASON 1

Meet Me on Jonathon Island (prequel novella)

Meet Me at the Grand

Meet Me on Lilac Lane

Meet Me at the Fudge Shop

Meet Me on Blueberry Hill

Meet Me at Sunset Cove

Meet Me at the Christmas Cottage

SEASON 2

Find Me in the Story

Find Me in the Blooms

Find Me at the Table

Find Me in the Lyrics

Find Me in the Spotlight

Find Me in the Wind

Find Me in the Stars

Find Me in the Harvest

Find Me in the Silent Night

JONATHON ISLAND
N
W
E
S
Jonathon Family Home
Sullivan Pumpkin Farm
MacBride Resort
Sullivan Hall
State Park
Lake Shore Drive
Airport
Jonathon Blvd
Quinn Ranch
Sugar Maple Ln
Blueberry Hills Neighborhood
LAKE HURON
Sunset Cove
Barrett House
Partridge Ln
Dahlia Dr
Lilac Ln
Zinnia Blvd
Poppy Place
Rose Rd
Blueberry Blvd
Pinnacle Dr
Blueberry Hills Park
GRAND HOTEL
Main Street
Downtown
Marina Way
Marina

One

ODAY MARKED THE BEGINNING OF AVA HARP-
er's new start. If Judson Wright was in a good mood, that was.

She walked through the newsroom toward her boss's office. Using her right hand, she gave a swift tug to the bottom of
the black blazer she wore over her slim, dark blue jeans. In her left
arm, she clutched a file folder tight. Her life was in that folder.

Or, at least, the life she wanted.

The clacking of computer keys and the voices of her coworkers
drifted over the tops of the chest-high cubicles laid out around
the room. Along the gray exterior walls hung selected front pages
from the *Chicago Herald* depicting significant events her newspaper had covered over the years. A scent of burnt coffee hung in
the air. She tuned it all out as she rehearsed the speech she would
give to Judson in a moment.

At thirty-five years old, Ava knew that if she wasn't focused,
she'd forget her whole agenda. Today wasn't a day for distraction.
Because, after searching for years—*years*—for a break, she'd finally

made a workable plan. She just needed Judson to see it that way too.

"Knock, knock." She paused outside her boss's open door. The small room held a desk, a couple of chairs, and a loveseat. Judson didn't have anything on his faded gray walls, but a framed picture of his grandkids sat on the corner of his desk. What he lacked in decor, he made up for in mess. Piles of papers and news clippings, and other detritus—was that a wrapper from the sub shop down the street?—lay everywhere.

"Ava, come on in." Judson half rose from his chair before plopping down again. His Albert Einstein hairstyle was especially on point today. And he wore the condiments of what looked like a hamburger on his white button-down. Many people made the mistake of underestimating Judson based on his appearance. Her first week on the job, Ava learned the truth. He had the sharpest newspaper mind of anyone she'd ever met. He ran the metro section of the paper with an iron fist and a sharp tongue. Her columns reviewing local eateries and giving cooking advice always came back from him bleeding red in edits. Yeah. Intimidating. "Shut the door."

Okay. Good start. Judson only shut the door for important meetings.

She glanced at the chairs in front of his desk. Piled as high with papers and other items as the rest of the space. Near the couch along the far wall—also covered with random stuff—a folding chair rested in its closed position. She grabbed it and opened it. It sank a good three inches as she sat. Great. Not exactly a position of power, but maybe that would be in her favor.

"Sorry, that chair has a broken seat." Judson ran a hand over his head, but it did nothing to lessen the impact of his wiry gray hair.

"No problem." She straightened her back.

"Sherry tells me you have a pitch for me." Judson's bulldog of a personal assistant took her job as bouncer seriously. Ava had had to beg and plead for this meeting. Sherry had finally caved after Ava brought her a slice of cheesecake from Studio 67, a restaurant where she'd been sent on assignment. She'd given the restaurant a great review in her column, Ava Harper Chows Down.

"I do." She pulled the top sheet out of her folder and handed it over. It was a printout from the Visit Us page of the Jonathon Island website. Judson glanced at it before setting it down on top of his desk. He folded his hands over his stomach and leaned back in his chair. "I know the *Chicago Herald* usually only covers local news, but I had a great idea for expanding our readership."

Judson nodded. "I'm listening."

Gulp. "Lately, our sales have been declining. Well, every newspaper is seeing declining readership. In exit polls, people have stated that they can find out these kinds of news items from anywhere."

"I'm well aware of the declining sales. I just had my ninetieth meeting about that this year, and it's only the beginning of May." He laughed, but there was little humor.

"Right. Of course. So, what if we gave the readers something different?" She took a deep breath. "What if I take my column on the road? I could work remotely, reviewing restaurants that are not just in the greater Chicago area. I could do other pieces too. Food-centered still, but like on food festivals, maybe food factories or something. Do you remember the Food Network show *Unwrapped*? It could be *Unwrapped* meets *Diners, Drive-Ins, and Dives*. Except I could review lots of places. Right now it's the beginning of May. Food festival season is just starting. I could get a jump on it." Her heart thumped. Could he hear it on the other side of the desk?

Judson's gaze sharpened. "I take it you're thinking of Jonathon Island?"

"I am. Jonathon Island in Michigan is having a food festival, Flavor Fest, in a few weeks, the first part of June. I thought that could be a trial run." She pictured the quaint village of Jonathon Island she remembered from her one and only trip there but pushed it aside. She'd stumbled across the contest advertisement while clicking around the town website and dreaming of living there. *Concentrate, Ava. No distractions.* "There will be two weekends of cooking contests with other activities in between. Cooking classes, demonstrations . . . even a fudge-tasting event. I could review the restaurants on the island as well as the contests themselves. Maybe do a few feature pieces on the chefs. I could get two weeks' worth of content from that event." She bit back the next sentence on her lips. Better to let Judson mull it over first.

"I know about Jonathon Island. My family has traveled there many times. Not lately, of course." Judson unfolded his hands and drummed them on his desk. "I don't know. Sounds expensive. The last time I brought the kids and grandkids there it cost almost as much as taking the family to Disney World."

She handed him another paper. "I've sketched out a budget and projected expenses. Their rates are low right now while the town is trying to garner new interest from tourists." She pointed at the bottom line. "But even if we weren't getting a sweet deal on lodging, I think we could reach a broader audience with these articles, and they'll pay for themselves. We could do hard copies first, then upload them onto our food blog. I've also outlined a couple other places I could replicate this experience."

"I like where you're going with this." Judson picked up a pen and marked a few spots on the paper. "Tell you what—I have to run this past the editorial team, but I like where your head is at. Let's consider Jonathon Island a trial run." He pointed the end of the pen at her. "If you can produce at least fourteen good articles and they garner some good traction, we'll consider letting you go remote full-time."

She stood, her insides feeling like they were filled with rising helium balloons. "Thank you, sir. I won't let you down."

"You never have." Judson turned his attention to something else on his desk.

Ava put the chair back where she'd found it. Her hand was on the cool doorknob when Judson spoke again.

"I see there's a charity competition here. Get signed up to cook for that. It's good press for the newspaper, plus it will give you an inside scoop." He stabbed a finger at the paper.

A few balloons popped and her stomach sank.

Judson went on. "The daughter of celebrity chefs Leah and Aaron Harper will make quite a splash. I bet you've been cooking since you were a toddler."

Now her heart was somewhere near her knees, which were in danger of giving out. "Actually, um—"

"I know you don't like to talk about your parents in your column, that's fine. But this is for charity." Judson waved a hand in the air. "And if you win, you can donate it to the *Herald*'s charity, Reading Is for Everyone."

Open your mouth, Ava. Tell him you can't cook. But the words stuck in her throat.

"I'll let you know what the board says, but in my mind, this charity competition seals the deal. Consider yourself signed up for all of it."

Gulp. Writing fourteen articles in ten days, no problem. Cooking anything more than a frozen dinner? Very much a problem.

She pushed the thought away. Time enough to deal with it later.

Sure, the job wasn't secure yet, but Ava felt a hundred pounds lighter after having her pitch over with. She beelined for the corner desk where she could see the top of her friend Emily's curly brunette head.

"I think he's going to go for it." She pitched her voice low, but Emily squealed.

"Ava, that's great!" Petite and always in a skirt or a dress, Emily Knox was the unlikely sports reporter for the *Herald*. The two had become friends after Judson sent them both on the same assignment, Emily to check out the Chicago Dogs, a local baseball team, and Ava to report on the food offerings at their park. Today, Emily wore a cream sweater over a calico sundress that brought out the blue of her eyes. "We're way past the minor leagues now. If it doesn't work out, you can always join me on the sports beat."

"Nah. I love my job, you know that." Ava shifted the folder in her hands.

"True. I don't think I've ever known someone to love writing about food as much as you do. Though sometimes I suspect you're in it for the free meals." Emily raised her right eyebrow.

Ava grinned at her. "You caught me. When someone can't cook, it helps to have a job where they're required to feed you." Except. Her heart seized. "One of the catches for this Jonathon Island assignment is Judson requiring me to sign up for a charity cooking competition." She grimaced. Would Judson really make her go through with it?

"Why are you making that face? It sounds like fun."

"You know I can't compete in a cook-off. Everyone will find out my secret." If her readers knew she couldn't cook, they would laugh her out of publication. Ava Harper Chows Down was peppered with cooking tips each week. Tips she didn't fully know how to utilize but had gleaned from the chefs she interviewed for her column.

Emily squinted. "How do you know you can't cook if you never even try?"

"The one time I tried, it was a disaster." She still woke up in a cold sweat sometimes, the fire alarm blaring from her nightmares.

"I'm sure it wasn't that bad."

"I mean, nobody died, and I didn't burn the house down, but the way my mom reacted, you would have thought I'd . . . Anyway, I decided cooking wasn't—" On Emily's computer screen, Ava spotted two familiar faces. Her gut clenched. "Emily, why are my parents on your computer?"

Emily fumbled with her mouse, and her screensaver came up. "I'm catching up on past seasons of *Life Afloat* over my lunch hour. I'm sorry. I should have asked you first."

Ava waved at the air. "No. It's fine. Are you on season three?"

"Yes." Emily's face became animated. "I love that they're on the same ship this time. You can really tell how much they love each other."

Ava stopped the automatic eye roll her eyeballs did whenever someone gushed about her famous chef parents, Leah and Aaron Harper. They'd been chefs on private yachts since long before she was born, and now they were regularly featured on the reality television show *Life Afloat*. An upstairs/downstairs-style TV program giving glimpses into the überrich lives of those who could afford luxury yachts and the staff that crewed them.

She didn't have the energy for them today. "Yep. Season three is a favorite for lots of people. Wait until you hit episode ten." Yeah, even though they never had time for her, she still made time to watch every episode. Really, sometimes it was the only way she could see them. Her parents were decidedly on the downstairs portion of the show, but the TV producers—and audience—loved them, so they were featured often, no matter which boat they were crewing.

"Did they really meet on a yacht?"

"Yep. Mom was the cook and Dad was a deckhand. She taught him everything she knew, and then they learned a bunch of stuff together. It's pretty rare they end up on a boat together now. Not too many yacht owners are looking for two highly trained chefs."

"Two chefs for parents, and yet you don't cook."

"Enough already." Ava waved off her words. "They gave me a love for good food and a talent for critiquing it—that's why I love my job so much—just not a talent for creating it myself." Her heart twisted.

"Hey, you know what you could do? Take a class at Escargot." Emily pushed a curl off her forehead.

"That French restaurant?" She'd heard good things about it but had never tried it out.

"That's the one. They give lessons there on Monday nights, when the restaurant is closed to the public." Emily tapped a few keys on her keyboard. "Yep. They have some the next few Mondays. I know they cater to beginners—my friend Michelle works there. I went to one of the classes for a girls' night out. I got some very helpful hints from the chef." Emily clicked around the website. "I just sent you the link to the sign-up."

"Thanks. I'll look into it." The band across her chest loosened a notch. "Enough chat for now. I'd better finish that article about Mainstreet Eatery. Maybe this will be the one to wow the editors into giving me everything I've ever wanted." A forever home where she could put down roots, plus the chance to chase the foodie stories she really wanted to tell? Yeah, she'd do anything for that opportunity.

There were times Zachary Sullivan knew he had the best job on earth. He whipped some horseradish into the hard-boiled yolk in front of him before spooning tiny dabs of the filling back into the quail eggs. Then he nested the filled eggs next to a prosciutto on rye open-faced sandwich. His take on open-faced ham sandwiches and deviled eggs. Needed some color. He added a sprig of watercress to one of the eggs and took a step back to see the big picture.

Like Picasso on a plate.

He'd dreamed up the food in the empty kitchen after closing time at Escargot. In the two years he'd been cooking at the French restaurant, he'd learned that the owner preferred leftovers to be eaten, not thrown out. It was fun to play around with the ingredients, trying out new recipes and flexing his creative muscles. Something that he never got to do when Chef Louie was around.

The kitchen at Escargot was quiet now. A hint of garlic, brown butter, and the lemon cleaner they used hung in the air. The surfaces of the workstations lined up in the middle of the room gleamed. Along the back wall, the top-of-the-line grills, oven, and deep fryer stood ready for service the next day. Someday he would run a kitchen like this.

He snapped a photo of his dish and texted it to his sister Dani.

Zach

Here's the elevated "church
potluck food" you challenged me
to make.

She probably wouldn't get the photo until morning, but he couldn't wait to prove he'd met the goal.

His phone chimed with an incoming text:

Dani

Looks great! A real winner. Wish I could do a taste test. I'll have to think of a harder task next time.

Zach

Are you still awake? It's midnight.

Dani

Can't sleep. Working on food festival details.

His sister was the tourism director for Jonathon Island, a small community in the middle of Lake Huron in Michigan. This year she had devised a full plate of festivals to welcome much-needed tourists to the island. Jonathon Island barely made it through the pandemic and the economic downturn. It didn't help that their main hotel, the Grand Sullivan, had nearly burned to the ground ten years before. Now that the hotel was being rebuilt, the town had begun a revitalization effort, and tourism was finally beginning to pick up again.

Zach
____

Good luck. Not that you need it.
The book festival and the Apple
Blossom Festival were successes.
I'm sure this one will be too.

As he tucked his phone into his back pocket, it started ringing.

"I think I'm in over my head." Dani's whispered voice came over the line.

"Really? You sounded so confident at your wedding." Zach massaged his forehead but couldn't stop the smile. Zach had recently catered Dani's wedding on Jonathon Island. The first time he'd been back there in many, many years.

Dani sighed. "Yeah, well, four weeks later and I'm not so confident."

"Why are we whispering?"

"Liam is asleep, and I don't want to worry him with this."

"But you'll worry me?" He transferred the call to his earbuds and stuck them in his ears, then began handwashing the bowls and measuring spoons he'd used to make the dinner. Chef Louie prized a clean kitchen. One of the few things they agreed on.

"You were already awake. Besides, I need your help."

"Sure. What can I do?"

"Come home for the festival."

"What? No." He'd already done that once this year, thank you very much. He had the scars to prove it. *You Sullivans think you're better than the rest of us.* Some cranky old man, one of the hotel groundskeepers, had grumped at him at Dani's wedding. *If it weren't for you, Jonathon Island would never have lost so many tourists.* And sure, the man's words meant little, except they confirmed all of Zach's darkest fears. He wasn't accepted and neither was his family. After all, it was his family that was responsible for the island's greatest tragedy.

"I just think I could use your moral support. I need this to go well. It'll set the tone for the whole summer. Plus, you could enter some of the contests." A rustle came from the other end of the phone. "Hold on, I'm going to move to the front porch."

"And what, compete against Martha Kelley? Or maybe Patrick? They'd love that. A Sullivan as competition." The Kelley family owned and operated most of the food places on Jonathon Island. Sure, Patrick was a good guy, but Martha gave Zach a sour look every time she saw him.

"Martha isn't competing, as far as I know. Besides, I have some others coming too. Val Anderson and Alicia Baird."

Huh. She'd pulled some good local chef talent. "Okay, fine. You have some heavy hitters."

"Please come. Did I tell you that Paul Hawkeye and Anne Green have agreed to be celebrity judges?" Her front door squeaked, and then a gentle thud echoed.

"You're kidding." The two television chefs seemed way out of Jonathon Island's league.

"Nope. Just got the confirmation today. They both loved the idea of being at a small-town festival."

"You know I wanted to work for Paul. It's one of the reasons I moved to LA after Seattle." He wiped a stray spot of egg filling off the plate in front of him. "Too bad I could never get a face-to-face with him."

"I thought that might get your attention. I'll ask again, please say you'll come."

"I'll think about it. I might not be able to get the time off since I was just over there for your wedding." He wandered over to the shared calendar hanging on the wall. "What are the dates again?"

"The first two weekends in June. Thanks, big brother. You're the best."

No one had requested that week off as far as he could tell. "I haven't promised anything yet."

"When have you ever said no to me?" Dani's smile came through the line loud and clear.

He laughed and hung up. Dani had a point—he had a hard time saying no to his family.

Jamie Randall, his six-foot-seven coworker who looked more like a Marine than a line cook, with his broad chest and close-cut blond hair, wandered over. He'd been working at Escargot when Zach first started. Unlike Zach, Jamie didn't care to move up in the ranks of the kitchen. He snagged one of the deviled eggs Zach had rejected. "Is this your new recipe?"

"Yep." Zach crossed his arms and leaned back on the counter. "I added a little horseradish and tarragon as well as mustard to the cooked yolks."

"Can I try it?" Jamie didn't wait for him to answer before popping the whole thing in his mouth. "Delicious. This should be on the menu."

"Ha. You're funny. Chef Louie would never go for it."

"Why are you wasting your talents here, man?" Jamie popped another quail egg in his mouth and chased it with a bite of ham. Suddenly, the big man snapped to attention. He gestured with his chin toward the kitchen door.

Zach turned in time to see two men enter. Marcel Boivin, the slight, silver-haired owner of Escargot and a head shorter than his companion, gesticulated widely as he walked and talked. The man next to him was the head chef of Escargot, Chef Louie Andrews.

"I just think we need a few new items on our menu," Marcel said, his French accent heavy tonight. "Ah! Hello, gentlemen." The old man clasped his hands together and nodded at Zach and Jamie. "Another excellent service tonight. Be sure to say merci beaucoup to the rest of the team." He advanced a step, leaving Chef Louie by the door, silent and glowering. Chef Louie, his chef's whites pristine and his brown hair gelled tight to his scalp, had sent the rest of the staff home after the kitchen had been scrubbed clean.

"Mr. Boivin, Chef." Zach nodded back. "I thought you'd gone home for the night."

"Chef and I had some business to discuss. What is this?" Marcel waved a hand toward Zach's elevated potluck food.

Zach stepped around the table, a lame attempt to block the food. "Nothing, sir."

"Nonsense. It looks good." Marcel selected an egg and ate it. His eyes widened. "This is fantastique. Chef Louie, you are a genius."

Wait a minute.

Louie's face cleared. "Uh, thank you."

"This is what I mean. New menu items. Chef Louie, why did you let me prattle on about it when you'd already prepared some things for me to taste?" Marcel ate one of the prosciutto on rye sandwiches. "Non. This one is pas bon. Not good. I don't know what you were thinking here. But I like that quail oeuf, I mean egg. Put it on the hors d'oeuvres menu."

Marcel breezed out, leaving Louie, Zach, and Jamie staring at each other.

Louie crossed his arms, eyes flashing. "You have been trying to undermine me ever since you stepped foot in this restaurant." Louie's French accent was not as thick as Marcel's, but it still cut through the air. "What were you trying to pull, having these things plated up?"

"I didn't even know he was going to be here tonight." But Zach's words didn't faze Louie.

"Since you feel you can upstage me, maybe you should teach the next Make-It-Monday series." Louie's hand flicked the air. "If this happens again, you're gone."

Zach sighed. "Yes, Chef."

Louie spun on his heel and stalked out.

"Chef Louie really has it in for you." Jamie carried the empty dishes to the sink.

"My first night here some big shot complimented my cooking, and Louie was offended. He's made it miserable ever since."

"Dude. What are you doing staying here and taking his mistreatment?" Jamie ran water over the plate. "Make-It-Mondays are like his idea of punishment. He only assigns them to someone on his hit list. Those classes are brutal."

A room full of people who didn't know how to cook coming in and thinking they could master it in a night? Yeah, the classes could be difficult, but he'd done them before. Shouldn't be a big deal this time either. The hardest part was being in front of all those people. "It's fine. I'm paying my dues."

"It's really not fine. He just totally stole the credit for your dish. And what dues? You've been a chef for a long time."

"His kitchen, his recipes. We all signed on to that when we came." He raised a shoulder. "And I've only been here less than two years. I'm still the new guy."

"It's not right, man. He's not doing it because you're the new guy." Jamie shook his head. "But whatever. It's your life." The big man patted him on the shoulder. "I'm taking off. See you tomorrow for another round of non-crime and punishment."

Except, maybe Jamie had a point. With Chef Louie in charge, his job was a dead-end.

He thumbed a text to Dani.

Zach

Fine. I'll come to Flavor Fest. Sign
me up for the contest.

Because maybe he could wow Paul or Anne and land himself a new position.

He needed to get out of this job.

Two

AVA HAD MADE A BIG MISTAKE NOT RE-searching the staff at Escargot. As she pushed through the doors to the kitchen after walking through the fancy French restaurant, she reiterated the reasons she was even here for the night. First, Judson had pretty much required her to go. Second, she needed these cooking classes if she was going to boil water without burning it and have any chance of her secret staying safe. Third, a distant third, if she ever wanted to cook half as well as her famous parents, she needed to stop microwaving frozen dinners and start preparing meals from scratch. She was thirty-five, for crying out loud. She should be able to cook something.

After Emily had mentioned that Escargot offered classes on the nights they were closed, and then "accidentally"—Ava heard the air quotes even if Emily didn't actually use them when she told Ava the story—shared that information in front of their boss, it was only a matter of time before Judson signed her up. He'd called her into his office when he broke the news.

"Harper. Good. I've gotten you into that cooking class tonight at Escargot." Her boss's hair appeared as though he'd stuck a knife into a power outlet. She'd always respected Judson. But she hadn't always appreciated his rule over her life. "I figured you could use the practice."

This didn't sound good. "Why do I need the practice?"

He looked up from the paper he was covering in red ink. Someone was going to have a bad day. "The editorial team decided to let you go to Jonathon Island for the Flavor Fest as a trial run."

She suppressed a squeal of delight.

"We also decided that you should definitely take part in that charity competition, so we signed you up for that."

"What? I can't do the charity competition." Seriously, she didn't think she was a big enough celebrity for the charity competition.

"We talked about this. You begged me to let you go to that festival, so I figured you should be in on the action and not just reporting on it. The editorial board agreed. Signing up for that competition is not optional." Judson had looked back at the paper in front of him and crossed out another line. "You'll be cooking for the good of mankind. Make us proud out there."

So, yeah. She needed to learn how to cook. And fast.

Still, all her reasons fled as she spotted the chef for tonight's cooking class. Zachary Sullivan. The same Zachary Sullivan she'd met years ago in Seattle before giving his restaurant a terrible review in her column.

This was the part of her job as restaurant critic and food reviewer for the newspaper that she hated: meeting the chefs in the wild. She valued honesty in her work, but she still cringed when she had to say that some recipe or another just wasn't working. It wasn't exactly the case with Zachary, but she still didn't like the idea of coming face-to-face with him. Besides, he didn't know that her review was . . . a mistake.

The scent of garlic cooked in butter wafted over her as she stood in the doorway, half in, half out. Ava looked around the kitchen. Gleaming stainless-steel cooktops lined the back wall. Several island workbenches stood in a neat row in the middle of the room. On each bench rested an assortment of cooking implements.

She should just leave.

She'd started to let the door swing closed when a gaggle of women pressed in behind her. They swarmed her and virtually carried her into the kitchen in their wake. The party of eight wore white T-shirts with pink lettering declaring them to be the Bridal Squad.

"Are you coming to this class too?" A tall brunette with *Bride* emblazoned on the sash across her chest grabbed her arm. "I'm so glad they offer these every month. I need to learn how to cook— and fast!" She smiled at Ava, and her eyes sparkled as brightly as the ring on her third finger.

"Um—" But she hadn't gotten any further before Bride tugged her forward.

"Hi," Bride said. "I'm Julia." Then she pointed out several members of her bridal party.

Swept up in the group, Ava soon found herself at the gleaming silver aluminum workbench.

Okay, she could do this. Maybe Zachary wouldn't even know who she was. After all, she'd signed up using her middle name. He stood with his back to them at the industrial stove, stirring something in a saucepan. Probably the source of the divine smell, if her nose had anything to say about it.

She sent a quick text to her mom.

Ava

> Guess who signed up for her first cooking class. 🤳

Mom

> Good job! Just don't burn the place down.

Thanks, Mom.

Though, it might be better than the alternative—Zach finding out she was here.

When she'd looked at this class through Escargot's website, they hadn't named the chef who was leading them. She hadn't even known that he was living in Chicago. And didn't he specialize in elevated Midwestern food, not French cooking? A photo on the wall opposite, nestled underneath several other photos of the staff, confirmed her first quick glance. Chef Zachary Sullivan.

He slid the saucepan to the back of the stove and turned to the group. "Everyone here?" His intense green-eyed gaze roamed over the assembled women. "I think we're expecting one more."

"I didn't think our chef would be so hot," one of the bride squad, a tall blonde wearing false eyelashes, whispered to Ava.

She looked closer at Zachary. Sure, he could be considered good-looking. If you liked eyes as green as new leaves in the springtime, hair dark and mussed, cheekbones so high and sharp they could double as knives in this kitchen in a pinch, and a hint of muscle showing under the rolled sleeves of chef's white. Yeah, if you liked all that, Chef Zachary was your guy. He oozed attractive charm, and she bet he knew it too.

"Ladies." He nodded at the group. "So glad you chose Escargot to celebrate tonight. It's always a pleasure to have a kitchen full of beautiful women." Several of the bachelorette party twittered. He seemed to have assumed Ava was part of the party because he included her in the nod. Perfect. She wouldn't disabuse him of the notion.

The kitchen door swung wide and hit the wall with a thunk. All heads turned to the young man who stood silhouetted in the frame. He bounded over to the middle of the room, where the rest of the group waited to begin.

"Sorry I'm late." He ran a hand through his red hair, standing it on end. "My shift just ended. I didn't think I'd make it at all."

Ava put her hand up to stop a giggle. The young man looked a lot like the main character from that movie where a rat worked in a restaurant. *Ratatouille*? That was it. He looked just like Alfredo Linguini.

"No problem," Zachary said. "You must be . . ." He looked at the class list. "RJ Edwards?" The kid nodded. "Fine. Try not to be late next time." The smile that accompanied his words didn't reach his eyes. "Welcome, class. Let's get started."

Okay then. Not a fan of latecomers. Good thing Ava herself was always punctual. No reason for her to stand out. Zachary began handing out aprons.

"Okay, people. My name is Chef Zach. Welcome to Escargot's Make-It-Monday." Zach moved back to the front of the group. He crossed his arms and leaned against the counter. "Tonight we will learn about the common utensils cooks use, the proper usage of pots and pans, and the concept of mise en place, or having everything prepped for cooking even before you start. We will end the night making a simple sauce. For those of you coming back next week, I will show you how to pair that sauce with three dishes for three completely different entrées."

Ava was definitely coming back next week. She needed to know a dish for her competition.

Zach stood up straight and began walking to one of the workstations on the far right of the room. "Follow me, everyone." Ava hung toward the back of the group. Someone had laid out utensils and knives on the bench in several long, neat rows. Zach began explaining each one and their proper usage. Ava could feel her eyes glaze over by the time he got to the third knife on the display.

Surely the knife you used didn't make that much difference, did it? She was here to learn to cook, not learn about utensils.

Reaching into her purse, she found a notebook and pen. Might as well make a few notes.

She jotted down some random words. Hopefully, they would make sense later.

She added a row of tiny mice chasing each other's tails along the bottom of the page. Then drew a cat ready to spring. She'd just started on a column of tulips when she realized the room had gone silent.

Everyone's eyes were on her.

"Did you care to join the class?" Zach stood in her personal space. He looked down at the mice and tulips. "If you're not interested in what we are doing here, perhaps this class isn't for you."

Ava's heart began to beat double-time. "I'm so sorry. Doodling helps me think."

"Really." He drew the word out. "What was the name of the final knife?"

"Um, cleaver?" She tacked on a smile for good measure.

He rolled his eyes so hard she worried he would sprain them. "Not even close. I just explained the use of the paring knife. A very important knife in a chef's arsenal."

She glanced at her notebook. Sure enough, near the end of the notes, she had circled and starred the words "paring knife." Her hands were listening, even if her brain wasn't.

"Again, I'm sorry. I meant no disrespect." Closing the notebook, she tucked it back in her purse. "I'm fully engaged." She needed to lock in.

His shoulders relaxed a notch, and he nodded once. "Good, because we're about to work on our knife skills. What did you say your name was again?" The room was still silent as the class looked from one of them to the other.

"Lea. Lea Harper." She swallowed hard against the almost lie. But she absolutely couldn't use her real name in case anyone recognized it from her column.

"Okay, Lea. Why don't you take first position? We're about to learn the proper way to chop vegetables. Using the chef's knife."

Chef Zach reached across the table and picked up a knife about eight inches long.

Properly chop vegetables? Seriously, who did this guy think he was?

But she knew from experience that Zach was an excellent chef. She'd be learning from the best. So, properly chopped vegetables must be part of that. Even though Escargot didn't take advantage of his talents, she certainly could.

Fine. If she had to chop a bushel of peppers in order to learn, she'd just have to do it. And she needed to focus, not lose track of what Zach was saying. Because she had to stay in this class. Her future depended on it.

Only a few more days and Zach Sullivan could kiss this job goodbye. As long as he wowed Paul Hawkeye or even Anne Green at the Flavor Fest in two weeks, he would be in high demand. Not stuck in this dead-end job where his boss all but guaranteed he would never advance to sous chef, despite his years of experience. Dani had been glad to hear he was coming. And since he'd said yes, she'd texted almost nonstop about details she was uncertain about.

Zach had a calendar in his apartment marking down the days until he was back on Jonathon Island. He could let his talents really shine. And hopefully ignore any snide remarks from the locals.

Tonight, though, he had to make it through yet another cooking class filled with beginners. At least this bachelorette party wasn't drunk like the last time he had led one of these. And the kid wasn't half bad. Speaking of which . . .

He made his way through the room. "RJ, can I speak to you for a minute?"

The kid's red head popped up, light-green eyes widened. "Uh, sure."

Zach tapped his clipboard. "My boss said you haven't paid the fee for this class and to make sure to collect the money tonight." In fact, Chef Louie had written in red ink and all caps: NO CHARITY CASES.

RJ ducked his head. "Can I pay it next week? I thought I'd get more in tips, but the front-of-house staff didn't share them all like they usually do, so I'm short this week."

How well he knew that feeling. There were plenty of lean weeks while he was putting himself through culinary school. "You know what? Don't worry about it. We had someone cancel and forfeit their fee. I'll apply that to your account." And if Chef Louie had a problem with it, Zach would figure something out.

RJ's eyes opened wide. "Thank you so much!"

Zach looked over the participants.

One of the blondes with the Bridal Squad wasn't wearing her signature T-shirt. He'd noticed earlier that she looked familiar, but he couldn't place her. He stole another quick glance. A smattering of freckles trailed across her narrow nose and the tops of her round cheeks. Gray eyes sparkled. Pretty. And he usually remembered pretty girls. She'd said her name was Lea Harper, but that didn't ring a bell. He looked her way again. She had her chef's knife in both hands as she mangled a red onion.

Pasting on a smile he made his way to her. "Here." He nudged her aside. "Let me show you."

She turned to him, knife forward. He put up both of his hands. "Whoa, there. Knife on the bench."

Her cheeks pinked. "Sorry." She laid the knife down and stepped back.

"You want to grip the heel end of the blade between your thumb and forefinger and use the rest of your hand to hold the handle." He demonstrated the technique. "That gives you better control and accuracy." He chopped one of the onions before setting the knife back on the bench. "Now you try."

She picked up the knife and fumbled with it a moment. "Like this?"

He reached over and adjusted her fingers so they gripped the blade more appropriately, her fingers cool under his touch. "There you go."

She sliced another onion, the pieces becoming more uniform as she worked.

"I think you've got it." He looked around the room. Everyone was making good progress. "Not a fan of matching outfits?"

"What?" She turned to him, knife out again.

"Have you got it in for me?"

Her eyes widened and she set the knife down. "Sorry. Again."

He gestured to the other women. "You aren't wearing your T-shirt."

Did her face just get pinker? How much darker could it get?

"Oh. I, um, I'm not with the group. I just arrived at the same time." She ducked her head and made a big show of carefully cutting a carrot.

"I don't mean this as a come-on, but do I know you from somewhere? You look familiar." The idea nagged at him.

"I'm new to Chicago." She started working on the celery. "I'm not from here."

Not really an answer.

"Neither am I. I've bounced around a lot." It was too bad none of those places ever felt like home. Chicago didn't either, but it fit the bill for now. "New York, Saratoga Springs, Austin, Seattle before that."

At the mention of Seattle, she paled so quickly he reached for her elbow. Couldn't have her passing out in the middle of class.

"Are you okay?"

She tugged her arm back. "I'm fine."

He let his gaze roam over her face. "Okay. Promise me you'll let me know if you aren't feeling well."

"Could you help me over here?" One of the bridesmaids waved a hand in the air. "I think my pieces are too big."

While showing the woman how to chop uniform piece sizes on onions, he kept one eye on the rest of the group. The kid, RJ, had moved so he was sharing a workstation with the non-bachelorette.

"First time here?" Lea asked him.

"I'm a dishwasher at The Lion's Lair, but I want to go to culinary school at Kendall Culinary." RJ set down his knife and adjusted his apron. "In the meantime, I'm learning all I can. You?"

"First time. This is quite a bit different than my day job."

"What do you do?"

The bride, Julia, called Zach over and he almost missed Lea's answer.

"... newspaper."

He helped Julia for a few minutes. Something nagged at the back of his mind like a mosquito you could hear but not see.

Wait a minute.

It came to him in a rush. Harper. Seattle. Newspaper.

The woman who had tanked his debut restaurant in Seattle had been a newspaper food critic with the last name Harper.

Could this be the same person?

One way to find out. "Ava?" he called across the room. She looked up and met his eye. Guilt immediately filled her gaze. Ducking her head, she furiously chopped at another onion.

His heart rate spiked.

He stalked to her bench.

"Ava Harper?" He pitched his voice low even though he wanted to howl. "You are Ava Harper, right?" She nodded. "I knew I knew you from somewhere."

She paled. "I don't—"

"Stop." He clenched his fist and tapped it on his thigh. One. Two. Three. Four. Keep it conversational, no need to involve the whole class in his business.

Ava opened her mouth. Closed it.

"Trying to tank this job for me like you torpedoed my restaurant? Why are you here?"

She put a fisted hand to her hip. "I would tell you if you'd let me get a word in."

A burning began in his belly. "Just answer the question."

"I didn't even know you were going to be here." She looked down at the workbench, then picked up her knife and began chopping again. "I signed up for the class, but it didn't say who the instructor would be. I didn't even know you lived here."

He barked out a laugh. "That's rich. Are you trying to make sure I never work again? To humiliate me with your skills?"

She set her knife on the bench with a slap. He winced. Expensive knives shouldn't be manhandled like that.

She jabbed him in the sternum with her pointer finger. On second thought, he was glad she'd put down the knife. "Look, I don't know who you think you are, Mr. Almighty Chef. No. I didn't follow you here to make you lose your job. Get over yourself. That thing in Seattle was six years ago. *Six years.*" She snapped her mouth shut and glanced past him.

Zach looked around.

Oh.

Nine pairs of eyes had turned in their direction. RJ stood mid-chop, mouth open. A few of the bachelorettes giggled.

He unclenched his fist and forced a smile. "Sorry, everyone. Sorry. I got a little carried away. Won't happen again." The class dropped their gazes and busied themselves with their work again. "Lea." He put a hard emphasis on her fake name, careful to keep his voice down so only she could hear him. "I should make you show us how to sauté our mirepoix for our first sauce."

She mumbled a response.

He looked at her. "What was that?"

"I don't know how to do that." Her voice was still only a little above a whisper.

He crossed his arms. "I don't believe you. Aren't your parents chefs? I saw them on that luxury yacht show. I looked them up after they started sharing all your stuff on social media." She nodded. "Don't you write a very successful column in the newspaper not only critiquing restaurants but also telling everyone else how to cook?"

She nodded again. Squared her shoulders. "But I never learned how to do it."

He glanced around the room again. No one was paying attention to them. He kept his voice low. "So, you're telling me you have enough pull to land a job at the *Seattle Courier* but you don't know how to cook?" The woman was unbelievable. "Why should anyone ever read your work or trust your opinion?"

She pulled herself together. "Please, keep your voice down." Her eyes pleaded with him.

"Of course, we wouldn't want anyone knowing you're a fraud." She couldn't be serious right now, could she? "It's okay for you to ruin my life, but I should protect yours?" As he spoke, the voice of his Uncle Bryan rang through his mind. *Real men protect the people around them.* Sorry, Uncle Bryan. He didn't think he could manage that with Ava-slash-Lea. Not after she'd taken down his restaurant and all his savings with it.

Her eyes flashed with hurt. Shoot. Regret curled through him. He should apologize. Be a better man.

"Lea, I—"

She spoke at the same time. "It wasn't like that. I—"

"I'm ready with my mirepoix." Julia appeared at Zach's elbow. Three bowls full of chopped vegetables jostled in her arms.

"Let's talk about this later," he shot over his shoulder and turned to show Julia the stove.

Somehow, he made it through the rest of the class. His gut

churned with anger. And guilt. He should have handled that better. Learned to forgive.

When there were five minutes left, he looked up from showing RJ how to finish off his dish with a pat of butter. Ava's workstation was empty. She must have ducked out early.

Hopefully she'd have the sense not to turn up for part two of these classes next week.

Three

AVA HAD SURVIVED THE COOKING CLASS the week before; now she had to survive this walk. Beside her, Emily Knox added a little bounce to every step she took, her brunette curls bouncing in sync with her skort.

Sure, Ava's ego had been stung when she realized that Zach still held a grudge against her for her review of his restaurant. But she figured she should give him a second chance. It had been a pretty bad situation. And yeah, she could see how he would blame her for the loss of his restaurant.

A week's perspective had helped her attitude. That and the good news she'd found in her email inbox the day before.

"My Realtor emailed me photos of a house on Jonathon Island in my price range." Ava pumped her arms in time with her legs as she power walked through her neighborhood. Tall apartment buildings rose up around them, making the street feel cramped and dark. Right now, in mid-May, she could still smell fresh air, but in the heat of the coming summer, the car exhaust would make walks like this less bearable. "I have them on my phone if you want to see them."

"Don't think that I will allow that as an excuse to cut this walk short." Emily shook her head. "You always want to quit early. I'm not falling for it this time. Besides, we're almost to Singing the Brews. You can show me over a nonfat latte."

"Nonfat? Why do you think I'm working so hard at seven in the morning? Give me full fat anytime." Ava had been lucky to find Emily at work the first week in her new job. The two even lived in the same neighborhood. "I don't know how I let you talk me into doing these power walks every morning."

"It's because you know you aren't getting any younger and you refuse to drink nonfat lattes." Emily tossed a smile over her shoulder as she sped forward a few paces.

"Fair." Ava increased her speed to match her friend's. A few minutes later, they entered the neighborhood coffee shop.

The morning sun had crested the tall buildings across the street in the time it took for them to step back out with their lattes.

"Should we sit at our regular table?" Ava gestured to the wrought iron bistro-style table at the end of the row. Early flowers bobbed in the planter box, marking the edge of Singing the Brews's property. The chair cooled Ava's heated muscles as she sat. She cupped her hands around her iced coffee, cooling her further.

She set her drink aside and pulled out her phone. After swiping it open, she navigated to the email app. The email full of photos from Mia Franklin rested at the top. "Look at this beauty. It even has a picket fence." She made the pictures full-size and held her phone out to Emily. "Swipe left to see them all."

Emily took the phone. "Oh, I see what you mean. Adorable."

"It's so much better than the drab apartment I live in now. I've been adding to the money Grandma set aside for me after Grandpa died. There's finally enough for a down payment. Especially if I get a small house like this one." Ava scooted her chair around until she sat shoulder to shoulder with Emily. Ava had memorized the twelve photos Mia had attached to the email. Four photos of the exterior of the small bungalow nestled in the older part of Jonathon Island, on Zinnia Boulevard. Six photos of the interior of the home, including the two bedrooms, avocado-green kitchen, and a Pepto-Bismol-pink bathroom.

The final two photos were of downtown Jonathon Island. The cobblestone streets, lined with clapboard buildings sporting cheery awnings and other bunting, invited her to come explore.

"Yeesh. That bathroom is a little scary." Emily grimaced.

"Yeah, it'll take some updating, that's for sure. Mia said the family who lived there have been there for many years, but all the kids moved away. The woman who owned it just passed away, and her kids don't want it anymore." Ava cupped her chin in her hand and rested her elbow on the table. "I can't wait to see it in person. I'll be putting in my offer when I'm there later this week."

"Remind me why you want to move to a remote island in the middle of nowhere?" Emily handed the phone back.

Ava gave her friend a light swat on the upper arm. "It's not that remote. It's a busy tourist area. Just because you have to take a ferry to get there doesn't make it the middle of nowhere. I went there once with my parents." A light breeze brought the scent of lilacs from a bush at the corner of the block. "It was a rare family trip. I don't know. I just kind of fell in love with the place. The charm, the sense of community . . . Nowhere else seems to measure up. And now that my grandma keeps threatening to move to Arizona, there's not much tying me to Chicago."

"Fine. I'm sure it's amazing. I don't see why you have to move away from me." Emily stuck out her bottom lip and made puppy dog eyes at her.

"Ha. May I remind you that you are moving away from me? You started it."

"Might be moving away. I might be." Emily held up her right

hand, second and third fingers crossed. "My last interview with the *Los Angeles Journal* is next week."

"It's going to be a slam dunk. You already know they want you. They wouldn't have contacted you if they didn't. Plus, it helps to have your old editor on staff." Ava stuffed her phone back into her pocket. "I'm going to miss seeing you when I walk past the sports desk."

"You'll just have to come visit me. Maybe on one of your trips jet-setting around the world, tasting food for money."

Ava laughed. "If I make it freelancing, I'll definitely add Los Angeles to the list at least once a year." She took a long pull of her coffee. The sweet creaminess canceled out the bitterness of the thoughts racing through her mind. *What if I can't hack it?* Her future hung in the balance.

It was a lot to hang on one week's worth of articles.

"Maybe while you're at Jonathon Island, you'll meet the perfect man." Emily saluted her with her cup. "It certainly sounds like a place straight out of Hallmark."

"Eh. You know I've given up on men." She rolled her shoulders.

"Please. One rotten dude should not put you off all of them. Elias is not someone you should base your opinion of men on." A car passed by on the street, its muffler loudly throwing out exhaust. "Elias Kemp is a terrible person. His name even sounds like a villain from an 1880s penny dreadful."

"I thought Elias was the one. Who dates someone for years only to dump them for no reason?" She crumpled up a napkin, the fibers rough under her fingers.

"A rotten person." Emily speared her with a look.

She sighed. "I can see now that he was just stringing me along. Using me. I shouldn't have been surprised when he left." After all, wasn't that what her parents did too? She should stop relying on people to stay. "No more men for me."

"Fine. I get it." Emily held both hands in the air, palms out.

"New topic. How was the cooking class?" She sat back in her chair. "Learn anything good?"

Ava's face grew hot. "I know you think it's silly that it bothers me so much, but there's something so dishonest to me about criticizing other people's work for something I never learned to do myself."

"I don't think it's silly. You have integrity. I admire that." Emily uncapped her cup and shook a few pieces of ice into her mouth.

"It went okay. I learned how to use a knife." Zach's arrogance flashed through her mind.

"Isn't that pretty standard for becoming an adult?"

"I guess I missed that lesson because I had a hard time mastering the skill." Her face felt as though it would light a forest on fire. "You'll never guess who was there."

"Judging by how red you are, I'm going with Brad Pitt." Emily grinned.

"I think you're the one who will be running into Brad Pitt." Ava raised her cup to her cheek, the icy dregs of her coffee cooling her face. "Zachary Sullivan was leading the class."

"Am I supposed to know who that is?"

Ava let out a long breath. "No. I guess not. I try not to talk about it."

Emily rolled her hand in the air. "Come on. Tell me now."

"Okay, but I might need another latte first."

"Cut it out. Give me the tea. Spill the beans. Need more foodie humor?"

Ava held up her hands. "No. Please. My first time writing my Ava Harper Chows Down column was in Seattle."

"That was when you were at the *Courier*?"

Ava nodded. "Yep. I was assigned to a new restaurant, Peach. Turns out it was Chef Sullivan's baby. It was his first solo place."

Emily leaned forward. "And it was this chef that was at your class last week?"

"He was leading it."

Emily held up a hand. "Wait. Let me guess." She closed her eyes. "You wrote him a glowing review, causing him to fall madly in love with you and beg you to meet him at the top of the Space Needle on New Year's Eve, but you couldn't go because you'd broken your leg in a car accident?" Her eyes popped open.

"Good guess, points for the movie reference, but you're way off." A strain of music filtered out from the coffee shop. The music group Miss Dahlia and Ariel sang about God bringing them to their destiny the long way. "The newspaper printed a bad review of his place."

"What didn't you like about the food?" Emily leaned in.

"That's kind of the problem. I actually did like the food. It was delicious." She could still taste the beef ragu in her dreams. "I briefly saw Chef Sullivan talking to another customer and thought he was arrogant, still do, by the way, much too pretty for his own good, but the food was amazing."

"So why the bad review?"

"Here's the thing." She shifted in her chair before bracing her arms on the table. "I didn't give it a bad review. Or not intentionally. I was still learning the ropes, feeling my way through writing my own column, and had some writer's block, so I tried out a writing prompt to get my juices flowing."

Emily's eyes rounded. "Oh no, something like 'describe an outing using only negative adjectives'?"

"Something like that. You know where this is going. By the time I'd written my real review, I was close to deadline on my first writing assignment. I got nervous, flustered, you name it." She twisted her fingers together. "So when I sent in my article, I sent in the wrong file. I didn't notice until I looked for it in the paper the next day. Then to make it worse, my parents shared the newspaper clipping on their social media, and it went viral."

"Ava, that's terrible. I'm so sorry." Emily placed her hand over Ava's. "What did he say when you told him?"

"I never talked to him again, until last week anyway. I was too embarrassed and young and naive." Only Emily's grip kept her from burying her face in her hands.

"Well, it's been what, six years since you were in Seattle? I'm sure he's over it."

She pictured the end of her class the week before. Zach getting in her face, green eyes flashing. "He's definitely not over it. The worst part is, I couldn't find another place for a class, so I have to see him tonight again. Unless he decided he couldn't stand the sight of me and got a colleague to fill in."

Emily gave her twisted fingers a squeeze before releasing them. "I'm sure if you just explain to him what happened, it will be fine."

"I tried to do that last time, believe me. He was not interested in hearing my side of the story."

"That's awful."

Ava took a long drink of her latte. The ice had all melted, leaving the coffee lukewarm. The sweet concoction soured in her stomach, and she straightened in her chair. "Anyway, I just need to make it through one more class, then I can focus on my trip to Jonathon Island. All that matters is that I learn enough to make it through that charity competition Judson signed me up for. Keeping my editor happy is at the top of my list."

At Escargot, she would keep her head down and learn everything she could. Because after tonight, she would never have to see Zachary Sullivan again.

Just get through the night. Zach's countdown for the last several days had turned into a mantra. *Just make it through.*

The kitchen waited, silent and ready, for the class tonight. Earlier that evening, he'd set up every station, lining up knives and mixing bowls and a pair of aprons at each spot, anticipating another full class. He double-checked the roster again. The bachelorette party would be back, this time missing one member. RJ was also on the schedule, as was Ava. He stifled a growl. He shut his eyes and breathed deep for a four count, then blew out his breath with a huff. No amount of deep breathing would change the fact that he was in this dead-end job because of Ava Harper.

His phone buzzed in his pocket. He pulled it out and glanced at the caller ID. His brother, Ollie. "What's up, bro?"

"I'm doing Dani a favor and confirming your arrival time for the Flavor Fest. You're coming in a day or two early, she said?"

"I'm counting down the minutes. I'll send you and Dani my flight info. I think I'll be able to catch the two o'clock ferry across." Zach straightened a knife that sat askew on the counter.

"Sounds good. Dani said to tell you she's got you all signed up for the contests you wanted. You're still staying with me, right?"

"Yeah. I appreciate it."

"No problem. You're welcome any time." A rustle came over the phone, and then Zach heard Ollie whisper something to someone on the other end. "Sorry about that." Ollie's voice rang through the line again.

"Everything okay?"

"Yep. All good. Eliza just had a question."

His brother had moved back to their hometown of Jonathon Island. He and his girlfriend, Eliza, ran a bookstore on the island. Zach hadn't seen them for a few weeks, not since Dani's wedding in April.

"Are you okay, though?" Ollie said. "You just sound a little off."

"It's nothing." Zach adjusted the spacing between two mixing bowls on the far workstation. "It's just . . . Do you remember that article that was super critical about my restaurant in Seattle?"

"The one that made the place a ghost town? Sure. I remember."

"The food critic was at my class last week." Zach rubbed his temple. "She's supposed to be here again tonight."

"Oh man. I can see why you're distracted. Don't let her get to you. Just be polite. I'm sure it will be fine."

Polite. Right. He could do that.

The restaurant's front door opened and closed with a bang. He cut a look at the clock. Class didn't start for another fifteen minutes. "Thanks for calling, Ollie. I need to get going—someone's here."

"See you soon, bro."

A moment later, RJ pushed through the swinging door. The kid's hair stood on end even more today. He had a grease stain on his gray T-shirt, and there was a red smudge on the knee of one of his pant legs. A paper bag swung from one fist.

"I hope that's ketchup." Zach gestured at RJ's leg.

RJ ducked his head. "Yeah. Sorry. I came straight from work. Today was a hard one."

"I'm sorry to hear it."

The kid shrugged. "I'm used to it. I wish I could work more, but they just cut my hours. I take every shift I can."

"I get that. But cleaning yourself up shows respect for yourself and for others." Zach put his hand on the kid's shoulder.

RJ's face brightened. "I brought you something. Tell me if it's any good. Be honest."

Inside the bag was a white foam container of soup. "Two spoons?" At the kid's nod, Zach grabbed each of them a spoon and lifted off the lid. With the first bite, an explosion of flavor hit him. "This is really good." RJ had balanced sweet yellow tomatoes with savory leeks and onions. "Seriously, this might be the best tomato soup I've ever eaten. A little browned butter in there?"

RJ ducked his head. "I'm playing with the recipe. My mom likes it, but I needed the opinion of someone who . . . isn't my mom."

"RJ, you know these classes aren't really meant for people who are serious about a career in cooking, right?" He handed him an apron. "They're more for dabblers. You seem like someone who wants more."

"I'm saving every penny that doesn't go toward my mom's rent for culinary school." RJ tied the apron on. "I was accepted at Kendall, but I couldn't afford it yet. They said there would be a place for me anytime I can come up with the tuition money."

Huh. Zach remembered those days. When his parents had cut him off because they didn't agree with his decision, he'd barely put himself through culinary school too. If it hadn't been for the scholarship . . . "Have you ever heard of the Silver Platter?" RJ shook his head. "It's a nonprofit that provides scholarships to low-income or at-risk people who are interested in pursuing a degree in Culinary Arts." He pulled out his phone and navigated to the Silver Platter's website.

Together they hunched over the small screen. Zach tapped on the Apply for Scholarship tab. The message "Awaiting Funds" in bold letters scrolled across the top of the page. In a smaller font the website informed them that they had awarded all available funds and were waiting for more generous donors.

"Well, that stinks." RJ ran a hand through his hair before shoving his hands in his pockets.

"I'm sorry, man." Zach tapped a few more areas on the website. "The Silver Platter really helped me out. It's not great to see that they're out of funds. I'm going to be in a charity cooking competition in a few days, though. The winner gets to name a charity to receive ten thousand dollars. I'd already chosen the Silver Platter even before I knew they were out of money."

Hope shone in RJ's eyes. "And you're a shoo-in to win, right?"

He laughed. "I don't know about that, but I sure hope so." Resolve straightened his back. Helping other young chefs while also securing himself a better job? Talk about a win-win. "Here, give me your cell phone number and I'll text you the info for the scholarship. Let me know if you need me to write you a reference."

As they exchanged information, the kitchen door swung open to admit the bachelorette party. Following close behind them trailed Ava Harper.

He almost admired the nerve it took her to dare show her face again. Though he noted that she'd chosen a spot farthest away from him.

Fine by him.

His conscience had nagged him all week about some of the things he'd said to her.

Okay, it probably was the Holy Spirit and not just his own conscience, but every time he thought about what she did to him, his blood felt like it was on fire. He shoved those thoughts to the back burner and pulled himself back into this class. He'd take a moment to apologize later.

"Welcome back, everyone. Tonight, we will be learning how to make a quick ratatouille, a twist on a classic French dish. You can get a ratatouille at nearly any French restaurant, but tonight's recipe is simplified for cooking at home." He'd developed this recipe for his main dish at the cooking competition, where he wouldn't have access to a gourmet kitchen, and practiced it every day this week. Now, he could almost make it in his sleep.

He watched the class chop their vegetables, guiding them as needed, then walked them through cooking the dish. He kept his distance from Ava. She didn't do too bad. She probably was exaggerating about how little she could cook. When one of the bachelorette party couldn't figure out the electronic kitchen scale, Ava showed her how to use it. Pretty soon their heads were bent together as they giggled over their ingredients. Later he spotted her soothing one of the women who was having trouble with her sauce.

The class passed in a blink. They all shared the fruits of their efforts, laughing and talking until one by one the group began to disperse.

"Ava, could you stay a moment?" Yeah, he caught the quick

widening of her eyes, but to her credit, she squared her shoulders and then nodded.

"Thank you for class tonight." She pulled her apron over her head and tossed it into the laundry basket provided. "And for not telling everyone who I am. My reputation is safe."

He waved off her words. "I have some standards. I'm not about to betray you. Even if we don't get along."

"Thanks?" Her eyes darkened. "I guess the feeling is mutual."

"Look." He ran a hand through his hair. "I don't want a fight. Actually, I wanted to apologize for how things played out last week."

Her shoulders dropped an inch. "Me too. In fact—"

"No, let me finish. I said some things that I regret. I apologize." He crossed his arms.

"Um, okay. I don't know if that's an apology, but I forgive you. Two-way street and all of that. I apologize too. I—"

Seriously? "Oh, so now you're a critic of apologies? I'm trying to do better here."

"You're right." She sighed. "I'm sorry. You just come off so . . ." She waved her hand around. "I don't want to say arrogant—"

"Then don't. I apologized. You apologized. Let's just leave it." His shoulders tightened. He rolled one, trying to release the tension.

Her phone dinged, and she stole a quick glance at it. "My ride is here, but I still have some things I want to say to you. Can we grab coffee or dinner somewhere to talk about this?"

No way he wanted to spend more time with her. "I'm leaving for an extended trip next week and have a lot to prepare beforehand, so I won't be around. Besides, I think we don't have anything more to say to each other, do we?"

She squinted her eyes at him. "I guess not." She held out her hand and he took it. "Goodbye, Chef Zach. I'll try to avoid your restaurants in the future." He shook her slim fingers once before dropping her hand and recrossing his arms. She spun on her heel and walked out of his kitchen.

And hopefully out of his life. He'd done his duty to his conscience and God and apologized. Now he could get on with the business of forgetting all about Ava Harper and focusing on the competition on Jonathon Island.

If he could win the charity competition, he could fund the Silver Platter for scholarships for kids like RJ. And if he could impress Paul Hawkeye enough in the regular competition, maybe he could even earn a spot in his kitchen. And then he could finally put down roots. He didn't even care where. Just a place that he could call home for more than a year or two. All he had to do was be flawless.

No pressure there.

Four

THE REST OF HER LIFE BEGAN TODAY.

A horn sounded on the ferry, and Ava looked out the window. Jonathon Island rose from the water in the distance. During the twenty-five-minute trip, she'd tried to ignore the faint fishy smell of the interior of this ferry boat, focusing instead on thinking through her plans for the next week and a half.

A plan that included buying the house of her dreams.

Her phone rang, and Emily's face popped up on the caller ID. "Hey, girl!" Emily said. "I'm sorry I didn't get to say goodbye before you left. Are you almost to the island?" Emily's trip to Los Angeles had been extended, and they hadn't had a chance to catch up over the past week and a half.

"Yep. Almost. I can see it out the window." She glanced out again, and a smile spread across her face. It looked picturesque under the June sun.

"How did your class go? Did you confess all to Zach?"

"No, I didn't tell him. He didn't give me a chance, in fact. Still arrogant." Ava rolled her eyes even though her friend couldn't see them. "Then my ride came. I asked to meet up with him again, and he said, quote, 'We don't have anything more to say to each other.' Unquote."

"I guess that's that, then." Emily laughed. "Unless you see him again."

"If I ever see him again, I'll give it another shot. But there's no reason for that to happen. He has a life in Chicago, and I won't be going into Escargot again. And soon, I'll have a life right here on Jonathon Island."

"I've gotta run. Good luck out there."

She ended the call with her friend, then laced her fingers behind her head and leaned back against her seat. She shoved all thoughts of Zach Sullivan out of her mind. She would forget all about the fight they'd had. And she'd definitely not spend any time thinking about his intense green eyes. She needed to concentrate on doing an amazing job here. No time for chefs with a chip on their shoulders.

The plastic of the teal seat squeaked under her as she dropped her arms and adjusted her position. A few moments later, the intercom squawked overhead.

"On behalf of everyone at Jonathon Island, we'd like to welcome you to the island. We'll be docking in just a few minutes, so please remain seated until the vessel has been secured to the dock and luggage carts have been unloaded. Please take this opportunity to collect your things. And lastly, please be courteous to your fellow passengers as you exit the ferry. Thank you and have a nice visit."

She slung the strap of her crossbody bag over her head and shoulder, then checked around her to make sure she hadn't forgotten anything. Her Realtor, Mia, had promised to greet her at the ferry landing so they could finally meet face-to-face.

Walking with the rolling gait needed on a boat, Ava made her way to the gangplank.

"Hello, Ava?" A younger woman in jeans and a light brown jacket waved at her from across the dock. Ava recognized Mia, with her long brown curls and friendly smile.

"Hi!" She waved back and crossed the few steps to Mia, dragging her luggage behind. She held out a hand, and her Realtor shook it. "You must be Mia. It's so nice to meet you."

"Nice to meet you too. Was your travel okay?" A light breeze coming off the lake ruffled Mia's hair.

"It was long, but fine." She'd been tired on the ferry, but finally seeing Jonathon Island in person felt like a shot of espresso straight to her veins.

"I'm glad you made it safely. This was perfect timing for me. My mom was able to have my kids for the morning." Ava knew from their emails back and forth that Mia had two children, a five-year-old boy and a three-year-old daughter.

"Thanks for meeting me."

Mia nodded. "Would you like to check into your room and drop off your suitcase before going to see the house? It's only a little out of the way to stop at the Grand first."

"That would be great." As eager as she was to see the house in person, lugging this suitcase around would be a pain.

"I'm thrilled you'll be here for the Flavor Fest. My cousin Dani is really excited about the festival season this year. As tourism director, she's in charge of all of that." Mia led the way up the street toward the main part of town. "It's been a long time since we've had this many tourists."

They turned left onto what looked like the main road going through the heart of downtown Jonathon Island. Ava stopped in her tracks. Main Street was just how she remembered it. Quaint, homey storefronts lined the streets. Awnings in bright colors stood over windows filled with treasures. Each one looked more delightful than the last. In the distance, she could see the top of the Grand Hotel. Her mouth lifted in a smile. She hadn't just imagined how perfect it all looked. Of course, living here would be different than vacationing here, but surely no one got tired of all of this charm?

She turned her head to look back at Lake Huron. The water sparkled in the early sunshine, each wave celebrating her arrival. Facing forward again, she caught up the few steps to Mia, and they began walking again.

"The timing was perfect for me. I was glad I spotted the festival information." Now she just needed to do the job justice and secure her remote position.

They passed by several stores. On the side of the road nearer the water, one of the signs read Martha's on Main.

She pointed to the restaurant. "Is Martha's as good as the online reviews say?"

Mia laughed. "Probably. I know I enjoy it. But you're the food critic—you'll have to decide for yourself." Mia gestured across the street. "While you're at it, you might want to check out the Fudge Shop on the Corner and Lily's Ice Cream truck. Both are local favorites."

Ava's mind spun with all of the possibilities for material for her articles. "Didn't someone write an article on the Fudge Shop on the Corner last year? Something about a contest for ownership?"

Mia laughed again. "Yep. Lily Hart and Declan Kelley were competing for ownership. Sort of a Romeo and Juliet situation, if you can believe it. The families are old rivals. Maybe more like the Hatfields and McCoys, I guess. Because Lily and Declan didn't die in a Shakespearean tragedy. They got married in January and are making fudge and ice cream together now."

Ava laughed along with Mia, her heart lifting.

Soon the Grand Sullivan Hotel loomed into view. She traced its graceful white lines with her eyes. Workmen swarmed over half of the structure while the other half looked original. A sweeping porch lined the entire front of the five-story building. A few piles of obviously charred lumber lay off to the side.

They walked up to the hotel and onto the grand porch.

"There aren't too many people staying here for the next two weeks. Mostly festival people, judges, chefs, and whatnot." Mia opened the front door. "There are only a few rooms available for use right now. As you can see, there's still a way to go in this renovation project."

"I'd heard you were rebuilding after the fire." The burning of the historic building had made national news ten years ago. Even then, it had been like a sucker punch to the belly to read about the tragedy at a place she'd visited as a child. "I can see the vision." And she could. She could picture families enjoying the veranda and picnicking on the lawn.

As they entered the lobby, a slim blonde turned from where she chatted with another woman behind the massive desk. She wore dark jeans topped with a T-shirt proclaiming *Jonathon Island First in Fudge*.

"Dani, hi! I'm glad we spotted you," Mia said. "This is Ava Harper. Ava, this is my cousin Dani."

Dani extended her hand to Ava. "Hi. Ava Harper Chows Down, right? I love your column. Looks like I dropped by at just the right time. It's nice to put a face to a name."

"It's good to meet you." Ava gave her hand a squeeze.

"I saw your name on the list for the charity competition next week." Dani clutched a clipboard to her chest. "I would have thought you'd try for the main competition. Considering your reputation, as well as your parents.'"

Ava's heart seized. "I—I'm just here to report on the festival, hopefully give Jonathon Island some good press." She tried on a smile.

"We're glad you're here." Dani's face lit up. "Actually, you could help me with something else. I need another judge for the main competition on Friday and Saturday this weekend. Since you didn't sign up for that one, would you consider being a judge?

With your review skills, you'd be great at it. Could make a good angle for your article."

Judging other people's cooking? She was back on solid ground. "I can do that. Just point me in the right direction."

"Great. There's a brief meeting tomorrow for everyone, and the contest starts the next day. Then, throughout the week, we have some cooking classes, a chili cook-off, and some other events before the big charity competition next week. Here's a list of activities." Dani unclipped a paper from her board and handed it over. "See you there." As Dani hurried out the door, Ava turned to the woman behind the desk.

"Ava Harper? Here's the key to your room. It's 207, just up the stairs." The woman handed over the credit card-shaped key with a smile. "Welcome to the Grand Sullivan Hotel."

The lobby swept upward in a two-story atrium. Lined with gorgeous wainscoting and, high above, detailed crown molding.

Ava turned to Mia. "I'll just run my things up to my room and then we can go again." Giving her luggage a tug, she headed for the grand staircase. Her feet sank into the dramatic carpet. Everything smelled new.

She hurried to her room and tucked her bag inside without stopping to look around. A few moments later, she rejoined Mia. "I'm ready, but I'm definitely taking time to explore later. This place is fantastic."

"They're doing great work restoring everything." Mia waved a hand at the furnishings. "They wanted to keep the Dorothy Draper style as much as possible. You can see it in the vivid colors and elegant lines. Dani and Liam really wanted to keep the classic look but update some things to be more modern."

"It's working." Her canvas shoes squeaked on the black-and-white tile as she followed Mia back to the front door. "Is there a restaurant here?"

"They're setting one up, but it isn't open for service yet." Mia held open the door, and the brilliant sunshine flowed in. "We can kind of take a shortcut through the lawn to Zinnia Boulevard from here, if you're up for it."

Ava's heart lifted. "I'm game. Lead the way."

"There are some beautiful gardens the other direction." Mia led her off the sweeping veranda and around the corner of the hotel. "We won't see much of that from this angle, but you should definitely check them out."

They walked through the grounds of the Grand, thick, green grass underfoot. On one side of the huge lawn, a row of canopy tents, open on three sides, flapped in the light breeze. In one large, pavilion-style tent, Ava glimpsed some portable stoves and white tables. The setup reminded her of that British baking show that was popular. Must be where the cooking competitions would take place. Passing a line of trees, they stepped onto a road.

"This is Jonathon Boulevard. The house I want to show you on Zinnia is just a little farther." Mia walked up the road.

Much like for the Grand Hotel, Ava vowed to do some exploring later. There was so much to take in. A hint of lilac hung in the air.

As they turned right onto Zinnia Lane, Ava's house waited a block or so down, a small bungalow, front door flanked with low bushes, white picket fence gleaming in the sun. Her heart began pounding in her ears. She snapped a photo and sent it to her parents.

Ava

This might be home. What do you
think?

She waited a moment but didn't get a response. Thumbing in Emily's number, she sent her the same photo. At least her friend would be in her corner.

Her phone buzzed. Yep. Emily.

Mia shot her a look and then grinned. "Excited?"

Not trusting herself to speak, Ava just nodded.

A few steps later, they were there. Mia unlocked the front door and stepped back. "I'll let you look around by yourself a few minutes." She held up her cell phone. "I need to check in with my mom and kids anyway."

Ava walked into the front room of the house. She blinked away a sudden pricking in her eyes. This home could be hers. Sure, the dated house wasn't everyone's cup of tea, but she loved it. The interior of the house looked just like the pictures, right down to the Pepto-Bismol-pink bathroom. She checked every nook and cranny, opening cupboard doors and peeking into the closets.

"Hello!" Mia's voice came from somewhere near the front door.

Ava walked out of the kitchen to find her. "My cheeks hurt from smiling. How soon can I put an offer down?"

Mia's face grew serious.

"What? Don't tell me you've already sold it. What changed in the past ten minutes?" She swallowed against a sudden tightening in her throat.

"I had a message on voicemail that there are several interested parties. There aren't usually too many houses in this price range on island, so this one is in high demand." Mia clasped her hands in front of her. "Is there any way you can put down a bigger offer?"

For her dream home? She'd scrimp all she could. She named a slightly higher number than what they'd already talked about. Her savings and the inheritance from her grandfather wouldn't stretch far. "I'm afraid that's all the higher I can afford to go." She bit at her cuticle.

"Hmm. I'll see if they're able to negotiate. But in the meantime, it might help for you to write a letter to the owners explaining why you want this house." Mia held out a brochure with the house photos and other specs on it. "Sometimes those things help. Even when the offer isn't as high as they're looking for."

Ava put a hand out to the nearby wall to steady herself. Then she took the brochure from Mia.

Sure. No problem. She made her living by writing.

Writing a letter to secure her house? How hard could it be?

From the ferry, the town of Jonathon Island looked like a movie set. It spread out before him as the ferry docked. Picture-perfect storefronts, with window boxes full of flowers, lined the streets. Several places had sandwich boards out front, advertising sales catering to the anticipated Flavor Fest crowd coming in over the weekend.

Zach took his first deep breath since the last time he was here. He walked up Marina Way and crossed onto Main Street, Jonathon Island.

"Zach!" A voice called from behind him. He whirled to see Ollie jogging toward him. "Hi! I was hoping to catch you." Ollie swiped a dark lock of hair from his forehead. He wore an Edgar Allen Poe T-shirt over his muscled frame. "I'll walk you to my place."

They turned to the right down the cobblestone road.

"Are you glad to be back so soon? Dani's wedding was only a month and a half ago." Ollie wove around a couple of tourists.

"Honestly, I'm conflicted." Zach tugged his rolling suitcase over a dip in the road. "But it's nice to be out of my suffocating job for a while."

"Is your head chef still insufferable?"

He recalled the criticism Chef Louie had given him a few days before. "He recently spat out a mouthful of a dish I'd made and told me that my sea foam was oversalted. Which is hard to believe, considering he never lets me create my own recipes and I have to follow his to a T. And he's always giving me the worst shifts."

"I'll never understand why you stay there."

"Well, the money is good. And you can't beat having Escargot and working with Chef Louie on your résumé." In the restaurant world, people expected some verbal abuse. Although if he ever had his own place again, he wouldn't tolerate it in his kitchen. "Plus, I don't really have any other options right now. At least I have a job."

"Hopefully, these two weeks will change everything for you."

"Fingers crossed." They halted for a moment to let another tourist family pass by. Their smallest child darted across the road, his mother chasing after him. "Good thing there's that rule about not having any motor vehicles here. No worrying about getting run down by a cab."

Ollie laughed. "No kidding. They should watch out for the horses, though. Conflicting feelings?"

"What?"

"You said coming home made you conflicted." Ollie waved at Patrick Kelley, who was rushing down the street in the opposite direction. The tall, slim older man was probably headed to his bar and grill, Kelley's. The Kelley family nearly had a monopoly on the food service in this town.

Zach shrugged. "I don't know. I just . . . How do you not feel like everyone is judging you all the time? Everyone knows our family's dirty secrets, Mom's affair . . . Dad burned down the hotel, for crying out loud." He tried for a smile. Hopefully Ollie didn't notice it was more like a grimace. "At least I was away at school when all the bad stuff was happening. Dani had to live here. And now you're back . . ."

Ollie shrugged. "I don't know. It's always felt like more people were caring about us than judging us. At least, once I gave them a chance."

Outside Smith's Hardware, Martha Kelley marched toward them, her hands on her heavyset hips and her gray-streaked hair frazzled. A firm line formed her mouth. "Zachary. You're back in town."

"Hi, Mrs. Kelley." He tipped his head to her. She frowned at them before passing by.

Zach raised an eyebrow at Ollie.

He threw his hand in the air. "Seriously? You can't judge the whole town based on Martha Kelley. No one ever knows what she's thinking anyway. Her face always looks like that, even when she's happy."

True. He remembered her sour face after her son took the best time in the rope climbing competition in fifth grade. "Fine. But you can't deny that people looked at us differently back then and still do. It's embarrassing."

Ollie crossed his arms. "Is that why you never come back to the island except under extreme protest?" He held up a hand. "Don't say it. I know you came back for Dani's wedding, but we all know it was only because Dani called you and begged."

"Look, Ollie, the truth is, a small part of me wishes I could come back home for good. But also, this place hasn't felt like home in a long time." In fact, nowhere felt like home. After finding out that his parents had split and he didn't have a place to come back to, he'd bounced around the country. Nothing ever seemed to stick. "Add in the judgmental—" He held up a hand to ward off Ollie's rebuttal. "Fine—the curious looks of everyone—I just need to forge my own path. I've been doing that for a while now, and it's all I know."

Ollie crossed his arms. "I dunno, man. I think it's all in your head. And I have almost two weeks to prove it to you." He moved ahead for a few steps. Zach gave his bag another tug over yet another cobblestone and followed.

"Wait up." He jogged a few steps. "The town looks amazing. It's even better than when I was here for Dani's wedding."

"Yeah, it's pretty great seeing tourists coming back. And most of the businesses are full too."

"Our little sister has done a great job. I'm proud of her." They walked in silence until they reached the bookstore. Zach trailed behind Ollie up the back stairs into his small apartment. "This looks even better than a few weeks ago too."

"I have to admit, the renovations were worth it." Ollie paused inside his door and put a hand to his hip. The butter-yellow walls on the large open layout contrasted with the white oak laminate flooring throughout.

"You have some new furniture. Last time I was here, I think you only had that couch and a bookshelf." Zach waved a hand toward Ollie's oversized beige couch. Now a low coffee table sat in front of the couch and a few end tables flanked it.

"Hey." Ollie moved into the room. "I also had a bed *and* a chair."

"Okay, okay. Please tell me you've also got some good cookware in that tiny kitchen of yours."

"It's not tiny—it's just not the size of the restaurant kitchens you're used to. And if you're going to insult my cookware"—Ollie raised an eyebrow at Zach—"you don't have to stay here."

"Fine." Zach held both hands in the air, palms forward. "You're right." He laughed. "I'll make up for it by cooking dinner a few times while I'm back."

"In that case"—Ollie walked a few steps into the apartment—"the couch is all yours." A stack of sheets and blankets sat on one corner of the couch. "Dad decided to stay at the hotel, so it's yours for as long as you want. I'll give you a key so you can come and go as you please."

Wait. What? "Dad is here?" Zach's stomach tightened.

"Not yet. But he'll be here in a day or two. I think he's staying for the whole festival." Ollie handed him a key. "He and Mom have started getting along again. Dani said he asked her to keep a room for him for several weeks throughout the summer and fall."

His voice was nonchalant. As if this wasn't the biggest bombshell he could have dropped.

"What do you mean, Mom and Dad are getting along again?" Zach ran a hand along the back of his neck. "You can't just drop that bomb. What's going on?"

Ollie sighed. "They started talking again at Dani's wedding. It took me a while to believe that either one of them wanted to be here." His mouth turned up on one side. "I guess they're friends now? I don't know. I try to stay out of it. But Dad's been coming back to Jonathon Island every once in a while." He shrugged.

Huh. "Maybe he wants to make amends?"

"Maybe. Anyway, I need to get going. I left Eliza alone in the store." Ollie reached out and punched him lightly in the shoulder. "Thanks for coming. The Flavor Fest is going to be so busy. It'll be good to have you around."

After he left, Zach dropped onto the couch.

Mom and Dad were getting along? How was Dad not still bitter about Mom's affair? How was Mom able to forgive Dad for nearly burning down the hotel? Not to mention never being around in the first place.

On the coffee table lay a flyer. He picked it up. "Flavor Fest" streamed across the top in a large font. He flipped it open and found the schedule of events for the next few days inside.

His heart rate picked up. This was what he needed to concentrate on. Winning the contests he was part of. No time to be distracted by his family drama. He had to focus if he wanted to make his dreams, and potentially the dreams of anyone earning the Silver Platter scholarship, come true.

Five

ONE MEASLY LETTER TO SECURE HER DREAMS.
How hard could it be? Hopefully, the homeowners hadn't
received any more offers since she'd seen the place yesterday.

Ava rummaged through the desk drawer in her hotel room.
After a sleepless night, she'd vowed to write the best letter of her
life. If that's what it took, that's what she would do. She'd wow the
socks off the owners of her dream house.

Her hand brushed the edge of a pad of paper, and she drew it
out of the drawer. The Grand Sullivan Hotel letterhead featured
an artist's sketch of the new Grand Hotel.

Perfect.

But first, coffee. Daylight streamed through the split in her
room's curtains. Gathering up her purse and the notepad, she made
her way out of the room. A beautiful day for a walk downtown.
She'd try out the lattes at Good Day Coffee. They were on her list
to review, anyway. Good thing Emily wasn't here to make her run
for the privilege of drinking them.

She opened the door and nearly ran into a young woman, probably in her late teens, in the hall. The woman wore a high messy bun and steered a cleaning cart featuring a stack of towels that threatened to tip over. A name tag declared her to be Olive.

"Oh. Sorry. I was about to knock," the young woman said. "Did you need services? Or clean towels?"

"I'll take a few fresh towels, thank you, but no need to clean the room or anything." Ava accepted a stack of towels. They were pillowy soft and still smelled new. She dumped them on a table just inside her room and then stepped out into the hall, closing her door behind her. Along the far wall of the hallway ran a line of photographs. "I didn't notice these last night when I checked in." She walked over to them.

"Yeah, they hung those up after they finished renovating this section," Olive said. "Like a history of the town or something."

Ava looked closer. She recognized a few local landmarks from her brief tour yesterday and from scouring the internet to find out more about Jonathon Island. One of the photos snagged her gaze, a familiar-looking dark-haired man surrounded by several others playing in the water. Then another of the same group in front of the hotel.

That was strange. "Do you know who the people in this photo are?" She tapped on the one in front of the hotel.

Olive looked at the photo Ava indicated. "Oh. That's the Sullivan family. The picture must have been taken before the hotel burned down. This is Zach, Oliver, and I think James. This one is Ashley, maybe? And their parents are in the back, Daniel and Becky . . ." The girl leaned close to the photo. "I don't remember all of them."

"Were they here on vacation?"

Olive gave her a puzzled look. "The Sullivans?"

Ava nodded.

"You do know this place is called the Grand Sullivan Hotel,

right?" The girl stopped just short of sarcasm in her tone. "They own the hotel. They live here. Or I guess they used to. Now it's just Dani." She tapped the face of the youngest girl in the photo. "Well, and Kate and Oliver."

Sure, she knew Dani Sullivan-Stone, obviously. She'd seen her name when she mailed in her application for the charity cooking competition, and when she'd done some preliminary research on Jonathon Island. As tourism director, Dani's name was all over the place. Ava just hadn't thought the similarity in last names—check that, the same last name—meant she and Zach were siblings.

Or that Zach was from Jonathon Island.

"Are you okay?" Olive put a hand on her arm. "You zoned out there for a second."

Ava plastered a smile on her face. "Fine. Thank you. Sorry." She adjusted her purse strap. "Thank you for answering my questions about these." She gestured at the wall of photos. "Now it's time for coffee."

"Oh, my Aunt Jill owns Good Day. I work there too when I'm not here. I'm Olive Kelley. You'll run into a lot of Kelleys on the island." Olive pushed her cart a foot, then stopped. "If you tell Aunt Jill I sent you, you might get a discount. See ya."

So what if Jonathon Island used to be Zach's home? He lived in Chicago now. No reason to think she would ever have to see him.

The daylight streaming onto the back terrace through the floor-to-ceiling windows beckoned to her, and she went out that way. She still needed to find a unique angle for her article series. Small-town festival? That seemed cliché, even if true. Maybe something about the return of the glories of Jonathon Island.

She paused halfway across the brick patio to jot down her ideas. Still not quite right. Her editor wouldn't ever approve her remote work if she didn't knock this one out of the park. Hopefully the festival would produce something so interesting she couldn't fail.

From the patio, she could see some of the festival tent canopies lining the side of the hotel. Their edges rippled in the slight breeze. A short detour on her way to coffee might be a good idea. That way she could scope things out before the crowds started to arrive. Maybe a good angle for her article would crop up.

The festival booths lined up along one central walkway, with a few dotting the rest of the side lawn. Several displayed banners proclaiming the name of the business using them. One read Good Day Coffee. Fudge Shop on the Corner was emblazoned across another. On the other side, a fish and chips stand nestled next to an omelet booth. A food truck boldly proclaiming to have the best ice cream on Jonathon Island was parked at the end. That must be the ice cream truck Mia had mentioned. By the looks of it, the festival staff had arranged all the food booths down this strip, and the others on the outskirts held other types of vendors.

At the far end and off to the side stood the huge pavilion-style tent where the cooking competitions were going to be. About twenty people milled around under the canopy, but the rest of the festival grounds were deserted.

Dani's distinctive laugh rolled toward her. So, the island's tourism director was somewhere in that tent. This would be a great time to do a little interview for the article. They hadn't had much time to chat last night.

As she walked closer, several people unloaded crates from a trailer connected to a dray wagon. The grassy tops of carrots flopped over the side of one black crate. Another looked like it held gallons of milk.

"Ava!" Dani's voice rang out from behind her, and she whirled toward it. The tourism director stood in a shaft of sunlight. Her casual jeans and Jonathon Island Flavor Fest T-shirt were perfect for the warmth of the beginning of June. "I'm happy to see you. Come and meet everyone." Dani looped her arm through Ava's and started pointing out the people around them.

A roar in Ava's head drowned out all the words Dani spoke. A dark-haired man bent to pluck a crate of cabbages from the cart. His muscles flexed under the short sleeves of his red T-shirt and along his back. He turned toward them. A flash of green eyes and high cheekbones confirmed what she suspected.

Zach.

Beside her, Dani trailed off.

A pressure on Ava's arm made her look at her companion. Dani had grabbed her bicep in addition to the arm she still had crooked around her elbow. Dani's eyes traveled between her and Zach. "Ava, is everything okay? You look pale. Do you need to sit down?"

"I'm fine." Not fine. Her mouth had dried. She really needed that coffee. "I, um, should really get going."

"Now? But you just got here. Let me at least introduce you to my brother." She tugged Ava forward.

Her skin cooled in the shade of the tent before warming again as they drew up next to Zach.

"Ava, this is my brother Zach. He's a chef competing in the cooking challenge. Zach, this is Ava. She'll be one of the judges." Dani dropped her hold on Ava's arm. Too bad because now Ava felt lightheaded enough to float away. Not only did Zach find her to be some sort of mortal enemy, he also knew her secret.

Zach narrowed his eyes. "One of the judges?"

Dani laughed, the sound light and airy in the air grown thick as roux. "Yep." She looked at Ava. "You have to promise not to give him special treatment just because he's my brother."

Zach barked out a noise that from someone else might have been a laugh. "I don't think we're in any danger of that."

What happened to his apology the last time they were together? Sure, she hadn't wanted to ever run into him again, but this was getting ridiculous.

Dani kept looking from one of them to the other. "Wait. Do you two know each other?"

Ava nodded. "I took his cooking class in Chicago." It wasn't up to her to let Zach's family know the rest of their history. If he wanted Dani to know, he could fill her in.

"Well then, you really will have a difficult time remaining unbiased. You already know what a great cook he can be . . ." Dani's tone was light, but Zach's intense glower seemed to talk her out of continuing her thought.

"I definitely know how good of a chef he is." Would Zach hear the apology in her words? She'd never really gotten to tell him how sorry she was for the events in Seattle. "Not only that, but he's a good teacher too." She tried for a smile. Failed. "There was a young guy there that Zach really took under his wing. I think he inspired all of us."

Zach's eyes lightened at her words. He cleared his throat. "Thanks for saying that." While his tone still wasn't exactly friendly, it was certainly less rough than a minute ago.

She had to get out of here. "It's true." She shifted her feet toward the entrance of the tent. "Well, I'd better run. Coffee is calling. Good to see you again, Dani. I'd love to set up an interview soon with you about your vision for this festival." She nodded at Zach before spinning on her heel and heading toward what she hoped was the waterfront.

Suddenly the assignment from her newspaper wasn't the only thing she was worried about. Now she also had to make sure Zach didn't reveal her secret. He could ruin everything.

So much for a quiet trip home. Zach looked around him, certain the world had shifted in the twenty-four hours he'd been on Jonathon Island. First, the bombshell about Dad being here, and now his nemesis, Ava.

Okay. Maybe not nemesis. But he found he couldn't think clearly when she was around. The old anger and bitterness he felt tangled up with his growing realization that she was a genuinely nice person. Bold and honest, but nice. Helping the other students in class, laughing and chatting all the time. Her easygoing friendliness had made the class run smoother, despite his prickliness toward her.

He looked over the people milling about, setting up all of the cooking spaces in this tent. He was definitely not watching Ava walk away. A morning breeze fluttered the edges of the tent flap. A beautiful Jonathon Island morning. If he listened closely, he could hear—or maybe just imagined—waves lapping at the shore not too far away. Under his feet, the spongy grass gave off a spring scent. He had spent the morning helping the volunteer festival crew unload the supplies for the cooking contest coming the next few days.

He tugged out the final crate from the cart. "Where do you want this?"

Cody Hart, the twentysomething fisherman engaged to Zach's cousin Mia, lifted his ball cap and ran a hand over his forehead. His dirty-blond hair ruffled in the breeze. "That one can go near the central refrigerator. Thanks for all your help."

Zach nodded. He wove his way through the groups of people tangling up the main walkway in the pavilion until he reached the central area. A pantry of sorts was taking shape as a few women unloaded everything. All the ingredients for the cooking contests were provided by Flavor Fest. After being prepped here, the festival committee would place the ingredients into the contestant's cooking station before the contest began each day. He'd already submitted his list for the first competition, but he'd need to submit the one for the charity competition by midweek in order for the ingredients to be available for him the following weekend. He recognized Allean Meyer, the librarian, with one of her signature crazy hats—a chef's toque today—and Janine Dirks, red hair and ever-present sweater. Dani had mentioned they were both on the committee.

"Ladies." He lifted the crate a little. "Where do you want this?"

"Oh, Zach. Thank you so much." Allean smiled at him. "You can just set it there by the crate of milk."

"I'm happy to help." Working as a team felt . . . nice. In the hustle of a professional kitchen, at least one run by Chef Louie, the sense of camaraderie was missing. Even surrounded by people working and shouting and all with the same goal, a professional kitchen could be lonely. "What else can I do for you?"

"I think we're good," Janine said. "In fact, you should probably make yourself scarce. We'll be setting up the individual cooking stations soon. We want to have that finished before the meeting in"—she glanced at her watch—"a little less than an hour. We can't have you hanging around gathering intel on what the other contestants are planning."

"Yeah. Shoo," Allean said. She waved a finger at him, ever the librarian. "I'm sure a chef as accomplished as you could figure out a lot about the dishes of your competition just by looking at the ingredients they requested."

He grinned at her. "Rats. You've discovered my plan. Here I thought I was being so sneaky."

Laughter rang out from the ladies as he walked away. Time to check out his own workspace. Dani had promised he would have everything he needed. What he really needed was to figure out what to do about Ava.

When Dani got back, he would definitely have to have a word with her. Sure, maybe it wasn't her fault. She probably didn't remember that Ava was the food critic who had taken him down. Maybe he could convince her to uninvite Ava Harper.

He shook his head. That would never work. They didn't have enough time to find a replacement. He would just have to suffer through having Ava as his judge. Again. At least this time she would be ruled by the criteria of the contest and not just her personal opinion of him and his cooking. Plus, she would have two other judges to balance her out.

He refocused on the task at hand, picking up his recipe card. He studied it for any mistakes. Satisfied, he took the card over to the cooking plate.

Another cool breeze lifted the edge of the tent, carrying with it a breath of the unique scent of Lake Huron, just out of sight on the other side of the hotel. Fishy and loamy with a hint of wet sand.

He glanced up, and his thoughts stuttered to a stop. His dad strode across the grass toward him. His tanned face beaming above a crisp white polo shirt and navy-blue slacks.

"Zach! I thought that was you." His dad ducked into the tent and reached for him. Did he want a hug? Zach stuck out his hand.

"Dad." Outside of Dani's wedding, he hadn't seen his dad in months, and he had avoided talking to him much at the wedding. While his mom had betrayed his dad with an affair, his dad had betrayed them all with his actions with the hotel. But then, he'd been aloof and unavailable for most of Zach's life, so Zach had given up trying to be chummy with him.

"Dani told me you were competing. I'll be sure to come and watch." His dad crossed his arms.

Really? Since when was he interested in Zach's profession? "Great, Dad. Thanks." He gestured at the table in front of him. "I've really got to get back to . . ."

A few people Zach didn't recognize made their way to the cooking stations at the other side of the tent.

His dad uncrossed his arms and then rapped the table with a knuckle. "Look, Zach. I hope we get some time to talk while you're here. But if not—"

Zach held up a hand. "No worries, Dad. We don't need some big conversation."

"No, really, Zach. I want to apologize. I'm really proud of how far you've come with this cooking thing. I wish I'd been supportive of you back when you were in school." His dad raised an arm like he was going to put it around Zach, but then dropped it again.

Zach lifted a shoulder and let it fall. "I managed." His dad's words at the time came back to him. *What do you want to waste your life cooking for? There's no way I'm going to pay for that. Come work with me instead.* Zach had refused, and his dad had refused to give him any money for school. "I got a scholarship from an organization called the Silver Platter."

"I'm glad you figured it out, despite my shortcomings." His dad ducked his head. "Maybe I'll have to look into this Silver Platter. Sounds like a good group."

Too little, too late, Dad. But he was supposed to be working on forgiveness. He rolled his shoulders forward and then back again before relaxing them.

"I know I've never come to your restaurants, but I always recommend them when I hear of friends traveling to your area." His dad chuckled. "Of course, it was hard to keep up with where you were at all the time. Maybe someday you'll be ready to put down roots."

Roots. Longing tugged at Zach's heart. Roots would be good. Amazing even. If only he could find a place that felt like home.

"Anyway, the friends who took my recommendations always came back with glowing reports."

"I'm glad they liked the food." Zach's chest expanded as he took a full breath. "Maybe someday I'll open my own place again. Then they can taste some of my original recipes and not someone else's."

"Whenever you're ready for that, I'd like to talk to you about investing." His dad's smartwatch buzzed, and he glanced at it. "Speaking of investing, I'd better check this email. Let's talk some more later, son."

Zach blinked several times as his dad made his way out of the tent. What even was all of that? His dad had asked for forgiveness, but Zach would need more time.

A tapping sound came over the speakers installed around the

tent. He looked to the center stage. Uncle Seb Jonathon—Mom's brother—was tapping at the microphone. Arranged around him was the Jonathon Island Flavor Fest committee. He didn't see any of the judges.

"If the contestants could come to the stage for a brief meeting, we'd like to get started," Uncle Seb said. As mayor of Jonathon Island, Seb would be Master of Ceremonies for the Flavor Fest activities.

A general murmur rose as everyone converged on the stage.

Uncle Seb, casual today, his shoulders broad under a light-blue short-sleeve button-up, laid out the plan for the next day. They would begin with an opening meeting and then there would be three rounds for the contest.

"You should have all prepared to cook an appetizer, a main dish, and a dessert," Uncle Seb said.

Around him, the other contestants nodded. Zach took a minute to assess them. It appeared to be a mix of local talent and some from outstate. He recognized Henrietta Hudson, the white-haired retired baker. She wouldn't be too much competition. Next to her, Patrick Kelley from Kelley's Bar & Grill squared up. The slim man with a bristling mustache already wore an apron. He would be one to watch. He was used to cooking under pressure. Three other women and two men made up the rest of the group. He didn't recognize any of them, but one woman, short, blonde, and probably ten years older than his thirty-six, wore a T-shirt with *Alicia's Kitchen* embroidered on the pocket, and one of the men had a cap with Moosehead Crossings. He knew those were two popular restaurants across the lake in Port Joseph.

Onstage, Uncle Seb was wrapping up. "Good luck to each of you. Whatever happens tomorrow, I'm sure the food will be amazing."

Zach would be bringing his A game. His future depended on it.

Six

ONE DAY TO PROVE HIMSELF. AT LEAST THE weather was cooperating. Zach looked out the rectangular window at Ollie's overlooking Main Street. The early morning sunlight glinted off the red awning on the building opposite.

His smartwatch buzzed an alarm. Time to make his dreams come true.

He swung his chef's white jacket off its hanger and made his way through town and to the festival grounds.

Patrick Kelley, mustache bristling, was setting out plates on his booth. "Hi, Zach! How are you feeling about today?"

"Confident, but hopefully not overconfident. I know I've got some tough competition, including you." After the meeting for the contestants broke up last night, he'd learned the names of two more. Kim Beebe from Trixie's and Enrique Perez from Fiesta.

"Yep. It's a good lineup. I'm not sure if I'll be much competition, but Val Anderson is a chef at Lion and Dragon. I hear they're up for a Michelin Star." Patrick reached under his booth and set out more plates. "You're not planning to stay on island, are you? With your skills, you'll give Kelley's a lot of competition. Do I have to worry about that?"

"Nah. No worries there." He wasn't ever moving back to this island. He wouldn't have even come back if Dani hadn't lured him in with the talk of impressing Paul Hawkeye and Anne Green. Maybe even to impress one of them enough to earn a permanent place in their kitchen. "I've got my eye on a different prize."

Over Patrick's shoulder, he spotted Ava positioned near his station. "Will you excuse me?" Not waiting for a reply, he dashed across the lawn to the cooking tent.

Ava stood with her back to him. "Ava, why are you lurking at my table?"

She whirled to him. Her eyes widened. "Lurking?" She put a hand to her hip. "I wasn't lurking."

"Sure could've fooled me." He was going for teasing, but his words came out hot. "I saw you hanging around my table. Are you looking for a way to sabotage me?"

Color crept up into her cheeks. "I *wasn't* lurking. Or looking to sabotage you." She dropped her arm and pinched her lips together for a moment. "I was trying to—"

"Trying to what?"

"Why are you always accusing me of things?" Her eyes flashed.

Shoot. She was right. He crossed his arms. "Sorry. Continue."

"I wanted to wish you luck. We're stuck together for a while, and I was trying for nice." She knit her fingers together at her stomach. "You're always assuming the worst about me. I'm a good person."

Oof. Now he really felt like a jerk. "I always seem to start on the wrong foot with you. I'm sorry. Again."

A smile spread across her face. "Forgiven." She reached out a hand to him. He took it and his mouth dried.

Boy, he was more nervous about this contest than he thought.

"Everything okay?" Ava's brow crinkled.

"Fine. Why?" He swallowed hard.

"I just would like my hand back."

He dropped his gaze to their hands. Had he rubbed his thumb across the back of hers? He let go as though she were the handle of a red-hot skillet.

Tucking the traitorous appendages into the pockets of his blue jeans, he went for nonchalant. "I'd better get my station set up. Big day." He brushed past her and concentrated on keeping his gaze firmly on his cooking equipment. When he finally turned around again, she'd disappeared.

Good thing too, because it would take all of his attention to perfect the appetizers he'd chosen for the first round. He'd made the sauerkraut meatballs many times, but they were very fussy. He'd decided to turn them into sliders for easier eating. He'd also chosen to make a quick ketchup and a horseradish sauce.

A squeal came through a speaker hanging nearby. "Contestants to the judges' table, please." Zach recognized his Uncle Seb's voice over the PA system again.

"Gather 'round, everyone," Uncle Seb said as the crowd surged to the center stage. Zach found a spot near the center. Seb briefly recapped the rules before introducing the judges. Joining Ava on the judging panel were the two chefs Zach wanted to impress. Paul Hawkeye stood with his arms crossed over his wide chest, signature silver hair cropped close to his head. Anne Green stood next to him, her petite frame dwarfed by the other chef. Her blonde head barely made it to his shoulder.

"Chef Hawkeye has asked permission to say a few words before we get started." Uncle Seb stepped away from the mic and gestured for Chef Hawkeye to take his place.

"Thank you, Seb." Chef Hawkeye nodded to Seb before turning back to the gathered crowd. "I love cooking competitions. I enjoy competing in them, but even more I enjoy judging them. Maybe because I have such strong opinions." A laugh rumbled through the crowd. "Seriously, though, these things are always a place to taste great food and to find new talent. That is why I've decided to add another layer to this contest. I'm prepared to offer a six-month internship, with the option to turn that internship into a full-time job at the Farm, to the winner of today's competition."

The crowd broke into a cheer.

Zach's heart sped. An internship at the Farm, Chef Hawkeye's flagship restaurant in San Diego, California, would be a dream come true.

Onstage, Chef Hawkeye clasped both hands on the mic. "So, to each of you competing today, put your heart into it. Take risks. Wow me. Go make something amazing. I believe in each of you."

Zach joined the crowd in a cheer before pushing his way through to his station. He'd just tied his apron around his waist when the starting bell sounded over the loudspeaker.

All eight of the cook stations under the tent were set up the same. Two long white tables formed two sides, while a makeshift pantry and dish cupboard formed the third. At the back, making the fourth wall of the station, was a small fridge, blast chiller, single-basket deep fryer, oven, and stovetop.

Zach picked up the recipe card for his sauerkraut sliders. He took a deep breath and squared his shoulders, then began gathering his ingredients. As he tossed his corned beef, cooked ham, and onion into a food processor, Chef Hawkeye's words rang in his ears. *Take risks.* How could he change up this dish to be even more edgy? He looked at his pantry, fully stocked with the ingredients he'd asked for. Not much wiggle room for spontaneous creativity. There! Two kinds of sauerkraut were lined up at the back. The original recipe called for regular sauerkraut, but he would add the red cabbage kraut instead. A brighter flavor, it would hopefully put his recipe over the top. He carefully measured out the kraut and added it into the processor, giving the whole thing a few pulses to combine. Then he tossed in several garlic cloves and a tablespoon of flour and added a few more pulses.

After the meat mixture was finished, he would turn them into sliders, dredging them in more flour and giving them a quick fry. He would plate them on Hawaiian rolls with horseradish and ketchup dipping sauces.

What the . . . ? Flecks of green and blue ran through his meat mixture. That wasn't right. He wiped his forehead with the back of his hand. His stomach cramped.

How did it get so hot in here? Too bad there wasn't a cool spring breeze coming off Lake Huron this morning. He grabbed a clean spoon and tasted the meat mixture. Hmm. A little salty, but otherwise fine. The frying process should even that out. Maybe it would take care of the weird colors too. Garlic sometimes did that when exposed to acid.

People milled about in the aisles between the cooking stations. Amid the din of voices, he could hear Ava chatting with some locals. He glanced up toward the sound of her voice. Her head was bent over a notebook as she jotted something down.

Looking back down at the bowl in front of him, he began forming the meat mixture into balls before flattening them into patties.

"Chef Zach, can you tell me a little about your dish?" Ava's voice jolted him from the rhythm he'd developed.

He glanced up again. Her gray eyes held curiosity, not animosity. "I'm making sauerkraut sliders."

"I don't think I've ever heard of sauerkraut sliders. Can you tell me a little more?" She had her pen poised above her notebook. He'd never heard her use that tone of voice before. Stilted, formal. Not her usual warmth.

"Is this for a newspaper article?"

Her cheeks pinked. "Yes. I originally came here to turn in a series of articles on the festival. Do you mind?"

He shoved aside the sudden irritation. "It's fine." He scooped up another spoonful of mix. "I first had these at a church potluck in Austin. I've modified them and added my own spin. I like to think I've elevated them." Shoot. That sounded so arrogant. "I mean, I've changed them up to appeal more to chefs like Paul and Anne." That wasn't much better, but at least the soundbite focused on the celebrities here.

Ava's wide-open gaze held him in place. She'd stopped writing. "You go to church?"

A band tightened around his chest. Yeah, he hadn't treated her like a man who believed in Jesus. "I try to. When I don't have a Sunday shift." Man, he really needed to be better at living out his faith. He believed in forgiveness, really, he did. But the grudge against Ava had been in his heart for so long. "Ava, I—" The alarm on his hot oil sounded. Time to get these patties in the fryer. This conversation would have to wait.

"Go." She waved him off. "I should get in a few more interviews anyway."

Working quickly, he dredged the patties in flour, then dropped them into the fryer. They foamed and bubbled. A moment later, they turned a beautiful golden brown. He set them aside to drain under the heat lamp.

Pulling six square plates from the shelf on his workstation, he dotted the horseradish sauce along one corner, then the ketchup. There. Excellent.

The five-minute buzzer sounded. He tuned out everything around him as he assembled his tiny sandwiches and got them on the plate.

A few minutes later all three judges stood in front of his space.

"Judges, I have sliders as my appetizer for you today." Zach's stomach tightened as the judges tried his dish. Paul grimaced and swallowed hard. Anne discreetly wiped her lips with a napkin, but he thought he spotted the bite of slider in the paper as she pulled it away from her mouth.

He glanced at Ava. Her eyes were wide, and her mouth formed a frown.

"Ah. Thank you, Zach." Paul tapped the table. "That was certainly an experience."

Zach heard the words, but they sounded a lot like the noise his dreams made when crashing to the ground.

What happened to Zach Sullivan, master chef? Ava needed a glass of water—and soon. The bite she'd taken of his appetizer was . . . not good. They'd been forced to give him the lowest score, and the blow had been obvious in the shock on his face. Did he really not know how terrible it had tasted? He'd need to make up a lot of points on the entrée and dessert rounds tomorrow to make up for it.

She'd eaten so many good appetizers this morning before ending up at Zach's table.

Now the crowd around them faded away as Zach turned an intense gaze on her. Whoa. Were his eyes always that dark green? He cocked one eyebrow at her.

"What did you think of my slider?"

"I, um . . ." She licked her lips, and his gaze flicked down at them. "It wasn't great." Really, what was she supposed to say? *It was the worst thing I have ever put into my mouth. I regret it with the regret of a thousand ants who join a picnic only to find out all the food is made with artificial sweetener.* Probably not.

"I already got the lowest score. Whatever you say won't be a shock to me." Zach picked up a towel and wiped his hands. "I want to know what you really thought of it."

Honesty would not be the best policy here, but she couldn't lie either. "I think it was the worst thing I've ever eaten."

A murmur began around her. She glanced left, then right. The audience who had been milling around the tent began to gather in a semicircle in front of Zach's cooking station.

A muscle jumped in Zach's jaw. "The worst thing, eh? C'mon, it couldn't have been that bad. There's loads of terrible food in the world." His eyes held amusement.

"One time, I had an assignment to cover the cooking class at a local high school. One of the kids made pasta and thought they could substitute ketchup for spaghetti sauce. That was better than this."

At her right elbow, a woman in a purple Flavor Fest T-shirt said, "Ooooh, are you gonna take that, chef?"

A lazy smile walked across Zach's face. He put his hands on the workspace and leaned toward Ava and the gathered crowd.

Was it hot in here?

"I happen to really like ketchup with my pasta."

"After tasting this appetizer, I can see why," she shot back. "You've obviously lost your sense of taste. Maybe you left your taste buds back home in Chicago?"

"You go!" someone called out from the back of the crowd.

There was no one standing near any of the other contestants anymore. They'd all massed around her.

"If I'd known there was going to be this much action, I wouldn't have disagreed with you about whether we should come," one man said to the woman he had his arm around. "This is actually fun."

Zach put his hands up. "Okay, I'll admit that wasn't my best effort. But any good cook knows you have to take risks to make something worthwhile."

"I'm sorry to break it to you, but that wasn't a risk worth taking." Ava put a hand to her hip. Was she actually enjoying this? Who was Zach Sullivan? Certainly not the person she'd thought he was. "And this is probably a silly question, but did you even taste your dish before plating it?"

"I didn't have time." Zach rubbed a hand along the back of his neck, leaving one lock curled out of place. Ava fought the sudden urge to smooth it back. "I didn't realize I would be interrupted so often, and I ran out of time."

That made sense. She wasn't the only judge who'd gone around asking the contestants about what they were doing. "And what about since then?"

"Yeah," someone hollered from amid the crowd. "Taste it!"

Others chimed in. Ava's stomach sank a little. Was it wrong that she was starting to feel bad for Zach? A muscle in his jaw jumped again.

"I don't negotiate with terrorists." A sparkle lit his eye as he spoke. He shook his head. "I don't need to taste it to know it was fine." He crossed his arms, the challenge evident.

"I hate to break it to you, bub, but coming dead last is a good indication that you are wrong." She crossed her arms too.

Now the crowd began to chant. "Eat it! Eat it!"

She held her breath.

His shoulders relaxed, and the hint of a smile appeared at the corner of his mouth. "Fine. I'll eat it." The crowd began to cheer, but he silenced them by raising his hands, palms out. "I will eat it, but only if Ava eats some too and tells me what's wrong with it." He raised one eyebrow.

She swallowed hard.

"You're on." She uncrossed her arms and nodded once. "Do you have some more stashed back there?"

"I happen to have one left." Zach turned to the back of his cooking station and cut the last slider in half. He plated the halves, added horseradish and ketchup, grabbed two clean forks, and handed one of the plates to Ava.

Ava speared the sandwich, dipped it in the horseradish and ketchup, then raised a brow at Zach. "At the same time?"

He'd done the same with his portion. "You're on."

The crowd around them began counting down from five. When

they reached one, Ava closed her eyes and popped the bite into her mouth. Everyone cheered.

She gagged. Yep. It was still terrible. Salty and metallic. And now it was cold too.

She opened her eyes. Zach's mouth was pulled into a frown. His eyes glittered. She forced herself to swallow. "Are those tears in your eyes?"

Zach's Adam's apple bobbed. He wiped his mouth. "That was so bad." He laughed. "I didn't think I'd be able to swallow it."

"Not to gloat, but I told you so."

The crowd began to disperse.

"Yeah, yeah. Don't rub it in." Zach tossed his dirty fork into a tub of sudsy water. "I don't get it, though. How could adding red cabbage instead of regular change it that much?"

Ava shrugged. "You're the chef, but I'd say there was an unexpected chemical reaction. Did you see how the color was all off?"

Zach rubbed the back of his neck. "I think the garlic turned green and the cabbage turned blue. That can happen with acids and alkaline ingredients. But that doesn't explain that metallic flavor." He poured them both a glass of water from the pitcher on his backline. "Here. Swish."

She swallowed the water in one gulp. "Thanks. So salty."

"Me or the food?" He raised an eyebrow at her.

"Har har." Amusement burbled up in her.

"I'm sorry I'm so prickly around you." He tucked his hands into his pockets.

"What?" She opened her eyes wide. "I hadn't noticed." His lips tightened and she relented, giving him a wink.

"Har har," he mimicked her. His gaze bored into her. A tightness crept across her shoulders. "I mean it. I feel like I'm always apologizing to you. But I—"

"Zach!" Dani wove through the crowd toward them. "I have an emergency, and I need your help."

Ava's shoulders relaxed. Dani had provided her a way out of this intense conversation. She backed away a step.

Dani caught her arm. "Please, stay. I think you can help me out too. You two can be my superheroes."

Help Dani out and become a superhero? How could she say no to that? "What do you need?"

"I just found out that a couple of people for the teams portion of the charity contest had to drop out." Dani's knuckles were white as she clutched a clipboard. She looked at Zach. "I have to totally rejigger the contest. I thought since you two already know each other . . ."

Zach crossed his arms. "I think I can see where this is going."

Dani blew a stray hair out of her eye. "So, will you do it?"

"Do what?" Unlike Zach, Ava had no idea where this was going.

"Compete in the charity competition." Dani brought her hands, still clutching the clipboard, up under her chin in a mock prayer pose. "Please, I'm begging you." She made a comical puppy dog face at her brother.

Zach laughed. "You don't have to look at me like that. You know I can't say no to you. I'm here, aren't I?"

This obviously had nothing to do with her. She was already doing the charity competition. Dani must have someone in mind to pair up with Zach. It looked like he was going to be the super-hero. Ava began backing away again.

Dani turned the puppy dog eyes toward her. "Is that okay with you?"

"Me?" Why did she have to give the okay? Zach was an adult. He could make his own decisions. "Me what?"

"Do the competition. As a team. A pair of chefs working to-gether. I know you signed up to do the singles portion, but I really need another couple's team. I thought since you two know each other, you might want to be on a team." Dani's tone turned plead-ing. "I saw you two just now. The crowd was eating it up. If you can bring that energy next week, it could really help. I could even whip up some new advertising for it." She traced a hand across the sky like she could read the ad up there. "Come and see the island's odd couple. Will they cook up something great, or will they grate each other apart?" Dani waved a hand between her and Zach. "You have chemistry."

Ava's face went hot. "I think—"

"Not *chemistry* chemistry." Dani laughed. "I mean the banter between the two of you just now. If you bring that to the charity competition, we could really draw some crowds."

Ava blinked at her, but Zach chuckled. "I think your slogan needs some work." He uncrossed his arms. "I didn't realize that the charity competition had a team event. I would have brought a partner."

"And now you don't have to," Dani said. "Ava can be your partner. I'll work on the slogan. It'll be great, I promise." She shoved a piece of paper at them. "Here are the rules." Without waiting for their agreement, she turned on her heel and dashed off.

"What was that?" Ava stared after her.

Zach smiled, but it was halfway to a grimace. "That was my sister. She always has plans for my life. Don't worry, I'll talk her out of it later."

"Talk her out of it? Why?" Sure, she had hoped to fly under the radar for the charity competition, but this could be even better.

"C'mon, Ava. We keep butting heads. Do we really want to cook together?" Zach put a hand to his hip. "Plus, I really want to do well in that competition. My charity could use the money. I know how reluctant you are in the kitchen." He raised an eyebrow. "Do you actually want to do this?"

She opened her mouth, but before she could say anything, he nodded once.

"I'll talk to Dani about it," he said, then turned and walked off.

Ava studied Zach as he walked away. His open posture, his

easygoing nature with his sister, his willingness to learn and grow. This Zach was not at all the arrogant chef she'd thought he was.

Suddenly, being his partner was very appealing indeed. Especially since being partnered with someone else held more risk of exposing her secret. At least Zach already knew her shortcomings.

She would just have to focus and not let Zach become a distraction. She had one purpose here on Jonathon Island. Everything depended on her writing articles that wowed her editor and won her the job of her dreams. Everything else was secondary.

Seven

AVA HAD NEVER BEEN SOMEONE'S SUPER-hero before. She'd barely been wanted by her parents, her ex, or anyone else. She needed to convince Zach that they could work together. She didn't want to let Dani down.

The scent of Zach's terrible appetizer from the day before still hung in the air. A sour note from the kraut, but also a hint of sweetness. The contest had been broken into two parts, so today they would have the entrée round followed by the desserts. Her mouth watered. Surely someone would incorporate the island's famous fudge in their recipe.

The crowd noise around her intensified as the guests waited for the next round of cooking. Ava turned into the slight breeze making its way through the tented pavilion. Heavenly in the heat that had only risen as the chefs prepared their spaces. She walked over to where Zach was prepping his small kitchen.

He stood behind the white folding table, chef's jacket pristine over pin-striped chef's pants. He'd rolled his jacket up to his elbows.

"Dani must be out of her mind." Zach untied and retied his apron.

"Good morning to you too." Ava rocked back on her heels.

"Good morning." His grunt strengthened her resolve to win him over into being a teammate.

"I think she just didn't catch on to the vibe between us. She's pretty busy." Ava pulled a rubber band out of her pocket and tied her hair back in a ponytail.

A half-amused expression bloomed on Zach's face. "Are you always like this?"

Her stomach squeezed. "Like what?"

"Finding the best in everyone? Looking for ways to be positive all the time?"

The tightness eased. "Me? Positive? Ha. That's a laugh. I'm super critical all the time. It's what makes me a good food critic. Maybe even a good writer." If he thought she was positive all the time, he had a lot to learn.

Zach shrugged one shoulder. "Other than the one very obvious time, I've never read anything you wrote that was critical without you jumping in to praise the chef as well. You look for the best parts of everything."

Ugh. That one article was going to be between them forever. She really needed to clear the air on that. "Zach, about what I wrote about your restaurant—"

The bell sounded for the five-minute warning.

"Sorry, Peter Parker. Now's not the time." Zach picked up a recipe card from the table in front of him.

He was never going to let her apologize and explain. She gritted her teeth. "Fine. But at least agree to be my partner in the charity competition. Also, Peter Parker was a photographer, not a columnist. You're thinking of Clark Kent, but I'm no Superman, er, woman."

He raised an eyebrow at her, his lips shut tight.

"C'mon. Say yes. We have to help Dani out."

He raised a brow, his gaze piercing. "So your charity can win, you mean?"

Probably not the time to tell him she hadn't even picked a charity yet. Yeah, she should probably choose the one her newspaper supported, Reading is for Everyone, but—"I'll donate my portion to your charity. There has to be something you care about, right?" Oops. She hadn't meant it quite like that. "I mean, do you have a charity you like to support?"

The line that had formed between Zach's eyes eased. "Actually, yes. The Silver Platter. They're a group that helps people pay for culinary school. They helped me out when my parents refused to."

"There you go, then." A warmth spread through Ava as she pumped her fist. See, Zach could be reasonable. "We'll play for the Silver Platter. They sound like a really worthy cause. I warn you, though, I'm very competitive."

"I'll take it under advisement. I'm guessing with your newbie cooking skills, I'll have to bring my A-plus game to the cooking table."

"Okay. Fair. But I make a great teammate. I'll do whatever you say with a 'yes, chef!'" This could be a great angle for her article. Winning a cooking competition to help fund a culinary charity. Plus, the view from inside she'd already planned on when Judson had signed her up. "If you ask me to chop carrots, I'll say 'how many?' If you want me to layer a sandwich, I'll ask 'how high?'"

Zach held up a hand. "Okay, I get it. You'll do what you're told. Somehow, I doubt that." His voice was easygoing. Flirtatious? No. Couldn't be.

The one-minute warning buzzer sounded.

"I should . . ." Ava threw a thumb over her shoulder. "Notes for my article and all that."

"Go." Zach shooed her away, but she found her feet had soldered themselves to the ground.

"What's your plan for this round?" She fumbled for her notebook and pen.

"I was going to make ratatouille, but I changed my mind. I'm making almond-crusted walleye with a side of potato confit."

"So fish and chips, then?"

Zach colored. Oh, he was fun to tease. His face broadened into a smile.

"Right. Fish and chips."

"Lucky for you, that's one of my favorites. Don't turn this one green." Her feet unstuck themselves from the ground, and she sped off to find someone to interview. Zach's laugh chased her all the way to the edge of the tent. She'd come back later to press him for an answer.

She stepped out from under the shade of the cooking pavilion and into the sunny midday. An aroma of caramel corn wafted toward her. The food on the midway smelled amazing.

Her phone chimed with a text. Emily.

Emily

Guess what? I GOT THE JOB!!!

A string of emojis followed her words. Several shocked faces, then balloons, then the fingernail-painting lady, five stars, then, weirdly, the cowboy-hat-wearing smiley guy. Ava smiled and shook her head.

Ava

**I knew you would! Congratulations.
I'm so proud of you.**

Emily

**They want me in LA by the end of
the month.**

Ava's heart pinched. She was happy for her friend. But now there was one less reason to stay in Chicago. She'd better make her letter shine. Too bad she couldn't come up with the right words. Every time she sat down with a notepad, her brain froze. Tomorrow she would have to buckle down and write something, no matter what. *Lord, please help me!* She couldn't lose this house. Not to mention write a series of articles that would win her a remote job.

She sent a few kiss emojis back to Emily.

Ava

Seriously, friend. I'm so thrilled.
You'll be amazing. I can't wait for
you to show me around the City of
Angels.

Her phone pinged with another text, and she braced herself to decipher Emily's emojis. Instead, her grandma's name popped up.

Grandma

Just heard from your mom. Her
yacht is being featured on *Life
Afloat* again. Sounds like that's
why she didn't make it home for
Christmas. The episodes will start
airing soon.

Ava suppressed an eye roll. There was always something. Grandma tried to put a good spin on it, but the truth was, her parents found their occupations more interesting and important than their daughter. Her mom could have chosen differently. The validation of the public and the glamour of her chosen lifestyle would win out over her daughter any day.

Still. No need to take that out on Grams.

Ava

Fun for her. Was Dad on this
season?

Grandma _________

Not this time, I guess. Your mom is
up by one.

She sent a thumbs-up emoji and then powered off her phone.
That was enough news for one day.

She took a deep breath and curled her toes in her running shoes.
She tipped her face toward the sun and closed her eyes. *Be present
in this moment.*

"Ava? Are you okay?"

Her heart jumped as she opened her eyes and slapped a hand
to her chest. "Dani!" Zach's sister stood in front of her, flanked by
an older man in a golf shirt and khaki slacks, his salt-and-pepper
hair neatly combed. On her other side was a taller man, closer to
Dani's age, with dark hair perfectly styled. Liam, maybe?

Dani confirmed her suspicions. "Ava, this is my husband, Liam."
She looped her arm through her spouse's. Liam gazed down on
her, his love evident in his eyes. She gestured to her other side.
"And this is my dad, Daniel Sullivan."

Daniel reached out a hand. "Nice to meet you, Ava. You're one
of the judges here?"

She nodded. "Yes, Dani invited me. I'm also writing a few newspaper articles covering the festival. I'm hoping to give your whole
island some good press."

"As the island tourism director, we appreciate it." Dani gave a
little half bow. "Are you enjoying yourself?"

"Other than having to eat Zach's terrible sauerkraut sliders, I'm
having a good time." Ava raised an eyebrow.

Dani hooted a laugh. "I'm sorry he inflicted those on you."

"Eh, they weren't that bad." Liar. "I know he can make amazing
things. That one was just a miss. I'm trying to be unbiased, but I
am looking forward to what he makes next."

"Yes, we're all looking forward to what is next for Zach." Dani
gave her a strange look, but Ava shrugged it off.

"Oh, look, there's Ollie and Eliza." Daniel waved at a couple holding hands and walking toward them. When they joined the group, Daniel gestured to the man. "Ava, this is my son Oliver and his girl, Eliza. They run the bookstore in town. Ollie is a twin to my daughter Kate. I don't know if you'll meet her this week. She's a photographer."

"Nice to meet you." Ollie pumped her hand once. Ava noticed his features were similar to his father's but more relaxed. His graphic tee advertised the bookstore.

Eliza tucked herself into his side. Straight dark-brown hair swung over her shoulders. Her brown eyes held a friendly curiosity. "Yes, nice to meet you. Welcome to Jonathon Island."

"Everyone is so nice here. Is it always like this?" Ava liked Eliza's shirt with its picture of a famous blue box. She'd watched a *Doctor Who* episode or two in college.

"Pretty much," Dani said. "Of course, I'm being paid to say that."

"No, you're right," Liam said.

Ollie threw an elbow into Liam's arm. "You have to say that, you're her husband."

Ava's heart pinched. What would it be like to have family where good-natured teasing was part of the fabric of the relationship?

Another man and woman joined their circle. Ava recognized her Realtor, Mia, but didn't know the tall blond man with her. Mia introduced him as Cody, her fiancé.

"Mia, are you nervous?" Eliza asked.

"Who, me?" Mia's laugh sounded a little high, but Ava didn't know her that well. "I'm only getting married next week—what do I have to be nervous about?"

The group laughed.

Mia put her arm around Cody's waist. "Seriously, though, I think I'm the luckiest girl in the world. I have two beautiful children, and now I get to marry my best friend."

Cody dropped a kiss on top of her head. "I'm the lucky one."

"Mia, I didn't know you were getting married," Ava said. "You should be concentrating on that, not on my silly housing needs."

Mia waved her worry away. "I've already taken care of most of my plans. Now it's just the waiting, and I'd rather stay busy."

"I told her I'd marry her any day and time. No need for any plans," Cody said with a cheeky grin. "But she insisted that we do things a more traditional way."

Mia gave him a little shove. "They're not even that extravagant. I just want my family around me and to honor our love and commitment to each other." They smiled into each other's eyes for a moment. Then Mia turned back to Ava, spearing her with a look. "Besides, your needs are not silly. They're valid and you deserve to have them met."

Oh. Ava blinked back tears.

"Plus, we could use the money to pay for our honeymoon." Cody's quip set off another round of laughter in the group.

"Have you finished your letter yet?" Mia straightened away from Cody. "It's really important that we get that in as soon as possible."

Gulp. She really needed to get that letter finished. "I'll get that to you ASAP." A buzzer rang out from the cooking pavilion. Ava smiled around the group. "I think that's my signal to head back. It was nice to meet you all."

If she could help Zach win the money for his charity, finish an article that satisfied Judson's demands, and write a letter that secured her a home here, her life would truly begin.

So. No pressure there.

If he could win the dessert section of the competition today and the other contestants failed miserably, Zach still might have a chance to take the whole thing. Sure, his appetizer yesterday had flopped. Big time. But he'd taken first in the entrée competition. And he was determined to finish in first again with this dessert.

He glanced around the competition pavilion for the space of the beat of a whisk. Across from him, it appeared Kim Beebe from Trixie's was building a napoleon out of ladyfingers and a cream of some sort. He flicked his gaze to the side. The chef from Fiesta was mixing something in a bowl. Flour flew everywhere. The crowd around Val Anderson's table laughed.

He tried to spot Ava in one of his quick looks, but her blonde head remained elusive.

Eyes on the prize, buddy.

Sure, it was a good idea to remind himself to stay focused. To not think about Ava and her plea to work together. To tamp down the conflicting emotions he felt at hearing his dad say *I'm proud of you.* Much harder to do.

"What are you preparing, chef?" A woman's voice pulled him out of his thoughts. A glance over his shoulder revealed Lily Hart and Declan Kelley.

"Lily!" He paused and turned to them. "Declan, good to see you."

Lily stood with her arm looped through Declan's. Her pale blonde head, with its purple streaks framing her face, only came to Declan's shoulder. Dani had mentioned last summer that the two old friends had become enemies for a brief time, only to team up to save the fudge shop on island. He'd also heard that they'd gotten married in January.

"I'm working on a sabayon to go with a peach tart." Check that, he was attempting to work on his sabayon. The mixture needed constant attention to fluff correctly.

"Sabayon, that's the sauce with champagne and sugar, right?" Lily said.

"Yep." Zach nodded once. "I saw your ice cream truck. I'll have to wander over for a scoop later."

"Maybe you can celebrate a win," Declan said.

"Here's hoping." Zach measured out the sugar he would need. "How is the fudge business?"

"Now that we're on the same team, it's going well. We're having a tasting later this week. I'll be showcasing my caramel bergamot fudge." Lily looked up at Declan with glowing eyes. "Stop by the shop while you're in town. We've got some new product. Maybe you can give us some ideas too."

"I'd love to." A timer chimed on his phone. "Excuse me. I've got to—" He gestured to his ingredients.

"Of course." Declan clapped his shoulder. "See you around."

Zach turned back to crack some eggs for his sauce. He mixed the eggs with sugar and then rested the bowl on top of a pan of boiling water on the stove. Whisking constantly, he added the champagne in a slow stream.

"Zach!" He stifled a groan as he turned to see Pastor Arnie Chamberlain standing on the other side of his workstation, hand extended. The red-haired, fifty-five-year-old pastor had been on the island for a long time. He'd officiated at Dani's wedding.

"Pastor." He rested his whisk against the inside of the bowl long enough to pump the man's hand once. "Sorry. This is delicate. Come around."

"Congrats on taking first place in the entrée round. I saw you yesterday too, and today was a nice recovery." Pastor Arnie shifted until he was in Zach's eyeline but still off to the side in the cooking space.

"Thank you." Zach lowered the temp on his burner. Too hot and the eggs would cook too quickly. "I always like almond-crusted walleye. I thought it had a nice nod to local flavor, and I'm glad the judges approved." He gave his sabayon another twenty strokes and took it off the heat. Dipping a clean spoon into the sauce, he gave it a taste. Sweet, creamy, with a hint of the champagne's bite. He dipped a second spoon and handed it to Pastor Arnie.

"This is amazing." Pastor Arnie's eyes opened wide. "With food like this, you're a shoo-in for the top spot."

Zach's chest grew lighter. "Thanks. Cooking always feels like a balance between confidence in my skills and terror that no one will like what I've made." At least this sabayon hadn't turned green or blue.

"Excuse me." He reached around Pastor Arnie for the plastic wrap, tore off a sheet, and laid it over the top of the mixture. A few minutes in the blast chiller would cool it enough to add the whipped cream.

"Sorry. I should get out of your hair." Pastor Arnie clapped him on the shoulder. "It's good to see you at home here. I know Dani was excited so many of her siblings would be here for this festival."

Zach flashed him a smile as the timer for his fruit tart buzzed behind him. As he opened the door on the tiny oven, the scent of warm peaches, cinnamon, caramel, and a hint of browned butter washed over him.

The crust of the tart, though alarmingly puffy, was a beautiful brown, and the peaches bubbled at the edges. Perfection.

We'll play for the Silver Platter. They sound like a really worthy cause. Ava's words from earlier in the day walked through his mind. Double the designations for the Silver Platter meant double the amount they would receive.

That settled it. He couldn't pass up a chance to offer other young people the opportunity to study the art of food. He would tell Ava and Dani that he was all in.

The warmth of the tart seeped through the oven mitts as he brought the confection out of the oven.

"Zach."

As he turned to the voice, someone jostled his arm. The tart slid from his fingers. Hot juice spilled on his wrist, and he dropped the whole thing. Molten peach lava spread all over a pair of tennis shoes. His gaze traveled up. Ava's shoes.

"Zach." She put her hand over her mouth, gray eyes wide. "I am so sorry. I didn't mean to startle you." She shook one foot out and then the other. "I can't believe I made you ruin your dessert. Ow. That's really hot." Her eyes turned red.

Zach's heart squeezed. "Here." He tossed her a towel. "Are you hurt?" He rubbed at the stinging red burn on his own arm.

She bent and wiped at the sticky mess. "No. I'm fine." She sniffed. "I'm just sorry for your pie."

"Tart."

She stood abruptly. "I'm sorry?"

"It wasn't a pie. It was a tart." Zach wanted the words back the second they left his mouth. She was hurt, for crying out loud. Now wasn't the time to correct her food knowledge.

"Tart, then." Her voice was neutral as she gave one last swipe at her shoes, but it was a losing battle. She grimaced and put the towel on the edge of his table near a pile of dirty dishes. She ran a hand over her eyes. "I feel terrible. How can I help make it up to you?"

"You actually didn't ruin anything." A buzzer sounded on his watch. "I made a second one. That's the timer now." He opened the oven door and found the second tart looking as delicious as the first.

Behind him, Ava hiccuped. He ignored her as he cradled the tart all the way to the plating station. He might need to cut the pieces a little smaller than planned, but he should still be able to salvage his dessert. Good thing he'd had the extra ingredients and the foresight to do something with them.

Ava hiccuped again.

He checked his watch. A few minutes before he had to mix the cream into the sabayon. The tart would need to cool anyway. He located another clean towel.

"I'm sorry about your shoes." He dipped the towel in a washbowl and bent down to wipe away more of the sticky residue. "I hope they weren't your favorites."

"Don't worry about them." Ava's voice was garbled. Still crying? He stood and searched her face. A glint of humor hid in her eyes. She put her hand over her mouth and hiccuped again. Or was it—

Wait.

"Are you laughing?" He crossed his arms and leaned away from her.

"I'm sorry," she said. A *he-he* escaped. She put her fist to her lips, then took a deep breath and straightened her features. "This is not a time to be laughing. The stress . . . you know. But"—and she let out a musical laugh—"these are my running shoes. I'll never be able to wear them again. You've done me a huge favor." Her laugh bubbled up again.

"I'm pretty sure you can buy more running shoes." He wanted to be upset about the spoiled dessert, but he had another one, and her laughter was contagious. Something unraveled in his stomach. A laugh leapt out of him. The ten-minute warning sounded, and he sobered. He caught her eye. "Ava Harper, you are nothing like what I thought."

Holding his gaze, she gave him a soft smile. "Zachary Sullivan, neither are you."

A heat spread across his chest. It was pleasant. Like a peach tart on a summer day.

"I decided to do the charity competition." He tossed the sticky towel into a pile of other soiled linen. "With you, I mean. We'll have to talk about that later. I've got to get moving."

She gave him a tiny salute. "Back to the judges' table for me."

He kept his eyes on the dessert plates.

He would not watch her walk away.

The contest called for six servings of each dish. He cut the tart into eight pieces. If he messed any of them up, he would have a backup.

After mixing whipped cream into the sabayon, he plated the pieces of tart, garnished each one with a healthy scoop of the champagne sauce, and then topped each with a fresh raspberry and a mint leaf.

He finished his plates just as the buzzer sounded.

"Chefs, be prepared for the judging." Uncle Seb's voice came through the speaker mounted over Zach's cooking station. He arranged his six plates so that the tip of each piece of tart pointed the same direction. He wiped his hands on the sides of his apron and stepped back.

Not too shabby.

Suddenly, his mom made her way through the crowd. "Zach, this looks beautiful." His mom looked poised and beautiful, as always, her auburn hair swept into a neat style despite the breezy day.

"Mom. Hi." His stomach plummeted. First a heart-to-heart with his dad and now something similar with his mom. He hadn't talked to either of them much over the years. Even recently at Dani's wedding, he'd been too busy cooking to really talk to anyone. And now, he'd been so busy with the festival he hadn't had time to check in with her. This was all too much too fast.

"I remember you cooking for us when you were a kid, but I never imagined you could do"—she waved her hand at his makeshift kitchen—"all this. It's amazing. You've really done well for yourself."

A smile tickled at the corner of his mouth. He didn't need his mother's approval, had lived for many, many years without it. But man, was it nice to hear her compliments. "Thanks, Mom."

"I know your dad already told you how proud we are of you. We had coffee together earlier, and we'll be watching you. We're rooting for you today."

Zach shifted his shoulders. Were they really getting along? His siblings had said so, but he'd had a hard time believing them. There was so much metaphorical water under the bridge for both of them that it was difficult to imagine them patching up their relationship.

The judges were wrapping up at local chef Alicia Baird's table. "I can't talk to you about Dad right now. It's almost my turn."

"Of course." His mom smiled. "We'll talk later." She disappeared into the crowd just as the judges and Uncle Seb made it to him.

"Zach, please describe your dish." Uncle Seb held out a wireless microphone to him.

"Judges, I give you a peach tart with a cinnamon reduction, topped with a fresh sabayon."

The pleased murmurs as they tasted his dish almost wiped out the memory of the shocked looks when tasting his appetizer.

Almost.

The next moments passed in a blur. Moving with the crowd, Zach made his way to the stage. He stood between Alicia and Patrick. All three of them bore war wounds from the day. Smudges of flour, cream, and other unidentifiable ingredients stained their aprons.

Alicia turned a bright smile to him. "Good luck, Zach."

"Thanks, you too." His insides churned. Was the one-two punch of his entrée and his tart good enough to overshadow his disaster of an appetizer?

Onstage, Uncle Seb recited the rules again. "Okay, I have the list of the winners." He held a white envelope in the air.

Zach searched the judges' faces for a sign of what the envelope contained. Paul's face was set in its usual stern lines. Anne smiled at each of the contestants. His gaze snagged on Ava. She wouldn't meet his eye. A rock settled in his stomach. That couldn't be good.

"In third place, and winner of a set of stainless-steel cookware—" Uncle Seb pulled a slip of paper from the envelope. "Val Anderson from Lion and Dragon." The crowd's cheers turned to a hum as blood rushed to Zach's head.

Okay. Not third, then.

Uncle Seb pulled the next slip out with a flourish. "In second place, and winner of this roll of knives." He gestured behind him.

"I know nothing about knives, but they assure me these are the good ones." The crowd laughed. Uncle Seb cleared his throat. "In second place, Zach Sullivan!"

When he heard his name called, his heart sank.

He'd taken second.

He'd missed his opportunity to work with Paul Hawkeye.

What was his reward for all of this labor? A set of kitchen knives.

Numb, he heard Alicia's name being called for first place, the cash prize and the internship. Uncle Seb called the winners onto the stage, and they all smiled for a photograph. Maybe they even bought that his smile was genuine. After the media moment was over, Zach made sure to shake the hands of the other contestants, giving each a compliment on their dishes. He'd sampled a few of them, and they deserved the kudos.

Uncle Seb handed him the set of knives. "Congratulations on second place. I know you were hoping for better. Maybe next time."

Zach tightened his jaw. He and Ava would need to cook their hearts out at the charity competition the following weekend, because he needed to win it. That was his only chance to wow Anne Green or Paul Hawkeye. His only chance to turn his life around.

Eight

CHALK IT UP TO ANOTHER POORLY THOUGHT-out decision. Ava tapped her pen on the legal pad she held. Did she really agree to compete in the charity contest with Zach? Yesterday had been a roller coaster with him, and in the waning light of a Sunday afternoon, Ava wasn't sure anymore.

She needed to win that contest. Being able to include the event in her articles would be a unique angle. They would have to learn to work together somehow.

Ava sat at a picnic table near the contest pavilion. Around her, the crowd that had gathered for the chili cook-off dispersed throughout the festival grounds. The setting sun cast long rays, coloring everything around her rosy gold. The smell of cooking oil lingered in the air. And did she smell popcorn?

She jotted down "popcorn" on her pad. The list she'd been making all day in between interviewing the chili contestants now read:

Fruit
Umami

Fat and salt
Buy Kleenex
Donuts
Rosemary
Popcorn

A jumbled list of random thoughts for picking out a dish for the competition. Oh, and an addition to her grocery list.

If only she could add "agreeable partner" to that list. Her shoulders slumped. Every interaction with Zach seemed fraught with misunderstandings. But they did promise to start over. Maybe it was time for her to make good on that promise.

She wandered toward the contest tent. Zach was in the spot where he had competed the day before. He hadn't competed in the chili competition, but he was here anyway, bent over, running a rag across the workbench. Huh. Generous with his time, even when he didn't need to be.

"I'm pretty sure they have people for that," Ava said. She leaned her hip against the table.

"I told Dani I could help out. She seemed tired, so I sent her and the others home after the chili cook-off. She hasn't spent much time with her new husband this week, and I don't mind cleaning up." Zach ran the wet cloth over the door of the tiny oven.

Ava spotted a bucket of soapy water, a second washrag hanging on the side. She picked up the rag, wrung it out, and began wiping down the other workstation. "Do you think they'll assign us this same space?"

He glanced at her, then back at the oven. "Maybe we can put in a good word with Dani. It would be nice to work in a space I'm already familiar with. As long as no one considers it cheating."

"I think we'll be fine. I didn't see anything about that in the judges' handbook." Look at that. Several sentences in a row, and no one was fighting. It was like a miracle. "Good effort yesterday.

I really liked your peach tart." She gave the table one last swipe. "Anything else need to be wiped down?"

"I think we're good. Thanks for your help. And your compliment." He dumped the bucket of soapy water onto the grass behind his station. "Are you heading back to the hotel? I'll walk you."

Ava blinked twice. Chivalrous Zach was new. "I thought I'd find the source of that delicious popcorn smell."

"Yeah, it's been tantalizing me too. I think Pop's Corn from Port Joseph has that booth. Follow me."

She hurried to keep up with him as they wove through the crowd. He stopped in front of a booth piled high with popcorn buckets. Along the back of the booth, popcorn machines held popcorn in all the colors of the rainbow.

"Two triple threats," he said to the teenager working the booth and handed her some cash.

"I can pay for my own," Ava said. "Wouldn't want anyone to accuse me of taking a bribe."

He grinned at her and her breath caught. "Nah, we're partners now, right?"

Right. Partners. And somehow, being partners with Zach Sullivan suddenly didn't seem too outlandish.

A few minutes later, they walked down the line of food booths. Ava clutched the warm bucket of popcorn to her chest. The scent of cheese, caramel, and butter drifted up from the three sections in the container.

"What are you doing?" The shocked tone of Zach's voice caused Ava to lose her grip on the popcorn pieces she held in her fingers. They fell to the trampled ground. Food for the birds now.

"What? What's wrong?" Her heart rate picked up.

"That's not how you eat a triple threat." Zach plucked one piece of popcorn from each section of the bucket and popped them all into his mouth at the same time. "The only way to eat it is by mingling the cheese, butter, and caramel." He closed his eyes as he chewed. "Mmm. Yep. Amazing." He cracked one eye open. "Try it. You'll see."

She obediently took one of each flavor and popped them into her mouth. "Oh! That's good." The flavors blended effortlessly. Cheese complemented the sweet caramel, and the butter flavor tied it all together. A few steps more brought them to the tables situated at the back of the hotel. "Want to sit?"

He nodded, then took a seat next to her.

"I saw a picture of you in the hall outside my room."

"The one with all my siblings?"

"That's the one." She tossed a few more popcorn pieces into her mouth. "You were all in front of the hotel."

He shot her a rueful smile. "I was like nineteen in that picture. Definitely going through an awkward phase."

A laugh burst out of her. "If that was awkward . . ." The deep, brooding look he wore in the photograph flashed into her mind. "You were quite intense."

"I thought that I was doing a smolder, but really I just look constipated." He chuckled.

"You looked pretty good to me. I bet all the girls thought so too." Rats. Had that been out loud?

He barked a laugh. "I'm sorry, Ava, did you just call me good-looking?"

"Nah. Just that you had a few good years out of high school. Not all of us are that lucky." Wait. Was she flirting with Zach, the king of arrogance? Except, today he didn't seem arrogant. Just confident. And funny. Plus, he'd been a gracious loser in the contest even though she knew it was important to him.

"Eh. I bet you were fine." Zach tossed some popcorn into his mouth.

She raised an eyebrow. "Do you mean fine"—she tipped her hand back and forth in a so-so gesture—"or *fine*?"—and waggled both her brows.

"I plead the fifth."

She laughed, then attempted to mimic Frodo from *The Lord of the Rings*. "All right, then, keep your secrets."

"What's on the notepad?" He jutted his chin at her legal pad.

"I made a few notes. I thought we should talk about our dish for the competition." She thought about his dishes from the day. Silly girl. Like she could contribute anything. "Of course, you're probably in a much better position to pick something out."

"I'd love to know what you have." He reached for the paper, but she held it back.

"Um, maybe I should just read it to you." Much safer that way. He nodded, then leaned his elbows against the table and closed his eyes. "What are you doing?"

"I'm listening and imagining."

Wow. This guy was full of surprises. "Okay. It's not like a big revelation or something."

"Ava," he said, eyes still closed. "Just read it to me."

She did. Her voice grew stronger as she read off each item, skipping the Kleenex, of course. At every word, he nodded. A ghost of a smile began on his face until, by the end of her list, it was in full bloom.

She cleared her throat. "That's it."

He remained still for another moment, then opened his eyes and turned to her. "That's a pretty good start."

"It is?" She rolled the pen between her fingers. "It's not really a recipe or even an idea for a specific dish—"

He held up a hand. "No, but it definitely invokes a feeling of a dish."

"A feeling of a dish?" She smirked. "Are you on the Cooking Channel or something? *The Philosophy of Cooking* with Zach Sullivan."

"Har har. I'm just saying, you could be really good at this if you let yourself try. You could be a chef instead of just critiquing everyone else's work."

And it should have felt like a dig, but his quiet confidence actually inspired something that felt more like pride. She loved her review job, but she would be lying if she didn't acknowledge the desire once in a while to make something delicious on her own.

"Thanks."

"Being a chef requires creativity. It's like art with food. You're creative, so we just need to figure out how to translate that into something edible." He rubbed at his chin.

"Ha. I don't know. It might take a miracle."

"Let's try something." He took the pen and paper out of her hands and set them on the table. "Close your eyes."

"O-ka-ay." She drew the word into three syllables.

"Just trust me. I'll close mine too."

She complied.

"Now, tell me about the best thing you ever ate."

She didn't have to think about it long. "Malfatti with browned butter and sage. I didn't even need to close my eyes for that." Malfatti, an Italian sort of pasta, sort of dumpling made from ricotta cheese and just a tiny bit of flour, then finished off in a pan of browned butter. Her breath hitched at the memory.

"No. Keep them closed." He covered her hands with his and her pulse leaped. "Tell me more about the dish. Why were you eating it? Where were you? Who were you with?"

In an instant she was back there. "It was the night of my high school graduation. Both of my parents were home. They wanted to make me something special to celebrate, so they made this malfatti. My mother had learned the recipe from a woman she had met in Tuscany. Mom had been so excited to show Dad what she'd learned." Her heart seized. They'd never been that excited to see her. "I remember my parents laughing in the kitchen as they worked together." A tear trickled down her face and she pulled her hands away to swipe at it.

"I'm sorry," he said. "I didn't mean to make you cry."

"Not your fault." She opened her eyes and cleared her throat. "It's just a bittersweet memory for me."

His gaze roamed her face. "Want to talk about it?"

Her stomach sank. She took a deep breath and then let it out slowly. "Both of my parents were—are—chefs. As you know, they work on luxury super yachts. That's how they met. They both worked a stint on the same yacht. Nowadays they usually work separately because they both have so much experience, but back when they started, they tried to get on as many boats together as possible." Which was sweet, she supposed.

"Quite the bohemian lifestyle." Zach's tone gave away none of what he was thinking.

"Exactly. After a few years of this 'lifestyle,' my mom got pregnant with me. They had a wedding ceremony officiated by the captain of the ship they were on at the time, attended by the rest of the crew. After I was born, they rented a tiny apartment and tried to figure out how to do life as a normal family." Ava shrugged. "Dad would take a six-week shift, and then Mom would go. It was like being in a divorced family with joint custody, except my parents stayed married."

In one of the trees lining the property, an owl hooted.

"Yeah. Anyway. When I was five, they decided they'd had enough of that and dumped me at my grandma's—my mom's mom. I guess they'd found a yacht crew that wanted them both, and they couldn't turn down the opportunity. They couldn't let their kid cramp their style. One shift turned into three and then more, and pretty soon, I'd lived with my grandma for thirteen years." The wound over being left behind never quite healed. Ava rubbed at her chest, but the ache held on.

"And they never came home?" Zach shifted in his seat.

"They'd fly in for a night or two and then jet off again. Once in a while they'd be around for a couple of weeks between seasons, but it was never predictable." She'd never known how long they were going to stay. If they would ever stay for her. "I always waited for the day that they'd say we would be a family again, but it never happened."

"I'm sorry that you went through that."

"Anyway, this is the long route to telling you why my favorite meal is bittersweet, and I don't mean the malfatti." She paused. Swallowed hard. "The morning after my graduation, I heard my mom and grandma arguing. My grandma said that they should spend more time with me. Then my mom said that she'd never meant to have a baby."

I never asked for that to happen. I didn't want it to happen. I love my daughter, but settling down with a husband and child was never how I wanted to live my life.

"That morning answered a lot of questions for me. I walked into the room where they were arguing. Turns out, my dad was in there too. He hadn't said a word. I guess he didn't want me either." She shrugged. "My parents pasted smiles on their faces, kissed me goodbye, and left that same day."

Zach rested his hand on hers briefly. "I'm sorry that happened to you. I know I said that already, but it's true. I wish it had been different for you."

"Sometimes I wonder what my life would have been like if they'd stayed home and taught me what they knew instead of dumping me in a retirement community with my grandma." She cleared her throat. Tried for a smile. "At least they taught me enough to be a good food writer. And their good genes gave me one thing that is essential for being a food critic."

"What's that?" A line appeared between Zach's brows.

"No food allergies." A genuine smile bloomed as he laughed,

though the ache in her heart stayed sharp. "Enough of my family drama."

"Trust me. I know about family drama." Zach stood. "Let's walk."

"Your family seems perfect. There are so many of you." She'd felt nothing but love from them as she'd seen them interact with Zach while she'd been here.

She'd give anything to have that kind of belonging.

It was getting really hard to hold on to a grudge against Ava Harper. And he no longer wanted to.

Her vulnerability in talking about her parents, her gentle teasing of him, even the times when she challenged him, were sculpting her into a very different person than he had imagined her to be all these years.

The bitterness of coming in second that he'd tried to hide was fading like a bad aftertaste. He still had plenty of time to wow Anne Green and Paul Hawkeye. He would focus on making their presentation at the charity competition the best it could be.

Zach led Ava through the French doors from the patio. Overhead, the chandeliers sparkled. "When I was a kid, this whole hotel used to be our playground. My parents owned it together."

Did he really want to drag this history up? The words burst out of him after being dammed up for so long. "My dad burned this place down."

Ava stopped. "I'm sorry. What?"

He turned and faced her. A stabbing sensation hit him between the shoulder blades. "My mom cheated on my dad and then married that guy here at the hotel. My dad got drunk and accidentally set the hotel on fire. That's why they're making so many repairs.

My sister Dani just got permission to rebuild it a year or so ago." Her mouth dropped open. "See what I mean about family drama?"

"But I met your dad. He's here. On the island." A line formed on her forehead.

He sighed. "Yeah. It's complicated. He's been living in Florida and running a hotel empire, but I guess he wants to make amends or something. Maybe it's something he learned in AA." Zach shifted his shoulders, but the ache between them held on. "We don't talk much. But this week he kind of tried to rekindle something. I don't know. It was weird. He hasn't tried to contact me in the past several years, but now he wants to chat?" Maybe he should have heard him out.

Ava began walking again. "That is complicated. You should give him a chance, though. I mean, he's your dad. The only one you've got."

He thought briefly of Uncle Bryan. His dad's brother had been a stable force in Zach's life, kind of like a surrogate dad at times. But she was right, he only had one father. "You're probably right. But it's hard to get started."

Their talk had brought them through the main lobby and to the kitchen, as though his feet only knew one way to travel. He pushed open the door to the renovated kitchen. When he'd been here to cater Dani's wedding, this part of the hotel had still been very much under construction. He whistled. "They've made a lot of progress since I was here in April."

To his left, ranges and ovens filled the wall, and to the right was the wash station. Shelves lined the other walls. In one corner were the doors to the walk-in cooler and freezer. Stainless-steel workbenches marched down the center of the space. Two stools rested near the sink area.

"Growing up, this kitchen was rarely empty. My love of food began here. I worked here through high school. There was a sense of belonging, of being on a team." He led her to the stools, then pulled them up to the nearest workstation. "One time my senior year, when the restaurant was closed, the chef said I could cook my family a meal as long as I cleaned up after myself. It was probably the most fun I've ever had. I spent a week designing the menu, then all day preparing it." He jutted a thumb over his shoulder. "The family gathered around the table out there, and I served them."

"That sounds like a lot of work."

"I was exhausted the next day, but that night was exhilarating. The looks on their faces were worth it. I'd never seen Mom look so proud, except maybe when I brought home straight A's. I knew that night I never wanted to do anything else." He braced his hands on the countertop, the stainless steel cool under his fingers. "Making good food for people you love is a kind of satisfaction you can't find anywhere else. The camaraderie you find in a kitchen is also unique."

"Your dedication to it shines through in your dishes." Ava sat on a stool and rested her elbow on the workbench.

"One of the reasons I'm here is to try to land a new job. I'm so ready to get out of Chef Louie's kitchen. I want to cook in a place that matters, that values its staff. Preparing someone else's recipes—and not even very good ones—for the snooty Chicago crowd Escargot draws in . . ." He shook his head. "Anyway. Enough about me. I have a thought about the competition." He stood and began pacing.

Ava crossed her arms. "Shoot."

"One word—pasties." He moved his hands like he was making a rainbow in the sky.

"Pasties?" Ava crinkled her nose.

"Don't tell me you've never heard of a pasty before?"

"That's the thing with rutabaga and beef in a pie, right?"

He put his hand to his chest. "You wound me! 'That thing with rutabaga'? It's so much more than that. It's practically the state food of Michigan. And it's perfect for this contest."

"Uh-huh. Convince me."

Fine. He liked a challenge. "We can take some of the food ideas you had, the rosemary and umami, and even some of the flavors from your mom's malfatti—browned butter and sage—and make an elevated pasty. We'd pair the traditional fillings of rutabaga and potatoes and beef with upscale seasonings. A simple food that we make shine."

As he talked, Ava leaned toward him. She jotted a few things down on her notepad. "I like where you're going with this. A local favorite made with a Zach Sullivan flair. You could even say a local favorite made by a local favorite."

Her words made his chest swell. But . . . "I don't think I'm a local favorite."

"Oh, please. I saw you with everyone out there." She waved his words away, then jotted down something else on her paper. "I think the whole town came to say hello to you today. You're Jonathon Island's golden boy."

"I think you're blind." He reached for her paper. "What are you writing down?"

She pulled the paper out of his reach. "Don't you know better than to take things that don't belong to you?"

"Sorry. You're right."

She gave him a smile. A dimple he'd never noticed before appeared on her cheek. "I'm just getting some ideas for my article."

"If you're going to call me a local favorite, I might have to protest."

"Fine, I'll just say the island's golden boy."

He groaned. "That's even worse."

"Sorry, not sorry. You're not my editor." She flipped the page. "Okay. What do we need to do to be ready for the competition?"

"I'll need to find a good recipe to riff off. I have one in mind, but I don't know if it's in the binder I packed for this trip."

Her mouth hung open.

"What?"

"Do you just, like, carry around a recipe binder all the time?"

He squared up. "I don't know. Do you just, like, carry around a pen and paper all the time?"

She looked him hard in the eye. Then her face softened. "Touché. You're right. Tools of the trade and all that. I wouldn't feel right if I didn't have something to write with nearby. You're probably the same about your recipes."

The clock on the wall ticked as a few seconds passed. "I know some people keep notebooks and journals with their recipes and inspiration, but I prefer to keep it all in a binder. Then I can add to it with various mediums, using those clear pockets and whatnot. Sometimes I'll jot a note in my phone, but mostly it's in the binder."

"I'd love to see it sometime."

"Maybe when you're ready to show me your notes." He raised an eyebrow at her.

She rolled her eyes. "Fine. Touché again." She yawned. "Do we need to discuss anything else? I'm beat."

He checked his smartwatch. How had it gotten to be midnight already? "I think we're fine. I'll plan the recipes and then check in with you tomorrow with my ideas. You'll just need to be my helper."

She patted him lightly on the shoulder as she passed him on her way out of the kitchen. "G'night, Golden Boy."

"Ha. Good night, Peter Parker."

Huh. Spending all that time with Ava had been fun. Too bad he was moving out of Chicago. He might have enjoyed getting to know her better. At least, he was moving as soon as he could. It was too late to win Paul Hawkeye's internship, but if he played his cards right, he could still earn himself a spot in Anne Green's kitchen in San Francisco. He could be on his way to restarting his failing career and finally settling down with a job he could be proud of.

A strange sensation, almost regret, filled him as he thought about moving to California, though. He'd started to feel almost at peace here on Jonathon Island. Like he'd come home.

Surely, if Dani had overcome the judgment of the islanders and made a home for herself after everything their mom and dad had done, he could too. Maybe his parents' shame didn't hang around. Was it possible, as his sister kept insisting, that the Sullivan family could come home to Jonathon Island? If so, maybe he could even come home to this kitchen, the place where his dream was born.

He turned out the lights and made his way to the hotel lobby. A group of young people stood around the front desk, chatting with Olive Kelley. He only recognized Emily Watson, the island's EMT, and Isaac Kelley, the younger son of Martha Kelley. Isaac leaned his elbow against the tall desk, his mouth working on a wad of gum. He straightened up as Zach got closer.

"Did you turn off the oven back there?" Isaac pushed back the hoodie covering his forehead. "We wouldn't want this hotel to be burned down a second time. Like father, like son. Am I right?"

A knife pierced his gut.

Emily swatted Isaac on the arm. "Not cool, Isaac. What did Zach ever do to you?" But she snickered with the rest of them.

"Aw, I was only joking. No harm meant." Isaac snapped his gum.

Zach brushed past them without responding. What would he say, anyway? Isaac was right.

Dani was wrong. Their family would never fully live down the shame of the past. It was baked into the walls.

Nine

A PERFECT MONDAY TO WRITE THE PERFECT letter. Hopefully she wasn't too late.

Ava walked across the brick-laid pathway of the grounds and up the three steps to the interior of the Grand's iconic gazebo and took a seat on a bench. Delicate woodwork traced its way around the top of the octagonal structure. Take one early spring morning, one cup of coffee in hand, mix well, and pour into an inspiring setting, and you had a recipe for a piece of perfection.

Focus on what you know. Ava looked down at the stationery in front of her. This weekend had been so full of activity that she hadn't had time to focus.

She bit the end of her pencil, adding another round of teeth marks to the ones already marring its surface. How was she supposed to start a letter that could change her life forever?

To whom it may concern:

Nope. She scratched the words out. Too impersonal.

Dear Homeowners:

Better.

A laugh just beyond the row of trees to her left caught her attention. She watched as an older couple strolled past, hand in hand.

Her chest squeezed. She'd always thought by now she'd be married. Maybe a few kids. Definitely a house. Something permanent.

Please help me make my dreams come true. No. No. No. Too desperate.

She double-tapped the pencil against her knee. Then tapped out the beat for "Yankee Doodle." Her eyes traveled the length of the pillared column directly across from her. Up to the ceiling, where the gazebo bristled with golden hanging bulbs. They must add an air of romance when lit on a summer evening.

Another couple came walking past, this time much younger. She recognized Dani by her blonde hair and waved.

"Oh, hello," Dani called. Then she tugged on the arm of the tall, dark-haired man next to her, and they made their way to the gazebo. "Ava, this is my husband, Liam. I can't remember whether I properly introduced you yesterday, as we got distracted with all the others."

"You did, although I don't think I had the opportunity to say 'Pleased to meet you.'" She stood and held out her hand to shake Liam's.

"You too."

"So, you're the mastermind behind the renovations on the Grand Sullivan." Ava jutted her chin to where the hotel loomed on the hill.

The side of his mouth turned up. "I'd say it was more of a joint effort with Dani." Liam wrapped his arm around his wife and tucked her close. Dani beamed up at him. Ava could practically hear the air crackling between them.

Sigh. With the birds singing in the row of pine trees, the warm, light, spring breeze tickling the tops of the grass, and the hint of lilacs just beginning to scent the air, it was a fairy-tale-like day for love. She half expected to see bluebirds flying over the heads of Liam and Dani.

She blinked the image away. "Well, you make a good team. Everything I've seen looks amazing."

"Thanks," Dani said. Her phone buzzed and she looked at it for a moment, her face creasing into a frown before her eyes opened wide. "Oh, shoot! I really need to get over to the festival grounds. It was nice seeing you, Ava. Thanks again for being willing to partner with Zach for the charity stuff. I know he really wants to win. The Silver Platter means a lot to him." Giving her a huge smile that faltered after a moment, Dani turned with Liam and hurried away, still tucked close to his side.

Ava watched them go for a moment and then returned to her bench, the seat cold underneath her.

After writing and crossing out three more sentences, Ava stood and walked a circuit around the inside of the gazebo. On her second turn around the interior, she spotted a familiar figure striding across the lawn toward her. The morning sun streamed over Zach's dark locks, highlighting a few golden strands she'd never noticed before. He wore a white button-down shirt, rolled to the elbows, and black jeans. A hint of his ankle showed above a pair of checkerboard deck shoes.

"Good morning," Zach said.

"Good morning, yourself." She stood in the doorway to the gazebo. A ripple of something unfamiliar zinged up her spine.

"Beautiful weather." Zach paused just outside the gazebo.

"Yeah. Nice day." Seriously? Talking about the weather?

He nodded toward her hands. "I see you have your ever-present notepad. Working on a story?"

"Not really." Just something much more important. But Zach wouldn't care about that.

"Notes for our competition?"

"You told me you'd take care of that. You made it very clear." She pointed at him with her pencil.

"True. And I have very good news on that front." Zach pulled a crumpled bit of paper from his shirt pocket. "I worked out a perfect recipe." He handed her the note. His bold handwriting ran all over the page, smudged in a few places, but still legible. And all completely unintelligible.

"I don't know what half of this stuff means." A pang ran through her stomach. Zach deserved to win. She thrust the note at him. "I should find Dani. Tell her to find you a different partner. One who can help you win." It was the right thing to do. Even if it meant tanking her article. It wasn't fair to saddle him with her incompetence. She would just have to find a new angle. That shouldn't be too hard.

But he shook his head and tucked the slip back into his pocket. "I'll write it out again, but clearer next time. We can win. I know we can." He moved a half step closer to her. "With your help and my skills, we're good partners."

She searched his gaze. "Okay. Partners." The thought rippled through her, making her heart flutter. "Did you come out here looking for me?"

He looked away. "Partly. I hoped I'd find you. I saw you walking in this direction earlier. I also have to find Dani." Zach tucked his hands into his pockets. "She asked me to teach a class, and I just saw the sign-up list. It's way too many people for one class, and I need her to split it into two groups."

"Dani was just here. She and Liam went to the festival grounds. I think there was some kind of emergency."

Zach's eyebrows rose. A muscle in his jaw jumped. "Emergency?"

"Festival emergency. I'm sure she's fine. She looked like she had everything under control."

"She's good at that." He nodded. "Um, I'm going to go find

her. Want to come along? Or are you busy with . . ." He gestured at her notebook.

She really should finish the letter, but maybe a walk was just what she needed to jump-start her creativity. "Lead on."

They fell in step across the spongy grass. "Okay. So. Here's what I'm thinking," Zach said. "We'll start by julienning some carrots."

She really should mention in the letter that she wanted to make the island her permanent home. And maybe also talk about how much she had been enjoying meeting the people who already lived here.

"Ava, are you even listening to me?" Zach stepped in front of her and tapped her shoulder. He walked backward in front of her for a few steps.

She shook her head. "Sorry. No. I was miles away." More like a half mile away.

"Want to tell me what's going on? I can't have you this distracted when we're working." He turned and fell into step with her again.

Right. She needed to be locked in for that. Partners.

She let out a long breath. "I'm trying to compose a letter to the current owners of a house I want to buy."

"Are you moving?" Zach's strides began eating up long stretches of grass.

"It's a cute little place." She double-timed to keep up with him. "Old but with a great layout. The bathroom is a Pepto-Bismol pink, but I actually might leave it that way. Keep some of its charm." She smiled and then sighed. "But I found out that there's a bidding war on the place. I can't afford to go much higher, but my agent advised me to write a letter. She said that sometimes people can be swayed by that."

He stopped suddenly, and Ava almost ran into him. "I admire you for wanting to find a place that you can make your own. Just tell them a little about yourself. I'm sure they'll love you." His shoulders hitched up a notch, and he began walking again.

Okay. Whatever that was about.

They reached the festival grounds. Dani stood next to the ice cream truck.

"Dani!" Zach jogged over to her, and Ava tried to keep up. "Tell me you didn't give me thirty people for my class."

Dani blew out a breath. "I didn't give you thirty people for your class."

"Are you just saying that to make me feel better?" Zach ran a hand through his hair.

"I'm just telling you what you want to hear," Dani shot back. She looked down at her clipboard. "I'm really busy, Zach."

"I can't teach that many people at one time. I need you to cancel half of them."

Dani's head whipped up. "No way. I can't cancel them. They all paid good money. I need this festival to be a success. For Jonathon Island." She stressed the last words. A muscle tightened in Zach's neck.

"Then split them into two classes. I'll just do the same thing twice."

Dani ran a finger down the paper in front of her. "Can't do that either. There's just no time for a second class. You'll figure it out. I know you will." She gave him a grin full of teeth and hurried away.

"Dani. Dani!" But she didn't hear him. Or, Ava suspected, she was ignoring him. He looked at her. "That sister of mine." But his growl didn't fool Ava for a minute. She could see the sparkle in his eye. He loved his baby sister and would do whatever she asked.

Zach stared at her for a long moment.

She felt her face heat. Did she have a smudge or something? "What?"

"You could help me with the class."

"What?" She'd never heard that kind of a shriek come out of her mouth before. She cleared her throat. "Um. I mean. Are you crazy? I don't even know how to cook, let alone how to teach other people."

"You'll be fine. I'm teaching the same stuff I taught at Escargot. You already know those techniques." Zach shrugged. "Besides, I mostly need someone for crowd control, and you're great with people."

"I don't know . . ." Wasn't she just in danger of showing off her incompetence?

"C'mon. It'll be great. Plus, it'll give us a chance to learn to work together more. I'll give you a refresher before the class starts. I already know you're a quick learner." Zach raised an eyebrow at her. "You could write about it for your article. A behind-the-scenes look at a cooking class or whatever. Say yes, partner."

Wow. He really believed in her. How could she say no to that? "Partner."

"Great. We'll see you in"—he looked at his watch—"twenty minutes."

Eep. She should have found out when the class started before agreeing to it.

How was she ever going to get her letter written if she kept being distracted by Zach Sullivan?

This might be Zach's best class yet, despite the fact that he'd had little time to prepare. It was fitting that Dani had scheduled this beginners class for a Monday. It seemed he would never escape Make-It-Mondays.

If only this favor for his sister wasn't distracting him from the real reason he was here on Jonathon Island: getting out from under Chef Louie's thumb and landing a job with actual prospects.

Zach did a quick status check. All under control. The honeymooners were giggling over their saucepan, the sisters from

Minneapolis seemed to be in a competition to see who could dice their onions the smallest. And the rest of the class occupied themselves with various tasks. He'd chosen to lead them through a boeuf bourguignon, the recipe simplified for home cooks. A fun dish for people to have in their repertoire that had the added benefit of teaching a lot of skills. Ava flitted from station to station, offering a positive word here and a gentle correction there.

Once, he even spotted her correcting someone's hold on a knife.

When Dani had told him earlier that day there would be thirty inexperienced people crammed into the hotel kitchen like the sardines they'd be using for the Caesar salad, he'd nearly hyperventilated. The kitchen was spacious enough to accommodate a well-trained staff of twenty or so, but newbies? They were lucky they'd been able to figure out how to move the group through the steps in shifts. If it weren't for Ava's help, he'd be drowning right now.

He caught her arm as she hurried past, ponytail swinging with her bouncing step. "Nice knife work. You're really learning."

"I pick things up quickly. Especially when I learn from the best." She whirled away to the next group.

He put a hand to his chest. That shot had hit home.

Was he . . . having fun?

When was the last time cooking was fun for him?

Here, in this kitchen tailor-made to his suggestions after his dad had burned down the last one, on the island he'd sworn never to return to, with the woman who had ruined his life, Zachary Sullivan was having fun.

The grin that slipped onto his lips felt good. Strange but good.

He clapped his hands. All eyes turned to him. "Okay, class. Time to get cooking. We'll have to take turns at the stove, but now is when the magic happens." He instructed the class to break themselves into pairs for sautéing their veggies.

The door to the kitchen opened and swung closed. In his peripheral vision, he caught a quick glimpse of a man in a blue polo and khakis. He finished explaining how they would use the cook-top, then glanced at the visitor. Then looked again. Paul Hawkeye had just taken a place near the door. "Keep gradually whisking in this flour," he told the sisters from Minneapolis, then walked over to Chef Hawkeye.

His stomach was doing loops. "Hello, Chef. I'm Zach Sullivan. We met at the competition over the weekend."

"Yes, I remember those abysmal sauerkraut sliders." Chef Hawkeye shook his hand. "Creative, but terrible."

"Sorry about afflicting your taste buds that way. I should have tasted the dish before serving it. I'm still not sure what happened."

"We all make mistakes. It's how we pick ourselves up again that matters." The other man leaned back and looked at him, gaze steady. "You show potential."

The stomach loops decreased. "Thank you, Chef."

"Please, call me Paul. Your sister Dani told me where to find you. I don't want to interrupt your class. It looks like you're reaching a critical part. A riff on a boeuf bourguignon, right?" Paul waved his hand toward the room. "Don't mind me. I like fitting in a little refresher here and there. I'm always open to learning." He crossed his burly arms and leaned back against the wall.

Yeah, no pressure there. Especially since this beef-and-vegetable recipe came almost directly out of Paul's cookbook *Stew*.

Zach turned back to the room. "Okay, everyone. We're going to take turns sautéing our mirepoix. Ava will lead one group, and I'll lead the other."

Ava's eyes widened, and he hustled over to her. "I thought I just had to be the encourager," she whispered.

"Plans change. I need your help. You can do this." He held her elbow until she met his eye. He needed this class to go well. At her shuddering breath, his own concerns fled. Forget Chef Hawkeye. Ava needed this class to go well. He held her gaze for a beat. "Ava, you've got this. You did great when you were in my class."

A murmur began around them. Ava took a deep breath, pressed her lips together, and nodded once.

"Attagirl." He squeezed her elbow and let go. "Let's form up into two lines."

The next thirty minutes passed in a blink. The aroma of onions and carrots and then cooked beef flavored the air. Soon each pair of students had a fragrant stew in front of them. "Now for the best part. Dig in, everyone."

Paul moved to the closest table. "May I?" He gestured at the pan. The honeymooners nodded. Taking a clean spoon, he dipped it into the soup.

Zach held his breath.

Paul closed his eyes as he tried it. His face became a fraction less stern. "Zach, I like the use of sherry here." He opened his eyes and leaned down to smell the soup, then straightened up again. "Normally it would overpower a dish, but the strong beef elements balance everything out."

The tightness in Zach's chest eased. "Thank you, Chef."

"Flat iron steak?" Paul raised an eyebrow.

"Yes. I like to use that one for my classes instead of a beef roast." Zach cleared his throat. "It's tender and well marbled, so you get the flavor of a long-cooking stew without needing to take as much time."

"Great idea. I might even make a change in my next edition of *Stew*." Chef Hawkeye dipped a clean spoon for another bite. "I'd credit you, of course. If it's okay."

"It would be my honor." His chest expanded. He faced the group. "Everyone, this is Chef Paul Hawkeye. You may have seen him on the Food Network." A titter ran around the room. "In fact, this recipe is an homage to his Beef All Day from his recipe book *Stew*."

Everyone clapped.

"Great recipe, Chef," one of the girls from Minneapolis called out. "We'd offer you a bowl of ours, but I'm afraid we already ate it all."

Chef Hawkeye laughed and raised his hands, palm forward. "Thanks, everyone. You had an outstanding teacher in Chef Sullivan here. I hope you all have a good time at the rest of the festival."

The class filtered out, and Zach started stacking dishes. Dani had told him she'd hired someone to clean up after class, but he didn't want to leave too big of a mess. On the other side of the room, Ava was doing the same thing. He heard a noise behind him and turned to see Paul also helping with cleanup.

"Sir, you don't have to do that." He lifted the dishes out of Paul's hands. "We have someone coming in for dish duty."

"No need to 'sir' me," the chef said. "I'm simply paying you back for the tasting I just had. Actually, I also wanted to talk to you about something." Paul glanced at Ava.

Ava looked between the two of them. "Right. I'll see you later, Zach. We should go over that recipe for the competition."

He was already looking forward to it. The room fell silent until the door closed behind her.

"Let me get straight to the point." Chef Paul leaned on his elbow on the workbench he'd just cleaned. "I'm opening a new restaurant in Chicago and am vetting candidates for head chef. Your name came up as a possibility."

Zach's pulse pounded in his ears. Chef Paul Hawkeye's restaurants were known to be overnight sensations. He'd hoped to work in one if only to climb his way up the ladder, but the possibility that he might jump straight to head chef boggled his mind. A dream come true. And ten minutes ago, he would have said a pipe dream.

"It was a coincidence that we are here together, but a good one. I'd planned on coming to Escargot next week, but this is even better." Paul straightened up. "I have to say, I'm impressed so far."

"I don't know what to say." Zach's lips felt frozen. Head chef in a brand new restaurant? A chance to set up his own kitchen and train employees without yelling at them all the time? Yes, please. "How can you be impressed when my cooking has been subpar?"

"That dessert wasn't subpar. This"—Paul waved his hand toward the rest of the room—"wasn't subpar. But you should know that being a great chef isn't just about your cooking. It's about your attitude. I've been watching you. You're a team player. You're usually good with people, and you have a command of the kitchen. These aren't things that can be taught."

Zach took in a deep breath. His chest filled with a warm sensation. "Thank you. That means a lot to me."

Paul's phone buzzed in his pocket, and he pulled it out. He tapped at it for a moment, the silence stretching thin between them. "Okay." He looked up from his cell and directly at Zach. "I've got to run. Nothing is set in stone yet, but I'll make some calls, talk to some people."

Did Zach want to stay in Chicago? He stacked the last of the bowls in the sink. If it meant working for Paul Hawkeye, how could he pass up the opportunity? Plus, Ava lived in Chicago. She was even buying a home there. He'd enjoy the chance to get to know her better. His thoughts buzzed, and he didn't trust himself to speak.

Zach walked with Paul to the door of the kitchen.

"Oh, I almost forgot." Paul paused just outside the door. "You don't mind if I call Chef Louie at Escargot, do you? He and I went to culinary school together a long, long time ago. We used to get into so much trouble."

Zach hesitated, but Paul didn't wait for a response.

"I just want to get Chef Louie's opinion on how you work under pressure. I always like to talk to someone who has firsthand experience working with my chefs before I make big decisions." Paul chuckled. "Though there's been plenty of pressure this week already." He reached out to shake Zach's hand. "I owe Louie a call anyway."

Great. The birth of a dream and the death of one all in the span of five minutes. Because if Paul Hawkeye was friends with Chef Louie and trusted his words, there was no way Zach would be landing that job.

Ten

WHAT ZACH REALLY NEEDED WAS A PLAN. He paced the length of Ollie's apartment and back again. From the chair in the corner to the two front windows overlooking Main Street, he could walk ten steps.

After his dismal second-place showing at the competition, he needed to win Anne Green over. The upcoming charity competition wouldn't be enough. He needed face time.

Just in case the possibility of working with Paul Hawkeye fell through. Which it definitely would after Paul had a chance to speak with his good buddy Louie Andrews.

He'd have to track down Anne and plead his case in person.

He opened his phone and thumbed in a message to Dani.

Zach

Are you at the Grand?

Dani

I'm in the contest tent. Why?

133

Perfect. I'll meet you up there in 5.

He ignored his jacket. Surely his jeans and polo shirt were warm enough for a June morning. Snatching up his keys, he dashed out of Ollie's apartment. As he pushed through the exterior door, a blast of wind raised goosebumps along his arms. So much for not needing that jacket.

He headed up to the Grand at a jog, dodging tourists and locals the whole way. A flash of blonde hair under the canopy of the contest tent told Zach where to go. He made a beeline for his sister and caught up with her with a minute to spare. In her light jacket, jeans, and Jonathon Island Flavor Fest T-shirt, Dani was better dressed for the weather than he was. She made a few marks on the clipboard in her hands as he approached.

"Dani," Zach said. "Can you tell me where to find Anne Green?"

"Hello to you too, big brother." Dani grinned at him.

"Hello. Now can you tell me where to find her?"

"What? Why?" Dani's brow crinkled.

"I need to talk to her." Zach's pulse pounded.

"You know I can't let you do that." Dani put her arm out and grabbed his bicep. "You're still in another contest. I can't let you speak to the judges for that contest."

Right. Dani would be a stickler for the rules. Best not to tell her about Paul seeking him out earlier. Her reputation was at stake. Well, so was his. Just not in the same way.

"I don't really care about that." Liar. He knew how much the Silver Platter could use the money. "Okay, I care, but I care more about landing a new job after this thing is over."

"And you think a one-on-one with Anne Green will do that for you?" A strand of her long blonde hair blew into Dani's eyes, and she released her hold on his arm to brush it away. "I can guarantee you that it won't work. She's not going to respect you for breaking the rules."

Her words punctured the hope that had filled his lungs, and he let out a long sigh. "You're right, of course. I just think talking directly to her is the best way to win her over."

"So do that. But not until you've completed your obligations." She glanced at her phone, then back at him. "Have you and Ava made a plan for the competition yet?"

He looked around the tent. Was she here? He didn't see her blonde head anywhere. "Um. No. Not really. I told her I would come up with the recipes. She just needs to be my helper."

Dani raised an eyebrow. "Isn't that a little . . . arrogant?"

Was it? He thought back over their conversation. Okay, yes. A little arrogant. But he hadn't meant it that way. It was just that he had the experience, and he knew Ava's secret lack of skills. He rubbed a hand through his hair. "You're right. I'll apologize. But we did come up with the menu together." Their evening spent chatting and planning had been the best part of his trip here so far.

Ava's soft voice filtered through his mind. *G'night, Golden Boy.* A warmth spread through his chest and up his neck. The wind flapping the edges of the canopy did nothing to cool him.

Dani eyed him carefully. "Wait. Do you like Ava? Ollie filled me in on your history with the review and everything from back in Seattle."

"Of course I like Ava." Zach attempted a laugh.

"No, I mean *like* like."

"I, ah. I don't know." Zach's stomach somersaulted. "I spent so long hating her, blaming her for losing my restaurant, that I forgot that she was a real person. These past few weeks since she first came to my class in Chicago have been . . . eye-opening. She's fun to be around."

"I think my big brother has a crush." Dani elbowed him.

"Stop." His fingers tingled. "It's not a crush. I'm just trying to give her a second chance. That's all."

"What's up, sibs?" Ollie appeared at Dani's side, Eliza next to him. They wore matching Island Bookstore T-shirts. Zach noted they had also checked the weather, Ollie in a brown cardigan and Eliza, a head shorter, in a jacket.

"Zach here has been telling me that he definitely doesn't have a crush on Ava Harper. Even though he's blushing."

"I'm not blushing!" But his sister and brother must not have heard him.

"He denies it's a crush, eh?" Ollie pretended to think this over, hand stroking his chin. "Do you look for her in crowds?"

That didn't mean anything, right?

"Do you try to find ways to brush her hand?" Dani put in.

Once or twice, but those were accidents.

"Do you find yourself wondering 'what would Ava think?'" Back to Ollie that time.

"Do you get sweaty palms when you think about her?"

"Does your heart race?"

They were going so fast now, Zach didn't even bother to reply.

"Or skip a beat?"

"Would you rather be with her than with anyone else?" At Eliza's quiet question, they all fell silent and looked at him.

"Ha ha, guys." Zach ran his hands down his pant legs. "Of course I have sweaty palms and a racing heart. You're giving me the third degree."

"Shakespeare would say you doth protest too much." Ollie punched his shoulder, then smiled down at Eliza. "I tried denying it too, but Eliza won me over in the end. I know you two have a rocky history, but it's obvious you like her. Life's too short to hold grudges."

Enough of this. "Did you come over here just to make fun of me, or did you have something else in mind?"

"Making fun of my big brother is always a positive bonus, but yes, I did have something else." Ollie turned to Dani. "Can I ask you a few questions?" The two of them moved away a couple of steps.

"Ollie likes having you around," Eliza said.

"He just likes to have someone to tease."

"That too. But for real. Your family loves you." Her face brightened in a wide smile, and then she stepped away to grab Ollie's arm. "All set, Ollie?" They walked away.

"Now, where were we?" Dani glanced at her watch. "I only have a couple more minutes before I need to go."

"It's fine. You've teased me and put me in my place. Feel free to go."

"I did have one other thing to talk to you about. I can spare another minute." Dani clutched her clipboard to her chest. "I wasn't going to ask until later, but then I thought you might want to have time to think about it."

"Think about what?"

"I need a chef for the restaurant at the Grand."

His heart rate picked up. Was she—

"I know you don't want to do it, you've turned me down before. I won't ask you again. But do you know anyone I could ask?" Dani rushed on. "I've been having a hard time finding anyone willing to move on island for the rate the hotel can pay them. They all say that with tourism being too slow, they can't trust that the restaurant will even last."

His heart stilled. He had told her no a few months ago. But now . . . "Someone would be lucky to run that place. It used to be the best place to eat on island."

"I know! We even had island people as regulars, not just tourists. I'd love for it to be restored to that, now that the hotel is almost back to normal."

"I have so many happy memories there. Like the time Kate and I made Mom that cake for her birthday."

Dani laughed. "I didn't know there was that much flour in the world. You guys made a royal mess." She paused. "Really good cake, though."

He smiled. "Worth it. But wait. Shouldn't James be the one to hire hotel staff?" Dani had finally convinced their older brother to move home and manage the hotel. "That doesn't seem like it would be up to you."

Dani brushed a hair out of her eye again. "I know it's not totally my job, but I just feel so responsible to make everything run smoothly. The Grand wouldn't even need a chef if it weren't for the revitalization efforts. It would still be a burned-out husk. I want to see every aspect of it succeed. We all need to work together to make Jonathon Island amazing again. I'd like to have some good options to present to James and his assistant, Josh. And soon. Everyone I've tried to recruit hasn't worked out."

Someone to run the restaurant at the Grand? Only the job he'd dreamed about for years when he was younger. But he had new dreams now, right? Between Chefs Anne and Paul, he hoped to land a major position. Plus, Dani wasn't asking him to do it, merely to suggest someone who could.

"I might know a few people." Saying the words felt like tearing out his heart.

"You don't have to answer me right now. But if you could give me a list of possibles before you leave for home?" Dani wrote something on her clipboard. "Oh, and if you have any more ideas for how to set things up in there so it's ready for service, I'd appreciate that too." She spun on her heel, but after two steps she turned back. "Notice I'm not saying anything more about Ava? We all like her." She grinned and spun again before he could reply.

Sure. He could help her get things ready to go. He could even suggest a few people who might be interested in a change of scenery and a life on an island in Michigan.

The harder part would be to figure out what to do about the things he was realizing about himself. Things like where was home? And what to do about these feelings for Ava that were definitely, absolutely, beyond any doubt, not a crush.

Doing something was better than doing nothing.

Ava tossed back the dregs lingering in the bottom of her coffee cup and then scooted out of the booth at Good Day Coffee. After waking early that morning, she'd come to the little shop for a breakfast sandwich and coffee and to write one of her articles. She'd been surrounded by the din of the coffee grinder and espresso machine.

The teal walls and quirky knickknacks of the coffee shop kept a smile on her face, and the atmosphere inspired her writing until articles number four and five were completed. There had been a constant stream of customers in the light and airy shop during the hour she sat with her iced caramel latte. A few, including Seb Jonathon and Cody Hart, had even stopped to say hi. Her heart felt warm and full. This was the community she was seeking, the small-town vibe she craved away from the rush of big city life. Hitting Send, she emailed Judson the finished copy.

Despite the delicious breakfast and even better company, she couldn't ignore the constant buzz at the back of her mind.

She'd finally finished her letter to the homeowners of the house on Zinnia and had given it to Mia on Monday. It was now Tuesday. Twenty-four full hours. The burble in her stomach every time she thought about the house threatened to turn into outright anxiety. Better to combat the what-ifs with some action.

She rummaged in her sling bag for her wallet, then extracted a few bills for a tip.

"See you later," Jill called. The bubbly, red-haired waitress had welcomed Ava and given her some local history while taking her order. As it turned out, she wasn't just the waitress; she also owned the place. Apparently, she was part of the Kelley family who operated many of the restaurants in town. That might be a good angle for a story. Ava jotted the thought down in her notebook. She had already arranged to interview Patrick Kelley. He'd promised to text her with a day and time that worked. She'd ask him about the family connections when she talked to him about his participation in the cook-off.

"See ya, Jill!" Ava waved, then walked out into the breezy street. The jeans and University of Wisconsin sweatshirt she wore didn't quite keep out the chill of the morning. She swiped open the weather app on her phone. Thank goodness, the afternoon would be much nicer. Maybe the wind would blow the clouds away and they could have some sunshine.

She navigated to her contact list and hit the button to call Mia. As the phone rang, she sent up a quick prayer. *Lord, if it's Your will—*

"Hello, Ava," Mia said. In the background, Ava could hear the high voices of two kids. "Finn! Stop crawling on your sister."

Ava laughed. "I'm catching you at a bad time."

Mia sighed. "No, it's always something over here." She gave a short laugh. "The only peace I get these days is when I'm in the office. And not always then, because I bring them with me sometimes. They're my whole heart, but they can make it hard to do my job at times."

Ava's heart ached at the domestic picture Mia painted. Mia was at least ten years younger than Ava, but she already had her life together. Two kids, a fiancé who loved her, and an established life in a beautiful community.

All the things Ava wanted for herself. She could start with the house.

"I'm just calling looking for an update on my house." She winced. Calling it "my house" maybe presumed too much. She began walking down the street. On her right, the windows of an antique store bristled with goodies. She peered through the glass, giving a little wave to the woman putting a doily on top of the chest of drawers in the window.

"Finn!" A rustle from Mia's end. High giggles sounded through the line. "That's it, mister. If you can't leave your sister alone, you need to go to your room. Sorry, Ava." Mia's voice came clearer through the line again. "I think I've bought a few minutes."

"They sound adorable." Ava put her arm over her stomach. The next storefront looked like a glassblowing workshop. The tinkle of a wind chime rang out over the street, and intricate glass bulbs hung in the window.

"They are adorable. And high energy. They're not usually naughty, just full of mischief."

"At least they're separated now. Can't get into too much trouble."

"Oh, give it three minutes, and Maggie will be crawling all over Finn in their room. They like to be together. Anyway, you called about the house?"

"Yes."

Mia sighed again. "I'm sorry, Ava. It's not looking good."

Ava stumbled on a cobblestone. Her heart sank all the way to her ankles.

"I gave your letter to the Realtor for the owners, and she said 'Oh, thanks, I'll add this to the others.' I guess everyone who is interested in the house is trying the same trick." Mia cleared her throat. "She did promise to get back to us in three days, though. Normally it would be faster, but since there are so many people making an offer, the sellers are wanting to really think it through."

"Okay." The next building stood empty, its dark windows looking over a dusty floor. The window boxes contained the remains of last year's flowers. "I'll have to leave it in God's hands, then." Easier said than done. She hadn't known anyone to come through for her. God Himself often felt very far away. "Are there other properties I can look at in the meantime?"

"I took the liberty of trying to find something for you," Mia said. "But I didn't see anything that met your wish list. Nothing in your price range, anyway."

A pricking began behind her eyelids. Ava blinked away the sensation. "How far out of my price range are we talking?" She could maybe afford a bigger loan—if she lived on ramen and toast for the next year. Mia quoted a number that made her eyes water anew. "I'm sorry, was that in millions?"

"Yes, I'm afraid so." Mia's voice dipped. "Most of the affordable housing got snatched up in our dollar housing scheme last year. Now it's mostly the larger homes left. And now that the island is becoming popular again, people are reluctant to sell. We could try to put in an offer on a house on Poppy, but you would be quite a bit below asking price." A stream of giggles sounded on Mia's end.

"Sounds like you better go." Ava put her hand to her temple. The pressure did nothing to relieve the building pain.

"I really am sorry, Ava. I hope you land that house, but I promise to not stop trying to find something for you."

"Mama, have snack?" A little voice echoed over the phone. Probably Maggie.

"Thank you."

"I need to get these kids a snack and into their clothes before Cody comes to pick us up for the day." Another rustle from the other end. "Just a minute, sweetie. Listen, Ava, I wanted to ask you if you wanted to come to my wedding."

Uh. "I don't know how long I'll be in town." Ava crossed one arm across her stomach and clutched at her elbow.

Mia laughed. "I think you will—it's tomorrow night."

"Tomorrow! On a Wednesday? I assumed it would be on the weekend. I know you said you wanted to keep busy, but shouldn't you be, I don't know, wrapping party favors or something?"

"It's going to be pretty simple. It's an outdoor wedding at Blueberry Hill Park followed by a picnic. Picnics are kind of our thing." A bumping sound came from Mia's end of the phone line followed by the distinctive noise of a cupboard being closed. "Here's a cracker." Muffled. "Sorry." Mia's voice came clear again. "Anyway, I don't want you to feel awkward or anything, but I'd love for you to be there. I already consider you one of the locals. The weather should hold. Six o'clock."

One of the locals? Overhead the sun came out from behind a cloud, painting everything golden. "How can I say no to a wedding and a picnic? See you there."

"I hope so." Mia's voice became distant. "Finn—" The phone clicked off. Ava smiled and shook her head. Happy chaos.

The walk during the phone call had landed her at the junction of Main and Jonathon Boulevard. She turned up the street. From here it would only be a short walk up to Poppy Lane. Mia didn't say which house was for sale, but surely it would be obvious. It would be the one with a For Sale sign in the front yard. No harm in looking at it.

Her phone chimed with a text message.

Patrick

I have some time today. Patrick

Ava

Great. In one hour?

Patrick

See you then. I'll make you a
burger at the bar and grill.

Hopefully by then she would have worked off her breakfast sandwich. One thing seemed certain. She would never starve on this island.

She found Poppy Lane and walked past several houses until she spotted one with a For Sale sign.

In front of her was a small house, set back from the road. White siding gleamed, and lilac bushes full of light-purple flowers ran along the sides of the craftsman-style home. A huge metal pole shed loomed behind the house, casting a shadow over the lawn. The shed must be twice the size of the house itself. No wonder they had such a high asking price. Someone would basically be buying two homes. What would anyone keep in there? Certainly not classic cars, with the ban on motor vehicles. Ava shrugged and turned back toward town. Mia was right. She wasn't interested in that property. At. All.

Her phone chimed again.

Emily
Fallen for any mysterious and
handsome Michiganders?

She laughed. Emily was always trying to set her up with some guy or another.

Ava
No. Everyone here seems taken.

Emily
That's the problem with a tiny
island. You should move with me
to LA. 😊

Ava
Not the vibe I'm looking for.

Emily
I know. You want the small-town

Hallmark guy with flannel and a
short beard.

Or maybe green eyes and chef's whites. Beard optional. She shook her head.

Ava

I'd settle for someone I can trust.

Her phone rang with a video call.

"You know the right guy is out there, right?" Emily got straight to the point. Her brunette curls sprang in every direction, and her eyes glinted with mischief.

"Hello to you too."

Emily rolled her eyes. "We were already in the middle of a conversation."

"Fine. You're right." Ava began retracing her steps back into town. Emily's face bobbed with every step.

"Ooh! Out for a walk? Turn me around so I can see."

Ava pivoted with her phone. "This is one of the residential streets."

"It's cute." Emily's voice held no trace of sarcasm.

"You'll never guess who is from here."

Emily closed her eyes. "Don't tell me . . . Chris Pratt. He's from the Midwest, right?" Emily opened her eyes again.

"I think he's from Minnesota." Ava tucked a strand of hair behind her ear. "No. It's Zach Sullivan. His family owns the big hotel, and he's back participating in Flavor Fest."

"The nemesis." Emily grinned.

"He's not my nemesis. If anything, I'm his."

"I don't think it works that way." Emily put her face closer to the screen. "How come you're always blushing when you talk about Chef Zach?"

"I'm not blushing." But she could feel that her face was on fire. Drat this fair skin.

"Do you like this guy?"

"I . . . don't know. He's different than I thought he'd be."

"Good different?"

Ava pictured his patience with the cooking class and the way he believed in her. "Definitely a good different."

"Maybe he's your lumberjack."

"What?"

"You know, your small-town guy." Emily waggled her eyebrows.

Too bad she wasn't here in person so Ava could give her arm a swat. "Stop. He lives in Chicago. And he wants to move to the West Coast. Nothing small-town about him. It doesn't matter if I like him or not. We aren't going to be living in the same place in a month or two."

"Ah, star-crossed lovers." Emily batted her eyes.

"I'm hanging up now." Ava grinned at her friend, then cut the call.

A moment later, a text chimed.

Emily

I'm not overlooking the fact that you said you like him. We are definitely going to come back to that later.

Ava wandered back to town, Emily's text ringing through her. She reached Kelley's Bar & Grill and pushed through the door. The scent of grilling onions and hamburger patties hung in the air.

Patrick waved at her from behind the long, dark bar. "Ava, over here. I hope you're hungry." Tall stools were tucked under the glossy surface of the bar counter.

A few patrons sat at the wooden tables scattered through the open space. On one wall stood a jukebox and a karaoke entertainment system.

As she walked across the scarred wood flooring, she scanned the other customers for a familiar shock of dark hair, heart pinching when she didn't see him. Silly to expect him to be here, of course. But this only proved Emily's intuition right.

She was falling for Zach.

Eleven

IME TO INVEST IN SOME NEW SHOES.

Ava sat in a folding chair near the back of the crowd gathered at Blueberry Hill Park for Mia and Cody's wedding. After spending the day on her feet, pacing as she rewrote her articles, as well as walking through town, it was a relief to rest her tired arches. If she was going to be a Jonathon Island local, she'd need to get better footwear than her current pair of casual shoes. Her tennis shoes hadn't survived their tart bath. So, shoes were definitely on a shopping list. Or maybe a bike. She looked to her right, where a line of bikes waited in a row.

Folding chairs spread out before her, arranged in rows for the outdoor wedding in the park. People occupied nearly all of the hundred or so chairs. A white runner split the chairs down the middle, ending at an arch covered in flowers. A tall pine stood sentry near the left front corner of the makeshift sanctuary. A little way off, picnic tables waited under a stand of trees.

Off to the side of the arches, a man with a shock of red hair was adjusting the sound system. Behind him, a younger person Ava didn't recognize held a guitar, and Olive Kelley sat on a cajón. At six o'clock on the nose, they started playing quietly. The opening strains of "'Tis So Sweet to Trust in Jesus" filled the air, wafting along on the pine-scented breeze.

The redheaded man, who must be the pastor, moved under the arch and was joined by Cody. No baseball cap tonight with his dark suit and purple tie. A murmur passed through the crowd before everyone settled again.

A woman bearing a strong resemblance to Ollie, a camera in her hands, moved to the front of the aisle and faced the congregation. Didn't someone say that one of Zach's sisters was a wedding photographer?

Three sets of couples made their way down the aisle, the men in jeans, white button-ups, and purple ties, the women in purple sundresses topped with a light shawl. One of the couples was Dani and Liam, but Ava didn't recognize the other two, one a woman with a streak of purple in her hair, and the other a slightly older couple, the woman bearing a small resemblance to Mia.

The music changed to a lively version of Pachelbel's Canon in D. A ripple of amusement ran through the crowd as a child—who must be Finn Franklin—dressed in a short-sleeve button-up shirt and a purple bow tie, walked down the aisle, a serious look on his face, a small tackle box in his hands. Behind him, his tiny sister, dark curls matted to her head, toddled behind, clutching a sprig of lilacs.

"Would the congregation please rise," the pastor said.

They rose and faced the bride. Mia, hand clasping her father's crooked elbow, floated on the music. Her cap-sleeved lace dress fell in an A-line to the white runner. In her hands, she carried a bouquet of lilacs and peonies. Keeping her eyes trained on Cody, she practically looked like the heart-eye emoji in the flesh. Seb gave the bride away and took his seat, as did the rest of the congregation.

"Welcome, everyone," the man with the mic said. "I'm Pastor Arnie Chamberlain. I'm so glad you came out for the wedding of Mia and Cody. They've requested we begin by singing "Tis So Sweet to Trust in Jesus.'"

The musicians transitioned back into the hymn, and the congregation launched into singing.

"'Tis so sweet to trust in Jesus,
Just to take Him at His word.
Just to rest upon His promise;
Just to know, 'Thus saith the Lord.'"

Ava let the song flow through her and into her heart. Trust. What a strange concept. Sure, she believed God *could* do what He said He would do, but she had little experience with people following through. After all, her parents—the two people who were supposed to love her more than anything—never had time for her. They would promise to come home and then not show.

As the song ended and the musicians sat down, Pastor Arnie lifted a worn black Bible from a music stand. "Our sermon text for tonight comes from Colossians three, verses twelve and thirteen. 'So, as those who have been chosen of God, holy and beloved, put on a heart of compassion, kindness, humility, gentleness and patience; bearing with one another, and forgiving each other, whoever has a complaint against anyone; just as the Lord forgave you, so also should you.'" He closed the book, leaving his finger marking the spot. "'A heart of compassion.' Those words always struck me. They are the basis for what comes next—the kindness, humility, forgiveness, and all the rest. Tonight, Cody and Mia, I encourage you to remember to have a heart of compassion for one another."

A familiar head of dark, mussed hair was four rows up and to her right. Zach. Ava's heart rate picked up. Teaching the class with him two days ago had been fun. He wasn't at all what she expected. She recognized what she thought was arrogance as a drive for excellence, and his self-centeredness was actually a cover for feeling socially awkward.

As though he felt her eyes boring into the back of his head, Zach glanced over his shoulder. Their eyes met. Ava's fingers tingled. He shot her a wink before turning back to face the front again.

He made her laugh, he was brilliant in the kitchen, and he was kind to his family. Uh oh, she might be a goner.

Around her, the congregation chuckled at something Pastor Arnie said. Whoops. Time to tune back in.

"And that is why I can trust Him. And so can you, Cody and Mia." Pastor Arnie gestured to the musicians. They moved to the front and began playing quietly. "Let's pray."

Shoot. She'd have to find out what she'd missed. She could use some wisdom on trusting God.

Pastor Arnie concluded his prayer and looked toward Finn. "Can we have the rings?" Finn held out the tackle box, and another laugh rippled through the congregation.

A longing filled Ava as she watched Mia and Cody declare their love for each other and promise to cherish each other forever. Would she ever know that kind of love?

A few minutes later, the ceremony wrapped up.

Ava hung back until the receiving line dissipated and then made her way over to Mia and Cody. "Congratulations and best wishes, you two! Finn and Maggie were the cutest."

Mia smiled. "I managed to keep that bow tie on Finn for the whole time. He was so excited to wear it for the last week, but when it came time to put it on today, he wasn't interested."

"He wore it well." Ava spotted the small boy weaving in and out of the crowd. Every once in a while, someone would stop him, and he would adjust his bow tie and grin up at them.

"I think everyone here is complimenting him." Mia's eyes

softened as she looked at him. "Now he'll never take it off." She tapped Ava's upper arm. "I bet he wears it to bed tonight."

Ava laughed. "I was hoping you could fill me in on Pastor Arnie's last point. I'm afraid my mind drifted off a little. But maybe your mind drifted too. You had a lot going on."

"Oh! No problem. He actually quoted one of my favorite verses. I asked him to include it. 'Trust in the Lord and do good; Dwell in the land and cultivate faithfulness. Delight yourself in the Lord; And He will give you the desires of your heart.' That's from Psalm 37. Verses three and four, I think."

Ava pulled her notebook from her leather shoulder bag and jotted the Scripture reference down. "Thanks. I'll look it up again later."

"This is probably really forward of me, but those verses reminded me of your house search." Mia lightly squeezed Ava's arm before dropping her hand. "Desires of your heart and all."

"Not forward at all. I thought the same thing as you recited them." The words resonated through her. "The hard part is the trusting."

Mia threw her head back and laughed. "Don't I know it! Oh, hi, Zach."

Ava's fingers tingled again as she looked to see Zach standing next to her. "Hi."

"Hi, everyone." Zach's lightweight green sweater made his eye color pop. He shook Cody's hand. "Congratulations, man." Then he embraced Mia. "Best wishes, cuz."

"Thanks." Mia swiveled her head as though searching for something. "Has anyone seen—Maggie!" She dashed off in the direction of the toddler. Cody grinned at them and chased after them.

Ava watched her for a moment, then turned to Zach. "That woman is a ball of energy."

"She has to be with those two. Their dad was on the track team, you know," Zach said. His smile lit his eyes an even deeper green.

How was that possible? "Thanks again for your help at the cooking class," he said. "I couldn't have done that without you."

Ava swallowed and looked out toward the safer view of the crowd clearing up the outdoor sanctuary, folding chairs and stacking them in neat piles. "No problem. It was fun."

"You're a natural with people. I wish I had that talent and your patience."

"You did great." Better than great, actually. He was the one who was a natural in front of the class. Why couldn't he see that about himself? "I was impressed with your ability to break down difficult concepts into manageable pieces."

Zach shrugged. "Eh, that's no biggie. I had to do it that way when I was going through culinary school. Cooking is really a series of steps anyway, so breaking it down is natural."

"Impressive, nonetheless." The crowd had dispersed now. She spotted Cody pulling a trailer full of chairs behind a golf cart. He had Maggie on his lap. "I was thinking I should explore the park a little before checking out the reception food. Care for a walk?" Hopefully, her feet would hold up. The ache had subsided during the wedding.

"Lead on." Zach held out a hand, and she gave a mock curtsy before heading toward the paved path a few steps away. The path traveled away from them and around the park.

"I love the small-town vibe here. It makes me feel safe." Ava pulled the strap of her bag up and over her head so it would stop slapping her with every step.

"Yeah, maybe. Safe in some ways, I guess."

"What do you mean?"

"I just have a hard time trusting people." Zach lifted a shoulder and let it drop.

"Why is that?"

Zach let out a long breath. "Probably because they will always betray you."

Her heart dropped. "Always? That's a little harsh."

"I've found it to be true in my life," Zach said.

"Maybe you're always pushing them away. Maybe you're misunderstanding them." She didn't trust easily either, but she couldn't just let his all-or-nothing statement stand.

"Oh, like the time in tenth grade when my friend persuaded me to tell him who I liked and then he spread that secret around the school? My classmates teased me for the rest of the year because the girl was way out of my league. Turns out he had done it to get back at me for something I didn't even do." Zach shoved his hands in his pockets. "Talk about betrayal."

"Zach." Ava paused on the trail. An old maple arched over them, the last rays of dappled sunshine painting the path. She waited until he met her eyes. "I hate to break it to you, but tenth grade was like two decades ago. I think it's time to move on." She raised an eyebrow.

He broke into a smile. "Fair point. I mostly mentioned it to show you that no one can be trusted. Up until that day, I'd thought that guy was my best friend. He showed me differently."

"Kids can be cruel." That old saying proved itself true daily.

"If only it were just kids. My ex-fiancée confirmed my hypothesis."

He had an ex-fiancée? They were back at the beginning of the walking loop, but Zach showed no signs of slowing down, so Ava kept pace as they began a second loop.

"Care to share?" The sun was hanging low on the horizon. From this point they could look out over Lake Huron. Silvery waves capped the surface of the lake, the wind offshore churning up dark, rough waves.

"Not much to tell." Zach stared straight ahead. "I caught her with my friend a few weeks before we were supposed to get married. I guess she wasn't interested in being with someone who was still finding his way."

"I'm sorry, Zach." No wonder it was so hard for him to develop relationships. His guard would have to be up all the time. "It was totally her loss. She threw away an amazing person."

"Really?" He looked at her out of the corner of his eye, one side of his mouth quirked up. "Ava Harper, what are you saying? Do you tolerate me?"

She felt the heat rise in her cheeks. He was being vulnerable. Maybe she should meet him with some vulnerability of her own. She swallowed.

"Actually, Zach Sullivan, I—I think I like you." She *liked* him? How embarrassing. What was she? Fifteen? The flush spread down her neck and arms. She quickened her pace and heard him scrambling to catch up with her.

"Ava, wait."

"I think this walk was a mistake."

He reached out and snagged her hand. "Just hold up a minute."

She stopped and faced him, cheeks burning. "I never should have said anything. You must think I'm ridiculous."

"I like you too."

Her heart stopped for a beat before leaping to life again. A smile spread across her face, matching the one on his. They stood and grinned at each other for a few heartbeats before Zach squeezed her hand.

"I guess we're both ridiculous." His low voice did funny things to her insides.

The ache in her feet no longer mattered. Not when she was walking on clouds.

Had he lost his mind?

He'd been drawn to Ava after the wedding like a hungry man to a buffet table. In her red capris, long blue shirt, with a leather bag slung over her shoulder, she looked more like an islander than an outsider.

From their perch near the Lake Huron overlook, they could see a few sailboats bobbing on the water. Zach blinked at Ava a few times. Had he really just confessed to having a crush on her?

Maybe it was Dani's and Ollie's teasing from earlier, maybe it was the intimacy of this walk they were on, or maybe it was Pastor Arnie's message tonight about trust, but something had shifted in him when she admitted to liking him. He couldn't hold back the truth.

He was falling for Ava.

Across from him, Ava's cheeks had pinked in a way that he found irresistible. The freckles scattered across her nose stood out even more. She gazed up at him from under her blonde lashes and gave two slow blinks.

"Why, Zach Sullivan." She imitated a Southern belle. Badly. "Would you say you tolerate me?"

He squeezed her hand and laughed. Wait. He was still holding her hand? Her slim, cool fingers wrapped around his and squeezed back. "It looks like I do."

He'd just outlined all the reasons not to have faith in people. But maybe it was time to try trusting someone again.

Around them, the light was fading fast.

"Should we walk back to the reception?" Zach let her hand go, then crossed his arms to keep from picking it up again.

"Sure," she said. They fell into step again.

The words Dani had said about his arrogance toward Ava being in the competition popped into his mind. They brought a stone to his belly. Yeah, he could see how he'd been a jerk.

"Listen, Ava." He cleared his throat. Good thing the light had faded. Easier to admit wrongdoing when Ava's piercing gaze wasn't drilling into his head.

"Mm-hmm?"

"I feel like I should apologize for my rudeness about you just being the helper for our charity team." His hands felt slick.

Next to him, Ava gave a low chuckle. "Yeah, I guess you were kind of rude, but I wasn't offended. If it makes you feel better, I forgive you. I'm well aware of what I bring to this team. Which is practically nothing."

"That's not true." The stone in his belly dissolved at her absolution and admission. "You bring enthusiasm, and heart, and ideas. That's not nothing. In fact, those are things that can't be taught." Her quiet thank-you sent a spear through his heart. "Seriously, Ava. You are pretty amazing."

He didn't realize she'd stopped until he was a few paces ahead. He looked back at her. Her gaze was soft. She blinked several times. "Ava?"

"Nobody's ever told me I'm amazing before." Ava clasped her hands in front of her.

"Well, it's true. You're not like anyone else, and you're amazing. I'll just have to keep reminding you. You did great in the class too." He admired her ability to chat with anyone and to find something positive to say about even the most terrible chopping skills. "You had everyone almost literally eating out of your hands. I don't know how you kept calm through all that chaos."

Ava caught up with him, and they fell into an easy walking rhythm again. "It can't be much different than a regular kitchen during the dinner rush."

"Sure, but at least then everyone knows what they're supposed to be doing." He held a finger in the air. "A well-run kitchen is a thing of beauty. A cooking class, that's just controlled chaos."

"You did pretty well too. Charming the ladies, building up the men." She gave him a toothy grin. "I think you could grow to enjoy the classes."

"Only if you're there to tame the crazy ones." They passed under a streetlight, and he glanced down at her. A pleased smile covered her lips.

If he stayed in Chicago, he could see that smile all the time.

"Have you heard anything back about your house?" They were nearing the beginning of the path. Maybe Ava would agree to another loop. He didn't want this walk to end.

"No. I'm not too hopeful. Sounds like everyone who put in an offer also had the idea of submitting a personal letter. I'm trying to keep my expectations low."

He could hear the defeat in her voice. "The right place is out there for you. I know it."

"Mia helped me find the Bible verse Pastor Arnie mentioned tonight. About getting the desires of our hearts," Ava said. "I told God I was leaving it in His hands, but I keep snatching it back."

He laughed. "I know the feeling."

For the first time, Zach felt a pang about moving away from Chicago. If he convinced Anne Green to give him a job and he landed on the West Coast, he'd likely never see Ava again. Then again, if the job with Paul Hawkeye panned out, he could be in Chicago indefinitely.

He should find out what neighborhood she was moving to. Maybe they would live closer now.

"Where—"

"Zach!"

He whipped around. His dad strode toward them. *Great timing, Dad.* Like always.

"I thought that was you." His dad looked like he'd just stepped off a yacht in his slacks and a sport coat. His hair ruffled in the wind. A gold watch glittered on his wrist. He'd spotted him earlier but hadn't stopped to chat. "And Ava, right?"

Zach suppressed a nearly involuntary grimace. "Dad, this is Ava Harper. She's a food writer for the *Chicago Herald* and my teammate in the competition this weekend." He gestured at his dad. "Ava, this is my dad, Daniel Sullivan."

Ava's eyes rounded. Was she remembering that this was the man who'd burned down the hotel ten years ago?

"We actually met earlier, though we didn't really get to chat. So much was going on." To her credit, Ava's mouth turned up in a smile as she extended her hand. "Nice to meet you, Mr. Sullivan. I've heard so much about you."

Zach's dad roared with laughter as he shook her hand. "I just bet you have. Don't worry. I'm a changed man. Or at least, I'm trying."

Zach's thoughts tangled. Anger, regret, and love all fought for dominance. He needed to sort these things out. Another person he would have to practice forgiving.

"Are you two walking back over to the reception? I'll join you." Without missing a beat, his dad fell into step beside them. "Ava, tell me something about yourself."

"There's not much to tell. I'm a food writer." Ava clutched the strap of her bag with both hands. "I'm hoping to move into a position that offers travel. My editor is basing that on how well my articles do from this trip."

"What's the worst thing you've ever eaten?" His dad's eager question made Ava laugh.

With a rueful glance at Zach, Ava answered. "I think it was whatever Zach was trying to serve last weekend. Sorry, Zach."

He put both hands in the air. "No harm done. I know it was terrible. Those flavors should have worked. But also, I never should have tried something new for a competition unless I'd already done it before."

"We're making pasties for the charity competition," Ava said.

"Ahhh." Daniel nodded. "Very Michigan. I like it. How about the starter course?"

"We're going with mushroom tarts for the appetizer," Zach said.

"Going traditional to showcase the very best parts of the Midwest and Jonathon Island."

The picnic tables for the reception came into view just beyond the space where the ceremony took place. Mason jars holding candles glowed in every available space between platters groaning with fried chicken.

"Smart."

"This competition means a lot to me." He squared up his shoulders. "I'd like to win for the Silver Platter. They could use the funds." Young RJ from his cooking class at Escargot flashed through his mind. If the Silver Platter got a fresh infusion of funds, they could help lots of RJs.

"Right. The Silver Platter. I looked them up. Great organization." His dad patted him on the shoulder, then did the same to Ava. "Best of luck to you both." He gestured to the dessert table. "Anyone need some chocolate cake?"

"Always," Ava said. "I'll walk with you."

Feeling like a very obvious third wheel, Zach trailed behind them, the silence amplifying his awkwardness.

"Ava," his dad said, "did anyone ever tell you about how Dani got me to agree to rebuild this place?"

Ava gave Zach a look of apology before turning back to his dad. "I don't think so."

"I'll give you the CliffsNotes version." His dad put an arm across her shoulder and led her toward the desserts. "Maybe you'd want to use it in your newspaper article."

Ava looked back at Zach over her shoulder. "Sorry," she mouthed.

His heart stilled. "It's fine," he mouthed back.

And it really was fine. Because on the walk, he'd realized that he had a big problem to sort through. Sure, he liked Ava, but was there any future for them? And did he even want one? What would a relationship look like if he moved to the coast to follow his dreams?

Twelve

HER STOMACH TWISTED AS SHE DRESSED FOR the day. Ava exhaled slowly, willing her nerves to settle. The walk and talk with Zach on Wednesday night had convinced her that if they were going to move forward, she needed to clear the air about the review her newspaper had printed.

Zach's dad had interrupted her before she could talk to him about the review. And then several other people wanted to chat. By the time she had a free minute, he'd already gone.

Yesterday, she'd concentrated on getting enough material for her article series. She hadn't run into Zach at all. But no more excuses. She couldn't keep sweeping that conversation under the rug. Maybe she could find a quiet moment after the contest today.

Today's events were going to be momentous. Was this unsettled sensation because she was worried about the contest or from the prospect of working in a small kitchen with the handsome chef she was finding herself falling for? No time to figure it out now.

But first, she had to keep the secret of her complete ineptness in the kitchen from being the only thing people talked about today. Right. She checked the mirror. She'd chosen dark slacks and a T-shirt for today and put her hair into a high ponytail. She squared her shoulders, then tugged her shirt straight. *You've got this.* If her parents weren't going to call and give her a pep talk, she'd have to do it on her own.

She'd make it through the day by doing everything Zach told her to do. She tucked her notebook into her shoulder bag and headed out the door. A few minutes later, Dani pointed her to the kitchen station Zach had used for the other competitions.

"I didn't think there was any harm in giving him the same one," Dani said. Today, the tourism director was in a hot-pink T-shirt emblazoned with the Jonathon Island Flavor Fest logo. It paired nicely with her whitewashed skinny jeans and Converse sneakers. "Most of the other contestants are repeats too, so they got their old spaces as well."

Ava looked around. She recognized Patrick Kelley, of course, and Enrique Perez. A few stations down, Val Anderson was prepping something. Their closest neighbor wasn't someone she knew, however. Time to introduce herself. She took a step in that direction.

"Coffee?" Zach's voice behind her caused her to whirl around. "Whoa." He pulled the two cups he held out of the way as her shoulder bag flew around with her. "You almost had to source your own caffeine." His white teeth flashed in a smile.

She took the cup, but her fingers nearly fumbled the hand-off. That stupid combination—chef's whites and black jeans—shouldn't be allowed. It was far too effective. "You're a lifesaver."

"I took a chance and ordered you a fancy coffee." Zach eyed her over the rim of his cup as he took a long sip.

"A fancy coffee?" She sniffed at the opening in the lid. "What is it?"

"Try it." His eyes held a challenge. "Tell me what you taste."

A long swallow revealed warm notes of spice and mellow coffee, lightly sugared with a foamy finish. "Hmm. Cardamom and raw sugar, maybe a light roast coffee . . ." She sipped again. "Is there pistachio in this cappuccino?"

Zach set his cup on the table and clapped. "Nicely done. I think you might have a future in the food industry."

"It's really good."

"It's my own recipe. I think Jill at Good Day thought I was crazy." Zach pulled an apron out from a box under the table. "Here, put this on. Wouldn't want to ruin that T-shirt."

"You might have a future as a barista." She patted his shoulder. "If this chef thing doesn't work out."

His laugh rang out as she tied on the apron.

A few minutes later, the competition was underway.

"Ava, chop those mushrooms smaller," Zach barked.

Ava stiffened. "I thought we could do them a little larger. It'll take less time to chop."

"You need to follow my plan. Too big and the mushrooms won't cook properly." Zach motioned to the instructions he'd printed out for her, Audrey's Mushroom Tarts written across the top.

Right. "Yes, chef." She saluted him and let the brief irritation go. She'd agreed to do what he said, and he knew best in the kitchen anyway.

"Did I tell you I first made a version of this dish in Seattle, fresh out of school?" Zach came alongside her and began chopping too. "A family who invited me home after church every week used to serve it."

"Nothing like a home-cooked meal after church." Not that she would know. It was usually a frozen potpie for her. "Do you have a church in Chicago?"

"I used to. But then I had to work Sundays for a while. I probably should start going again. It's hard to be motivated when I don't feel like any place I live is permanent."

"I get that. My apartment in Chicago isn't anything special. It certainly doesn't feel like *home* home." Ava's heart pinched. "Of course, I'm hoping to change that when I move."

Conversation ceased as Zach cooked the mushroom mix on the stove, then they both worked together to fill tiny dough cups with the filling before topping them with cheese and popping the tarts into the oven.

"We should have time to wipe everything down while we wait." Ava reached for the bucket of soapy water Zach had stashed under the side table.

"You know I always love a clean kitchen," he said.

The timer on Zach's phone chimed. He pulled the pan of mushroom appetizers out of the tiny oven at the back of their station.

"Audrey always finished this dish with just a dash of Himalayan salt. She said it was love." Zach sprinkled a small amount of pink salt across the tops of the tarts. "I've tried making it without that final step, and it's never the same."

Ava tried a quick bite. They only had minutes before the round completed. "Zach, you might not be able to share your feelings with words, but you put your heart into everything you cook."

"Plate up, sous chef." Zach's growl made a grin spread across her face.

Their appetizer was met with oohs and aahs from the judges.

"You'll be moving on to the next round tomorrow morning," Anne Green said. She clapped her hands lightly before heading to the next cooking station.

Ava squealed. Zach picked her up and spun her in a circle, laughing.

He set her down. His gaze drew her in, a hint of gold ringing Zach's pupils.

She swallowed hard, then put her hand on his chest and pushed away from him. "I need to talk to you about something."

Zach's brow crinkled, but his eyes still danced. "Don't you know how ominous it sounds when someone says 'I need to talk to you'?"

She couldn't help the smile that crossed her face despite the pounding of her heart. "Sorry. But I do need to talk to you. Hopefully, somewhere more private?" She gestured at the crowds still swarming the tent.

"Gazebo?" He jutted his chin in the direction of the structure. "Gazebo."

They were quiet as they walked across the spongy grass. With every step the damp grass released the scent of spring—loamy, fresh, green. Ava's hand brushed Zach's, but she tucked it into her pocket. It was better if he heard her out before they held hands.

Thankfully, the crowd at Flavor Fest hadn't drifted over to this area of the hotel grounds. The gazebo waited for them without other people around.

The air cooled by a few degrees as they entered the shade of the wooden structure. A few steps in, Ava turned to face Zach.

"I think we need to talk about the review in Ava Harper Chows Down."

Zach's eyes clouded. "I don't think that's such a good idea."

Ava rubbed her clammy hands on the front of her jeans. "I just wanted to explain—"

"Ava, I'm having a hard enough time putting the whole thing behind me without you dredging it back up again. Can't we just leave it?"

"I don't think I can spend any more time with you until we hash it out. Plus, I think you'll appreciate what I have to say."

"Fine."

Zach's grunt left her unconvinced, but she forged on. "Do you want to sit down?" They sat, Zach's back ramrod straight. Ava fought the urge to put her hand on his and massage the tension away.

She cleared her throat. "When I worked at the *Seattle Courier*, it was my first real column out of journalism school. A column with my own byline. I couldn't believe I'd landed the position. It was a way to stay connected to the food scene without being in a kitchen myself."

"So, you thought you'd score off me?" The hurt in his voice sent a spear through her. "Sorry. Still working on the forgiveness thing."

"No. Just listen to me." Ava put out her hand. "I went to your restaurant and ate close to the best meal of my life. I thought one of your waiters would have to roll me out, I ate so much that night."

Zach's mouth dropped open. "What are you saying? How could you write those things about me, then?"

"At one point you came out of the kitchen, and I heard you talking to another patron. I don't remember exactly what you said, but you sounded so full of yourself, talking about the 'proper way to do things.' I know now that it was your commitment to excellence talking—and maybe some self-doubt."

"Ava." Zach's voice was low, dangerous. "I fail to see how any of this is supposed to make me feel better. You wrote a critical review because you thought I was stuck-up."

"No! I didn't write a bad review. By the time I got home, I'd decided to ignore my observations of you and just focus on the food." She needed air. "But then I sat down in front of my computer and froze. I couldn't think of a thing to say. So"—she swallowed hard—"I tried using a writing prompt from school where you write the opposite, or at least something different than what you plan to say. It unlocked my brain from having to be perfect so I could write the real thing."

"The real thing." Zach leaned forward. "So, the review printed in the newspaper was the real thing?"

"No!" She was mangling this explanation. "That was the result of the writing prompt. My real review was a glowing one. Five stars. Or five forks, I guess, since that was the rating system the *Courier* used."

Zach fell back against the bench. "Let me get this straight. You came to my restaurant, loved the food, didn't care for me, went home, wrote a terrible article about my restaurant, then wrote a good one, but somehow the bad one ended up in the newspaper?"

"That's about ri—"

He held his hand up. "And then, your very bad review—the imagery is still seared into my brain, by the way, vivid—tanked my restaurant, which led to bankruptcy, caused my girlfriend to break up with me, and sent me on a series of dead-end cooking jobs in order to get my life back on track? And now you're telling me it was all a mistake?"

Hearing it all together like that—the restaurant, the bankruptcy, the breakup—made the whole thing ten times worse. And it was already very bad. Her lungs felt tight, like she couldn't get enough air.

Zach sighed. He rubbed his temples. "I can see why you wanted me to know all of that. I wish I could say it makes me feel better, but it just doesn't." He stood and paced a few steps. Then he tapped his fist on his leg three times. "I just want to put this whole thing behind me. I have some good opportunities in front of me if I can just focus on them."

Not forgiveness. Not really. But it was close enough. The band around her chest loosened by one notch.

How was it possible that she felt both better and worse? She had thought that telling him would make him feel better, maybe even forgive her faster. Then they could move on and . . . what? Be together? But she was moving to Jonathon Island, and he wanted to live on the West Coast. There was no future there. Whatever had been developing between her and Zach wasn't meant to be.

Ava hadn't intended the bad review? One of the most pivotal

events of his life, arguably *the* most pivotal event, and it was all a mistake. Not only that, but the woman he'd spent the past six years being angry at wasn't who he expected at all.

It was all leaving him confused.

Her quiet words had torn the scab off a wound that still festered. And yet, he couldn't square those old feelings with the new ones he was acquiring.

He ran a hand through his hair and took a minute to compose his thoughts. Shouts of laughter occasionally drifted from the festival area, disrupting the quiet around the gazebo and surrounding hotel grounds. The scent of hot oil and caramelized sugar also drifted over. His stomach rumbled, but he didn't think it was only because of hunger.

"Do you have any questions for me?" Ava looked at him as though she were afraid of what he would say.

"Why didn't you tell me this before? Like back in Seattle?"

"I tried to get the newspaper to print a retraction, but I was so new that they wouldn't go for it. That review got tons of hits online. And then my parents shared it with their fans . . ." Her lips twisted in a grimace. "After trying for a few weeks, I finally decided to come see you for myself, to apologize and explain. By then, you were already gone."

That tracked. "I moved to Austin two months after Peach failed. What a dead-end job that turned out to be. A line cook in a catering kitchen where the recipes included barbecued beef and pretty much only barbecued beef." He'd begun cooking on autopilot. Living on autopilot.

Moving to Saratoga Springs and even New York City hadn't helped. And now at Escargot, with Chef Louie blocking him whenever he could, he was on the same trajectory. In fact, since Seattle, he'd been on autopilot in all areas of his life. Romantically, financially, and spiritually.

He was tired of it.

Time to get out of this stale half-life of his.

He looked at Ava. Over the last few weeks, he'd learned that she was nothing like the monster he'd built in his head. He liked spending time with her. He wanted to fully forgive her, to trust her. Like Pastor Arnie said in his message the other night, just as the Lord forgave you, and all of that.

Maybe he needed to take drastic action.

"Ava, would you like to go on a date with me?" Okay, not his smoothest proposal, but the words were out there. They hung in the air for a moment, and his chest grew tight with the breath he was holding.

Ava raised her eyebrows. "You really want to go on a date. With me."

"Look, I'm not going to deny that all of this has thrown me for a loop. I'd rather just forget the whole thing, but instead I'm going to work on forgiveness." Bitterness wasn't worth it, he was learning, except when needed for balance in a dish. "And despite a big mistake from a long time ago, I like you, Ava. I'd like to see if we have any kind of future."

"Then, yes, I'd love to go on a date with you."

He looked at his phone. "We're free for the rest of the day. Want to get together in a few hours?"

"Tonight?" Ava hadn't stopped staring at him. He patted his shoulders and then the top of his head. "What are you doing?"

"I'm checking to see if I grew a second head." Oh, he liked teasing her. "The way you're staring at me . . ."

"Sorry." She bent her head to either side, almost to her shoulders.

"Now what are *you* doing?"

"Checking to see if I have whiplash. This conversation took such a sharp turn." She laughed and stood. "Okay, if we're really doing this date thing, I'd better go freshen up."

He wanted to tell her that she was fine just the way she was, but he needed a moment too. More than that, he needed someone to debrief with.

After Ava walked away, Zach pulled out his phone. "Uncle Bryan, can we talk?"

"Hey, Zach!" His uncle's voice sounded warm and strong. "I've got some time. What's up?" For as long as he could remember, his dad's brother had been a mentor to him. If anyone could help him work through the problem of Ava, Uncle Bryan could.

"Can you meet me at the gazebo at the Grand? I need to hash some things out."

"I'll be there in fifteen."

When his uncle arrived, he wrapped Zach in a hug, his thick forearms and working man's body a solid mass. He'd recently moved back to Jonathon Island with his wife Mary to run the family's pumpkin farm. "Good to see you." Uncle Bryan slapped Zach on the back and then pulled away. Zach motioned to the benches lining the walls of the wooden structure and they sat.

"Thanks for coming over." Zach led him through the story of how he and Ava met, their subsequent lives, and now his growing attraction to her. "Except, every time I think I'm ready to move past what happened, something brings it all up again."

A crowd of people approached, walking in the direction of the food festival. Among them were his mom and dad. Strangely, his dad had his hand on the small of his mom's back, guiding her over a dip in the lawn.

A chill wind swept over the trees, bringing a hint of lake water. Zach rolled his shoulders, then began pacing inside the gazebo.

"Hmm. That is a tough one." Uncle Bryan cocked his head to the side, the way he always did when thinking through a difficult situation. "Forgiveness can be hard, but we're called to do it any-way. Let's walk." They headed out across the lawn, passing outside the festival grounds and into the magnificent gardens someone had restored for the Grand.

"Yeah, Pastor Arnie was talking about that the other night. I'm not sure I can forgive like Jesus did. He was perfect. I'm so not." He shrugged. The fact he couldn't let this go was a perfect example of that.

A laugh rumbled out of Uncle Bryan. "I can attest to that. None of us are. The good news is that we don't have to be."

"I just don't think I can forgive and forget. I mean, I know Ava's review wasn't intentional now, but the consequences of it are all tangled up in what happened afterward. I essentially lost my restaurant because of her." Their strides took them off the hotel property and out along the water on the west side of the island. Waves crashed against the shore, carrying leaves and bits of sticks with them. Overhead, a seagull cried its discordant call.

"One bad review was all it took? Maybe you need to take a closer look at your memories from back then." Uncle Bryan cleared his throat. "But either way, we know God is sovereign. He takes our bad situations and works them for the good of those who love Him. He is more concerned with our hearts than our comfort. He allowed that article to be published, and while that might be a tough bite to chew on, He has a purpose in it. We have to trust Him." He clapped Zach on the shoulder. "Plus, I have good news for you. Forgive *and forget* isn't in the Bible."

Zach halted, shoulder to shoulder with Uncle Bryan, at the edge of Lake Huron. The lake stretched to the horizon. Sunlight glittered across its surface. "I'm pretty sure it's in there." Hadn't he heard that in Sunday school or something?

"Sure, the Bible tells us God will forgive us and not remember our sins. That means that any sin that He washes away He won't hold against us. And it says we shouldn't keep a record of the ways people have wronged us." Uncle Bryan cleared his throat. "But that just means we don't hold on to our hurts, counting them over and over. We release them to the Great Healer and trust Him to work in our hearts. The concept of forgive and forget has been warped into something God never intended."

A wave rippled over the sand, taking some of the debris with it. "Huh. Okay. So I don't have to forget, but how do I forgive?"

"Fake it 'til you make it."

"What?"

Uncle Bryan laughed. "I just mean you keep acting in forgiving ways, not bringing up old hurts, not using those things as weapons. Sometimes it helps me to say the words 'I forgive you' out loud, even if it's in the privacy of my own space."

Zach suppressed the urge to laugh out loud. Just say "I forgive you" and it would all be over? Not in this lifetime.

"So, I what, just keep pretending she didn't do anything wrong?" They began walking back toward the hotel.

"Nah, you don't ignore the wrongdoing, but once you've decided to forgive, you act as though your heart is following suit. I know it sounds a little nutty, but it's always worked for me." Uncle Bryan paused as a squirrel ran across their path. "Of course, this isn't an excuse for someone to walk all over you, but maybe that's a conversation for another day. It sounds like this Ava is sincere in her apology. Take her at her word and start acting like you forgive her. The rest should fall into place."

"I guess I can give it a try." Couldn't hurt. At least it was more than what he was already doing. And hadn't he just decided that he needed a different trajectory in his life?

"I'm going to head into town." Uncle Bryan waved toward the main drag.

"Thanks again. Tell Aunt Mary hi for me."

"Will do. I'm praying for you, son."

He checked the time on his phone. Whoops. He'd better hustle if he wanted to be ready in time. But what kind of date could he pull together in such a short time? He turned and headed up the hill to the Grand, a breeze off Lake Huron at his back.

He didn't want to take her to Kelley's Bar & Grill. The place would be overrun with tourists. Best to keep this to a place he felt more comfortable.

The hotel rose up in front of him. His steps faltered. The site held so many memories, good and bad. Despite the recent history, the hotel had always felt like a safe space. Right. It could make a good date.

He thumbed a text to James.

Zach

Okay if I use the kitchen tonight?

James

It's all yours.

One problem down. Now what to cook together?

Their conversation from when they planned their contest dish came back to him. Right. That sage and brown-butter malfatti her parents had made. It shouldn't be too hard to recreate a similar dish. He'd just need a cookbook with the pasta in it so he could get the proportions of ricotta cheese and flour correct. The sauce would be simple.

Okay. So all he needed was to find a cookbook, preferably one from Italy, source the perfect ingredients from the island's tiny grocery store, and forgive the woman who blew up his life.

Easy as chicken potpie.

Thirteen

LIFE WAS UNREAL SOMETIMES.

If someone had told Zach a month ago that he would be taking Ava Harper on a date, he would have laughed in their face. But now he could barely keep himself from whistling as he buttoned up his light-green shirt.

He'd turned his uncle's words from earlier over in his mind, looking for flaws, but the recipe seemed sound. He just needed to work on putting it into practice. Starting tonight.

He checked the mirror in Ollie's bathroom. His dark hair stood on end as if he'd been in a hurricane. Nothing a comb couldn't handle. He dialed Ollie downstairs at the bookstore and put the phone on speaker while taming his hair.

"Hey, man. How late are you open tonight?" Zach dunked his comb under the tap.

"I'm just about to close up. Why?"

He ran the dampened comb through the worst of his hair. "Shoot. I was hoping to walk down there in a few minutes."

"Are you looking for something specific?"

"Do you have a cookbook section?"

"Yeah, we have a small one. Mostly for local stuff. But there's all kinds of things."

"Any chance you'd stay open late for your favorite brother?" He turned his head, checking the sides. An errant lock stood straight out, refusing to be tamed.

Ollie laughed. "Don't let our other brothers catch you saying that. If it's for a good cause, you can convince me."

The memory of Ava's smile and the sparkle in her gray eyes filled his thoughts. "Oh, it's for a good cause all right." Funny, he didn't really want to share with Ollie what that cause was. Must be a knee-jerk reaction to the teasing he was sure to endure.

"Need a recipe for the second half of the contest?"

"Not exactly."

"Zach, I've known you all my life." Ollie's voice lifted. "There's something you're not telling me."

"Fine. I'm taking Ava on a date, and I thought we could start at your bookstore."

"A date?" Zach was pretty sure they could hear his brother's crow over in Port Joseph. "I *knew* you liked that girl."

Zach finished his hair and smiled at his reflection in the mirror. It came out more like a wince. "She's pretty, she's kind, she's hardworking, and she has a razor-sharp wit. What's not to like?"

"You're playing it casual, but I know how weird this must be for you. You said yourself that Ava was the one who wrote that critical review of your restaurant all those years ago."

"She actually apologized for that. I forgave her. Am forgiving her." Zach put both of his hands on the bathroom sink. The cool porcelain anchored his hands from running them through his freshly combed hair. "I don't really know the semantics, but I'm trying to move past that. Ava is a cool woman, and I want to get to know her better."

"I'm proud of you. Forgiveness like that isn't easy. I definitely think this is a good cause. I'll hang out until you get here."

"Thanks, brother."

As Ollie was hanging up, Zach heard him holler. "Eliza, turn on the romantic lighting and mood music—my brother's bringing a date."

Zach's smile stayed firmly in place across town, through the lobby of the Grand, and all the way until he knocked on Ava's door. She opened it, and his breath caught. Ava's lavender sundress nipped in at the waist, then flowed out and skimmed the middle of her shins. She'd topped it with a light-gray sweater thing. A little gray purse hung over one arm.

"Wow." His heart beat double-time.

"I hope that's a good wow." A line appeared on Ava's brow.

"Definitely a good wow. You look amazing." Zach held out his hand. Ava took it, and he led her out into the hall before coaxing her into a spin. "My sisters would approve of the twirl on that dress."

"Every girly girl loves a good twirly dress." Ava squeezed his hand. "You clean up nice yourself. I always like your chef's whites, but that shirt is doing all kinds of good things to your eyes." Ava's eyes sparkled. Adorable. "What do you have planned for us tonight?"

"Are you always this impatient?" They walked down the stairs and out the door. The early evening sunlight still warmed the air.

"What? I can't ask what you have planned?" She put a hand to her hip.

"Maybe you could extend a little trust. Weren't you listening to the pastor at the park?"

She barked a laugh. "Fine. I'll trust you."

His heart soared, a lightness flooding him at the unexpected words.

"First stop, the Island Bookstore."

"Oh, I love a good bookstore. That's the one your brother owns?"

"Yep. The only one on the island. He's keeping it open for us, so we'd better leg it over there." He glanced down at her feet. "Will those shoes be okay for walking?"

She looked down. "They should be fine for tonight. I knew about the no-vehicles thing here on Jonathon Island, so I tried to only pack my most comfortable shoes."

"Shoes, plural? How many did you bring?"

"None of your business."

Their chat carried them through the grounds of the hotel and down to Main Street.

"Ollie's store is on the other end of the main drag." Zach dropped Ava's hand. Walking down Main with Ava was one thing, but holding hands felt too exposed.

"Oh, good. That'll give me a chance to take a few snaps for my newspaper article."

As they passed Kelley's Bar & Grill, a scruffy Jack Russell terrier ran out from between the buildings. He stopped in front of them and sat on his haunches, tipping his head to the side.

"Hello." Ava bent down and scratched him under the chin. "And who are you?"

"That's Jack." Jack leaned into Ava, tail wagging. "He's kind of the town dog. He doesn't belong to anyone, so everyone feeds him."

Jack yawned and trotted off.

"He's very cute." Ava straightened up. "A dog like that in Chicago would get taken to the pound."

"One thing that is true of Jonathon Island is that they take care of their own." Saying the words out loud made them ring true. But if it was the case that Jonathon Island cared about people, why didn't he feel that way? Could it be only in his own mind that they judged him poorly? Maybe he'd taken the heavy emotions the town had felt after the Grand burned down too personally. Other than that poor attempt at a joke by Isaac Kelley and the dig the old-timer had gotten in at Dani's wedding, everyone had been genuinely kind to him recently.

They fell silent, pausing a few times for Ava to take some photos.

Light spilled from the window of Oliver's bookstore, welcoming them. Ollie stood at the door in a T-shirt and jeans, bow tie at his neck, holding it open.

"Hello, sir, madam. Welcome to my establishment." He bowed at the waist before extending an arm to point the way. "Please make yourselves comfortable. We have the very finest selection of books for you this evening."

Eliza stood with a towel over her arm. She held a cookbook with both hands, extending it as though it were a wine bottle. "Vintage 1982. I think you will find that the flavors are very complex." The cover featured a grandma-type woman in a frilly apron holding out a chocolate cake.

"Ha ha." Though heat crept up the back of his neck, Zach couldn't wipe the smile from his face. "Very funny. Ava, I apologize for my brother. He thinks he's hilarious. Apparently, he's dragged Eliza into it too." Though, this lighter side of Ollie was new. Last time he'd been home, Ollie had been . . . grouchier. Maybe it was Eliza doing the influencing.

Ava laughed. The sound, light and carefree, went directly to his heart. "Don't worry about it. I like being teased. I never had siblings, so it's fun to be treated like I belong."

Ollie moved to stand next to Eliza. "Seriously, guys. We'll leave you to it. Want me to direct you to a certain shelf?"

Zach glanced down at Ava. He still hadn't told her what they were up to. "Cookbooks." A black-and-white patterned runner drew a line over the dark floor to the register. Rows of bookshelves stood behind a large round table displaying the dark jewel-toned covers of the book series by the fantasy author Victor Holt. Pendant lights lit the space. Ollie had done well for himself.

"We have a bunch of them over on that shelf." Ollie thumbed toward the back of the store. "Help yourself." He grabbed Eliza's hand, and the two of them disappeared somewhere else in the store.

Zach led Ava to the shelf of cookbooks. Ollie wasn't kidding. On the shelf a wide variety of options waited in a line.

Ava tugged at one. *Blueberry Delights.* She showed him the cover. A lattice-topped blueberry pie sat on a table surrounded by lilacs. "Yum."

He ran a finger along the shelf. "How about *32 Ways to Use Spam?*"

"Gross. That's not a real thing."

He grabbed the book and showed it to her, the iconic blue-and-yellow can featured prominently on the front. They laughed. As he replaced the book, he found one that might be what they needed. A French cookbook from this year. He flipped it open and checked the table of contents. Jackpot.

"See anything you like?"

"These are all Greek to me," Ava said. She handed him a copy of *The Greek Table, A Mediterranean Cookbook.* "Seriously, though. I'm not sure what I would do with a cookbook."

"You're a smart cookie. I know you can learn to follow a recipe." He tucked the Greek cookbook and the French one under his arm and headed for the checkout. "We should let Ollie close up."

Ava trailed behind him.

After they paid, they went next door to Doug's Market. What the old-fashioned grocery store lacked in selection, it made up for in charm. Stepping inside was like stepping back in time. Thankfully, they had an excellent cheese counter.

Gary Jacobs, a fiftysomething man who looked like he'd be more comfortable as a football linebacker than a cheesemonger, waited to help them.

"I need some ricotta and a pound of Parmesan," Zach said. "And then can you point me to the flour?"

Gary sliced them a neat hunk of Parmesan from the wheel on top of the counter, then pointed at the stack of ricotta tubs. "The flour is down aisle four," he said before turning away to wash the tools he'd used for the Parmesan.

The sage he needed should be in the next row over.

After he'd picked out some semolina flour, Ava blocked his way out of the aisle. She put her hands to her hips. "I'm beginning to suspect what this date is all about."

"Really," he said. "What gave it away?"

"Cooking? Really? That seems to be all we do lately." She scowled, but he caught the glint of amusement in her eyes. Plus, her dimple gave away the smile lurking below the fake frown.

"Can I help it if cooking is my love language?" Oops, did he just say *love*? It was way too early for that kind of word. "Uh. I mean . . . it's what I'm good at."

Ava eyed him. "I know."

And what did she mean by that? He swallowed against a sudden dryness. "If you're not having fun by the end of the night, you can plan the next date."

"I've got news for you, Golden Boy. If I'm not having fun by the end of the night, there might not be another date." She kept the mock scowl a moment before her face softened into a smile to match the light in her eyes.

"Challenge accepted."

"I'm assuming you have a plan for all of these ingredients?" She waved toward his shopping basket.

"Prepare to be amazed." Zach paid for the groceries, and a few minutes later, they were on their way back to the Grand.

The kitchen lay quiet and still. He'd come down earlier and

gathered up some of the tools they would need for their supper. He dropped the bag of groceries next to the mixing bowl he'd found.

"Okay, the recipe for malfatti is on page one hundred and two." He flipped open the French cookbook.

Ava blinked at him, her eyes shining.

"What?"

"Malfatti? You remembered my story." Her mouth slowly pushed up into a half smile. His heart pumped double-time.

"It isn't the easiest recipe to learn cooking skills on, but I thought something with meaning to you would be motivating." Shoot. He'd ignored the bad memories connected with this dish for her. What if she didn't want to relive all that? "We can totally make something else—"

"No. This is perfect. I'm honored you want to make this with me." Her smile pushed up into her freckled cheeks. "Thank you. Now, tell me what I can do."

He gestured to the cookbook. "Find something we can hold this open with."

Ava banged around the kitchen a moment before reaching above his head and plucking a ladle hanging over the center table off its hook. "This should do it." She leaned over his shoulder. "Is that our recipe?"

"Sort of." He tucked the ladle onto the book. "We'll use the base pasta and then make our own sauce." He turned his head to look at her face, inches away from his own. His breath caught. From this distance, he could smell her shampoo. Something floral and bright. "Ah. I'll show you how to roll the pastas into shape."

She blinked slowly. "You make cooking almost fun." She moved a step away from him.

"It is fun." Suddenly he could breathe again. "Although, my ex never thought so." Why did he bring her into it? Maybe he was subconsciously comparing the two women. But he knew better.

Ava was nothing like that selfish, grasping woman he once thought he'd loved. "Never mind. I don't want to talk about her."

Because right now, all he wanted to do was focus on the woman in front of him.

Who would've guessed cooking could be this much fun?

The scent of sage curled through the kitchen, warm and earthy. The past hours she'd spent with Zach felt surreal, like something she'd dreamed up but never thought could be real. Shopping with him had been a blast, and the playful teasing from Ollie and Eliza at the bookstore had only added to the charm. Ava couldn't shake the feeling that Jonathon Island might just be where she was meant to be.

Having spent thirty minutes perfecting miniature cheese clouds, she and Zach had triumphed, and he was now finishing off the malfatti in the pan.

Zach moved the pan off the stove and gave the dish one last stir. He dipped in a spoon and captured one pillow of savory cheese. His lips drew her gaze as he blew on the pasta. Then he lifted the spoon to Ava's lips.

The flavor of the buttery sage exploded on her tongue. Unexpected tears sprang to her eyes as she remembered the last time she was wanted. She swallowed the bite past the lump in her throat. "That's amazing. Just how I remember my mom and dad making it."

"Aw. I didn't mean to make you cry." Zach put a hand on her shoulder.

She brushed at her eyes. "No. It's good, actually. It reminded me that even though my mom and dad weren't good parents, there were times they showed how much they cared for me." Or at least, there were times they wanted to show off their cooking skills, but she would cling to the former thought. Even though they didn't want her.

"Want me to plate up the rest?" Zach squeezed her shoulder before dropping his hand.

"Yes. Absolutely."

He split the food between two plates and drizzled the butter from the pan over them.

She picked up the plates. "Want to eat out in the dining room?"

"Nah. Let's just eat here. It's a little more private." He gestured to the long stainless-steel workbench running down the center of the room. "You're fun to be around, and I don't want to share."

Flutters pooled in her stomach. "No one has ever said that to me before."

Zach paused, fork halfway to his mouth. "Really? None of your boyfriends told you that you're fun?"

"I actually haven't had many boyfriends." The fan above the stove kicked on, its whir filling the silence between them. She traced a finger around the edge of her plate, catching an errant bit of sage.

"You're good-looking, funny, and smart." He jabbed his fork in the air to emphasize each point. "I find it hard to believe you didn't have men knocking down your door."

"I've kind of avoided being in a relationship." Ava looked at the ceiling. Did she really want to drag all of this up? The ceiling didn't offer any help. But if Zach could open up about his love life, she could too. "If you really want to know, I was engaged once too." She took a huge bite and made a show of chewing.

"What happened?"

The sage turned bitter in her mouth. Elias. The lump of malfatti turned to mush, and she swallowed it. "Not much to tell. He strung me along for several years until I finally had the nerve to confront him about setting a date." She closed her eyes for a moment, then stared at the table. She ran a finger through a drop of butter that had spilled, smearing it a few inches. "Elias led me on, always bragging about my job with the newspaper and bringing me to all his events." She swirled the butter again. "I'd had doubts about him for a long time, but I didn't listen to my gut. And then he proved that I was right all along. He said I was nice to have around and he liked me a lot, but he had no intentions of marrying me. That he wanted something different out of life. When I broke it off with him, he immediately got engaged to someone else. As far as I know, he's never married." She shrugged and then wiped her fingers on a napkin. "Since then, I haven't seen the point of getting into a relationship. No one sticks around, anyway." Her heart squeezed.

Zach stood and then pulled her to her feet. "C'mere." He wrapped her in an embrace. He smelled like pine and pepper and a hint of lemon. She sank into his arms, resting her head on his chest, his chin tucked on the crown of her head. His heart beat a rhythm beneath her ear. "No one should have treated you that way." His voice rumbled through her. "You are worthy of being loved and cherished." His words resonated within her, deep and comforting. They spread to fill long-empty spaces in her heart.

She pulled back to look at him. "I could say the same about you, you know. The way your ex treated you was terrible. You deserve to find love and happiness."

His gaze searched her face. She reached up and stroked an errant hair off his forehead. He glanced down at her lips. Her breath caught, her heart stumbling over its next beat. She tipped her face up. The air in the kitchen stilled as he dipped his face closer to hers. His arms tightened around her.

"Ava," he murmured. Then, finally, his lips met hers.

Warmth bloomed in her chest. Zach kissed her as though she were something precious, something to linger over. His thumb traced a circle on her shoulder blade.

Forget belonging on the island, she was beginning to feel she belonged right here. In Zach's arms.

He tasted of spice and browned butter. A flavor she associated with home.

She curled her fingers into the back of his shirt. Holding on as if he would fly away at any moment.

Because that's what people did, right? Left her?

She broke contact with him, breathing hard.

He rested his forehead on hers.

"What are we doing?" There was no way this could work between them, right? "Just a week ago you hated me. Are we really trying to have a relationship?" She let go of his shirt and stepped back out of his arms.

"Ava, wait." Zach reached his hand toward her, but she moved out of his reach. "I think with a little more time and . . . and . . ." He raised his hands, palm up. "I don't know, the right ingredients for a relationship. We could really make something between us."

She couldn't help the smile. "Right ingredients? Once a chef, always a chef."

"Guilty as charged." He crossed his arms loosely. "What do you say? Want to give it a try?"

She crossed her arms, mimicking his stance. "Just what do you consider the right ingredients?"

"Off the top of my head? Spending time together. Extending understanding. Not betraying each other. Maybe following through on promises?" He uncrossed his arms and counted them off on his fingers.

"That sounds like a pretty good list. I'd add finding things to agree on." Picking up her purse from next to her, she pulled out her notebook and pen.

Zach laughed. "Is that a tiny notepad and minuscule pen? Really?"

She gave him a cheeky grin. "I've told you I always travel with paper."

"Doesn't that get to be a bit much? Why don't you just use the notes app on your phone?"

"I feel better writing things out longhand. It has more emotional meaning to me that way." She jotted down the things they were talking about.

"Are you really taking notes on our conversation?" Zach leaned back, crossing his legs at the ankles.

She looked up at him before glancing away. Her cheeks heated. "I tend to forget things, even important things. I wanted to be sure to note what is important to you." She pointed the end of her pen at him. "You're growing on me, Golden Boy, and I want to show you I care about what you care about."

"That kind of talk might earn you another kiss."

"I'll take you up on that." She tossed her notebook down.

An hour later, Ava made it back to her room and collapsed on her bed, limbs heavy with exhaustion. Tonight had been wonderful. But . . . her head spun.

She wanted to believe Zach. To trust that he meant what he said. But every time her heart leaned toward him, her head yanked her back—reminding her of all the times she'd let herself believe before. People always said the right words. That they wanted her. That she mattered. And yet, time and time again, their actions told a different story.

She needed clarity.

She pulled out her phone and dialed Emily.

"Ava, what's the emergency?" Emily's voice was thick with sleep.

"Sorry, did I wake you?" She hadn't even looked at the time.

"It's no problem." Emily cleared her throat. "What's up?"

"I kissed Zach. Or maybe he kissed me. Zach and I kissed." Shoot. Now she really sounded like a teenager.

Emily squealed. "What? That's amazing. Was it amazing?"

She remembered the sense of belonging she'd felt in his arms. "Yes."

"Okay, but I don't think you'd just call me because of an amazing kiss. Even if it has been years. What's really up?"

"I just don't know if I can trust him to stay with me. And what about me moving to Jonathon Island? And he wants to move to the West Coast. And what if he just wants to have a good time and not commit?" Her thoughts pinged around faster than the blades on a blender set to high.

"Whoa, slow down. One thing at a time." There was a rustle on Emily's end. "Okay. First, you're just starting out in a relationship. Trust takes time. Second, sure, you're moving, but there are many ways to stay in touch these days. Third, see point two. Fourth, as I keep telling you, not everyone is like Elias. There are good guys out there. Maybe Zach is one of them."

A few minutes later, Ava hung up. Emily's words rattled around in her mind.

Had she found someone she could rely on? Or would he let her down like so many had before?

Fourteen

ZACH REALLY NEEDED TO GET HIS HEAD IN the game.

Last night's date with Ava had been amazing. The walk, the cooking, and the mind-blowing kiss.

Even Ava's tic of writing everything in that notebook of hers seemed cute today. It was hard to remember the depth of her previous mistake, considering how much closer they had become. Maybe Uncle Bryan was on to something after all.

He thought he'd given up on women after his fiancée's cheating, but Ava had made him rethink, well, a lot of things, actually. Maybe some people would pull through for him. Maybe some people would be there for him and care about him.

Right now, he was the one who had to pull through. They were an hour into the main course portion of the contest, and he couldn't concentrate. And he needed to concentrate if they had even a prayer of winning this contest. The Silver Platter couldn't operate without the money the winnings would bring in.

An acrid smell reached him. Someone in this tent was burning their onions.

"Zach!" Ava's shout brought him back to the pavilion tent where their cooking station stood between two of the other teams.

Oh. On the stove in front of him, the pan smoked. A charred mess clung to the bottom. "My bad." He scraped the burnt onions into the trash before grabbing a clean pan and starting over.

"It's a good thing I chopped extra with the knife skills you taught me." Ava pointed toward a bowl of onions ready for the skillet. He tossed them in the pan before setting it on the burner.

Zach's gaze lingered on Ava as she chopped carrots, the rhythmic motion mesmerizing. A sharp sting jolted him back—heat seared his palm. Shoot. He yanked his hand away, barely catching the pan before it clattered to the ground. When had he let his hand drift so close to the burner? With Ava in the kitchen, it was hard to focus—the swish of her high ponytail, her deft fingers chopping the vegetables, and her humming were all competing for attention. He kept making rookie mistakes.

Right. Get back on track. After setting the onions aside to cool, he checked his recipe card. "Time to work on the dough." Mixing up a rough pastry dough wouldn't take too much concentration. He could practically do it in his sleep. Some days on the job he almost had.

"I'll just move these things out of the way." Ava cleared a spot on the workspace that faced the aisle. Just beyond the white folding table, the crowd milled about, watching the contestants as they worked.

The judges had come past earlier too. Paul Hawkeye and Anne Green were joined by Martha Kelley for this round of the competition. Was it his imagination, or had Paul been cooler toward him than he had in the past? His smile had definitely been more coldly polite than the warmth he'd shown earlier. He must have made that call to Chef Louie after all.

Fine. He still could win over Anne Green. She'd liked his appetizer yesterday. She'd probably appreciate the Michigan staple they were making today.

If he could land a job in her kitchen, he could get out from under Chef Louie's thumb and finally have the freedom to do some real cooking. Maybe he could even convince Ava to move to the West Coast. But being so far from his family would be difficult now that they were finding their way back to each other.

No time for those problems now.

Zach grabbed flour, salt, lard, and butter, then moved up next to Ava. She was jotting some things down in a notebook but put it aside as he joined her.

"What do you want me to do?" Ava looked at the task list.

"If you could start the roux for the sauce, I'll get this dough working."

"The roux—are you sure?" Ava's eyes clouded. "I only just learned how to do that. I don't know—"

He put his hand on her arm. "You'll be fine. I watched you demonstrate it several times in class to our students. I'm confident you can do it."

She put on a smile, but it wavered. "Okay."

"Seriously, you'll be fine. Here." He scooped out the amount of flour she would need for the roux and dumped it into a clean bowl. "Remember, it's one part butter to one part flour."

She frowned and turned away. Her whispered words floated to him. "One part to one part."

His mouth turned up on one side. Pretty soon her humming started up again, and he began to hum along. His shoulders relaxed. The day was smoothing out like the dough he was mixing.

"Sweet Caroline," Ava belted out.

"Bah, bah, bah," he sang along. He was locked in now. Back in the sync they had discovered during the cooking class.

Ava sang the next line in the popular song.

He glanced behind him. Ava was swaying to the music as she whisked the roux.

Someone in the crowd sang out the next part of the song.

Twenty or thirty people formed a half circle around their space. A singsong murmur rippled through the crowd as they picked up the next lyrics. Suddenly his parents were in front of him among the crowd.

"Hands, touching hands . . ." Those weren't the next lyrics, but okay.

"Reaching out . . ." He tapped his foot in time, keeping his eyes on the dough he was kneading in time to the music, not daring to look at his mom and dad. From this viewpoint, however, a small glance upward revealed his parents holding hands.

What?

Maybe it was just in response to the song. That must be it. Not an indication of anything else. A quick glance to either side showed many people holding hands and swaying.

Shoot, he'd lost track of how many turns he'd given the bread dough. Between his attraction to Ava and now his parents' complicated relationship . . .

The crowd shouted the nonsense line.

"So good! So good!" His dad sang out.

After a few more Sweet Carolines and other mangled lyrics, the song drifted into confusion. The crowd laughed and began to disperse. He did another hand check on his parents. They still had their fingers laced together as they walked away.

A low rumble passed through his belly. His good mood evaporated. Was he happy for them? How could his dad forgive his mom for cheating on him?

He punched the dough a few more times. It felt overkneaded but hopefully would soften as it rested. He put it in a bowl to rest until the filling ingredients were finished.

The five-minute distraction Ava had started with that sing-along could derail their whole day.

His phone chimed with a text. What was Chef Louie doing texting him?

<u>Louie</u>

I heard you were looking for a new job from Chef Paul. If you're so unhappy about being here, you don't have to come back. You're done.

His heart fell to somewhere just above the grass trodden flat under his feet. Sure, he didn't like his job, but at least it was work. Now what?

"Zach, something is wrong with this." Ava's voice cut through his thoughts. "The roux isn't coming together like it did in class. It's all gloppy."

"Does someone have paprika?" the contestant from two tables over called. "I can't find any paprika."

Ava turned from the stove and snatched their container of paprika from their small pantry area. "Got it!" She hustled past him, leaving a waft of her floral shampoo in the air. He felt a tug in his gut. If he had known that kissing her would leave him this distracted, he would never have done it. Or maybe he would have at least had the good sense to wait until after this extremely important day was over. Even more important now that he'd lost the one stable thing in his life. *Focus in, Zach.*

He looked into the pan on the stove.

"Ava! What is this?" But she was already gone. He stirred the glue-like roux in the pan before glancing at his watch. Drat. Not enough time to make a new one. Here's hoping it would be fixed as he added the beef broth. Pouring in the broth and stirring as though creating a storm on the lake, he couldn't quite get all the lumps out. Maybe he could strain them.

Ava came bursting back into their area. "Saved the day!"

Her cavalier attitude stuck a hot poker through him. They weren't putting out their best work and she didn't even care. Never mind landing a job with Anne Green. There were people who needed the prize money. Kids like RJ Edwards would never be able to afford schooling if the Silver Platter went under.

He huffed out a breath. "What happened to this roux?"

"I'm sorry," she said. "I had it going and it seemed fine, but then I had to jot down an idea about what I wanted to write for my newspaper column. I turned away for only a second, I swear. And then it got all lumpy. I'm so sorry."

"You should have been concentrating on this. You know how important it is. But. Whatever," he said. "I'll fix it or at least I'll give it my best try. Find something we can strain it into. There should be a mesh strainer somewhere in the pan section."

Behind him, Ava rattled the pans. "Got it." She held out a colander.

"That's not a mesh strainer." But what was he going to do? Run to the store and buy one? He had to make do with what they had in front of them. Hopefully, it would be good enough.

Because this day was turning into a disaster.

Cooking with Zach during a competition was nothing like cooking with Zach for fun.

He had been on edge all day. Truly, she had too. That kiss last night had set every nerve on fire.

She didn't know what to say or do around him anymore. It felt like she was sixteen with her first real crush all over again.

They'd finally felt in sync with the singing, but that ended abruptly, and she didn't know why.

Yeah, she probably should have waited to write those things

down for her article, but she really didn't want to forget them. Once things settled down after this round of the contest, she could explain to Zach. He would understand, she was sure of it.

She handed Zach the colander she'd found sandwiched between a skillet and a stock pot.

"Seriously? This is all they had for us?" Zach looked at the dish like it was a rotten tomato. "That's a colander, not a mesh strainer."

"Yep. This is the only thing like it."

"These holes are so big. I don't think I can strain all the lumps out." He sighed and took the tool. "If you can mix the veggies together, I'll try to get the gravy into something edible."

Her mouth dropped open. "Excuse me?"

He looked at her for a moment. Comprehension must have hit a second later because his eyes opened wide. "Oh no. I promised myself if I ever ran my own kitchen, I wouldn't treat anyone like Chef Louie does, and yet, his voice just came out of my mouth. Sorry."

"I forgive you. We're under a lot of stress." And it was fine. Really. She had seen him be better, do better. This day must really be throwing him off his cooking game.

He nodded once. "Assembly time. Got those veggies ready?"

She pulled the bowl of mixed veggies toward them.

"Gah!"

She jumped at his voice. "What?"

"I forgot to slice the meat." Zach tugged on a pair of black gloves.

She grabbed the two pieces of beef out of the fridge and slid a chunk onto his cutting board. "I'll help." After grabbing her own gloves and cutting board, she began working on the other piece. The crowd noise faded away as she concentrated on slicing the meat into small, even pieces.

Pain seared through her finger, and she sucked in a breath.

"What is it?" Zach asked.

"I cut my finger." She removed her glove. Blood spurted from the tip of her index finger, dripping on the meat on her board. "Oh no!"

Zach's lips pinched together. "Let me see." He took her hand and gently probed the cut. "It's not too deep." He wrapped the finger with a small piece of paper towel and handed her another glove. "Restaurant trick for when there are no Band-Aids."

She eased the glove over the makeshift bandage.

"We'll have to throw this away." Zach was already back at his cutting board. He pointed the tip of his knife at her board.

"I'll take care of it." Her stomach felt sick. So much time and materials wasted, just because she couldn't handle a knife. She scraped the meat into the garbage and put the cutting board with the other dirty dishes. "Will we have enough left?"

"We'll just have to hope for the best." His curt tone cut more than the knife had.

The cramped space of the outdoor kitchen felt like a cage. Ava kept bumping into Zach, and he moved like an elephant. A sigh escaped Ava's lips as Zach's foot landed heavily on her toes again, the dull ache mirroring the hurt in her heart.

She'd liked it better when they were singing.

"We should have practiced this instead of making the malfatti last night." He reached for another ball of dough. "You're not giving each of those pies enough crimps. It should be exactly twenty for each one." He pinched another couple times on each of her pasties.

She sighed and tried again. The dough stretched into a circular shape under her hands. When it was as wide as a dinner plate, she dropped some of the filling into the middle. Drawing up the edges, she crimped them, murmuring a count to herself. There. Twenty crimps. The pie went next to its brothers on the baking tray.

After a lifetime, they had ten meat pies lined up like soldiers ready for battle.

Zach checked his phone. "Okay, we should have enough time to get these baked and ready to plate. While they're in the oven, we can work on the apple chutney."

She picked up the tray. The cut on her finger throbbed with the weight. Bracing herself for the blast of hot air, she opened the oven door. Except—"Zach, did you preheat the oven?"

"Yes, I turned it on when the round started." He came over to stand beside her.

"It's stone cold." She put her hand on the door.

"I turned it on." Zach gestured to the knob, which was pointing at the appropriate temp. "It worked yesterday. What happened between then and now?" His face grew stormy.

She turned the knob, but nothing happened. "It's like it's not getting any power."

The back of the oven butted up against the tent wall. She followed the oven cord to where it plugged into a long orange extension cord. Check that. Where it *should* be plugged into the extension. Someone had kicked it or something, because it was hanging by only one prong.

She shoved the two ends together. "Try it now."

"Got it."

The next hour passed in a tense silence as they chopped apples, walnuts, and dates for an apple chutney. As Zach gave the mixture a quick cook on the stove, she took the opportunity to write down a few things for her article. Her readers would eat up the details of the sights and especially smells of the day. From Enrique Perez's direction, she caught the distinct smell of hot peppers. Her eyes watered even from this distance. How could he stand to be working directly with them? A question to ask him later.

She now knew that the chef next to them was Alicia from Alicia's Kitchen. The short blonde was standing around, chatting with her partner and a few festival goers. Her bright pink apron, adorned with delicate white embroidered hearts, swung gently as she moved. Alicia held a clean spoon and seemed to be using it to illustrate the story she was telling.

"Chef Alicia, what are you making?" Hopefully she wasn't interrupting, but she needed to get a few quotes for her article. "It smells amazing." Underneath the spicy peppers permeating the tent, she could smell the piquant scent of olives and chicken wafting over from Alicia's station.

Alicia turned a bright smile toward her. "It's a family recipe. Every generation makes it a little bit different in order to claim it as our own. I call it Sweetheart Chicken because I fixed this dish for my first date with the man who would become my husband." Alicia pointed toward the dish with the spoon in her hand. "Next thing I knew, he was my sweetheart. Now I make it for our anniversary every year."

"Aw, that's the cutest story. I love that. Thank you for sharing it with me." She wrote furiously. "Do you mind if I quote you?"

"Go right ahead. I love telling that story. Just don't ask me for the recipe." Alicia gave her a wink before turning back to her partner.

Ava began sketching out the essence of her article. She glanced at her phone. Only a few more minutes before the last push of the contest.

When the timer for the oven beeped, she took a deep breath. It wasn't enough to loosen the band around her chest.

Zach drew the pasties out of the oven. His groan told the tale. He thumped the pan next to her. An acrid scent rose from the baked goods.

"Over half of these leaked." He grunted.

The gravy from the leaky meat pies had soaked into their neighbors, the shallower pools of it looking charred and smoky.

"Can we save any of them?"

"I'm going to try." He pointed a spatula at the bowl of chutney.

"We have exactly three minutes to get those into bowls and plated with these."

A stack of ramekins waited for her to fill with the sweet side dish. She spooned mounds of the warm apple dish into each one. The spicy hint of cinnamon and cloves rose up around her.

At thirty seconds, the crowd began counting down. She chanced a quick look around. The teams near them also looked frantic, their hands moving in a blur. Only one team stood still, already having finished.

"Ava, focus." Zach's bark made her heart leap.

At the five-second mark, she placed the last ramekin of chutney on the last plate. In her rush, she spilled some out the top. Too late now.

"Hands up, contestants." Seb Jonathon's voice came over the loudspeaker. "We'll be coming around to judge your dishes in a moment."

She tried to catch Zach's eye, but he engaged in conversation with some bystanders. She walked up next to him and waited for him to acknowledge her.

"Good job, chef," the bystander, a woman Ava didn't recognize, said.

"Oh, I'm not a chef," she said. "Zach here is the one with training. I just follow orders."

"Sometimes," he muttered.

"Excuse me?"

"Nothing." He tipped his head at her. A quick nod. "We made it through." The woman wandered off. Probably picked up on the vibe.

Why was he being so weird? Sure, they'd had a rough time, but that didn't excuse his behavior.

"Good job, Zach." Maybe if she reached out she could figure out what was going on. "I can't believe we pulled that off."

He gave her his full attention then, his gaze hard into hers for a moment. "Yep. We sure did."

Where was the tender man from last night? "Have I done something wrong?"

He opened his mouth to answer, but just then the judges made it to their table.

Ava groped for Zach's hand as Paul Hawkeye, Anne Green, and local judge Martha Kelley bent over their bites of the dish, but he took a step away.

It didn't matter how they did in this contest because somehow she'd already lost something far more precious. And she didn't even know why.

Fifteen

HE'D FALLEN SHORT. AGAIN.

"This gravy has lumps," Anne Green said. The short chef poked at a piece of the pasty on her plate. "It's got good flavor, but some of the liquid has leaked out, and now my pasty is soggy."

"That's better than mine," Paul Hawkeye said. He looked at Zach. "One edge of mine is burnt. The leaked gravy burned this part here." He speared the offending piece of crust and set it to the side. Leaning slightly away, he crossed his arms, his biceps bulging. "I understand you had some trouble with your oven?"

"Yes, Chef." Zach tried to keep his tone upbeat. This was no time for excuses. "Someone unplugged it, and we didn't notice until we tried to bake the pasties. I bumped the temp up a little to try to regain some ground." His stomach churned.

Ava stood at his side. He could feel the tension rolling off her. He should reach out and take her hand. It was right there. But he couldn't get himself to cross the distance.

"Hmm. Risky. It might have worked if your gravy hadn't leaked. Too bad." Paul tasted some of the chutney. "This is good. But unnecessary. A pasty is a meal on its own."

"I'm not sure about the rosemary in here. Very . . . unique," Martha Kelley said. Zach's heart sank. *Unique* was Midwest code for *not good.* "And personally, I'd like to see more meat in these pies. Did you cheap out?" Beside him, Ava gasped. She opened her mouth to speak. Not a good idea. He grabbed her wrist. She rightly took that as a signal to remain silent. There was no use in defending themselves. The judges were right.

The dough was soggy.

The edges were burnt.

There wasn't enough meat.

The chutney was an extra flair, just there to show off.

And it had all flopped.

His heartbeat thrummed in his ears as the judges moved off to finish their critiques. Ava tried to talk to him again, but he couldn't bring himself to hear her pity.

A few minutes later, they waited in front of the stage in the center of the cooking tent.

Uncle Seb stood at the microphone, holding a paper in his hand. "In first place," Uncle Seb said, "Enrique Perez from Fiesta and his partner, Lottie Holmes. Chefs Perez and Holmes have named Second Harvest as their charity." The crowd erupted into cheers. Uncle Seb held up his hand for quiet. "The contest committee will be sending them twenty thousand dollars. Many thanks to the sponsors for their donations to the prize money. In addition, Chef Paul and Chef Anne also pledged to donate an extra five thousand dollars, bringing the total to thirty."

Thirty thousand? The Silver Platter could have made good use of that money. Zach's failure pressed his heart into his stomach.

Uncle Seb read off the other winners, and he and Ava had taken third. He'd never make it to the top if he was always being held back. He spun on his heel and began weaving through the crowd to get back to clean his kitchen. He felt Ava fall into step behind him.

"Zach."

He couldn't turn and face her. He didn't know what would come out of his mouth.

"Zach." They'd reached their own space now. The roar of the crowd surrounded him, but he tuned it out. He bent down and grabbed the bucket of soapy water under the table, moving it up.

Ava hovered at his elbow, but he still couldn't look at her.

"I need to write down a few thoughts for my article, but then I want to talk to you." Ava moved past him.

Her words turned his blood into shards of ice. He rounded on her. "Your article?" His teeth clenched so hard his jaw ached.

Her eyes went wide. "I just had a couple of thoughts, and I don't want to forget them. My editor will need this article before the end of the day."

"Sure. We definitely wouldn't want you to forget anything about this day. We certainly don't want you to publish false information. At least not on purpose." He let the arrows fly and watched as the words hit the mark.

Her face darkened. "I don't know what's gotten into you today, but I think there's been some misunderstanding." She picked up a notebook and pen.

Seriously, did she have those things stashed everywhere? Was she writing her article when she should have been concentrating on helping them win?

"I'll just be a minute."

A surge of anger threatened to swamp him. The sight of the notebook clicked something into place. A nagging suspicion at the back of his mind pushed its way out of his mouth.

"Did you do this?" His stomach boiled with acid.

Her head snapped up. "What?"

"Did you tank our chances in order to have a more interesting article for the paper? A way to land your dream job by sacrificing mine?" The thought made a lot of sense. "Or maybe you had to throw the game because it wouldn't be believable for you to win."

Ava's mouth made an O.

"That's it, isn't it? You made us lose on purpose."

"I'm sorry?" She put her hand to her hip. "I'm super confused. Just how exactly do you think I could throw the game?"

"Oh, let's see. You started a sing-along instead of concentrating on cooking." He began ticking the evidence off on his fingers. "You ran off in the middle of making the roux—to help our competitors, no less—completely ruining the dish. No." He held up a hand to silence whatever she was about to say. "You're right. It was already ruined. Your pasties leaked everywhere. You keep writing in that notebook instead of concentrating. I wouldn't be surprised if you unplugged the oven too." He couldn't believe he hadn't suspected earlier. He'd been so distracted by their fun evening the night before, he hadn't thought Ava could be this calculating.

"Did you hit your head as a child?" Her eyes blazed fire.

He crossed his arms. "What kind of question is that?"

"Do you realize how insane you sound right now? Accusing me of all of these wild actions." She threw her arms in the air. "I don't even know where to start."

"Just answer the question." His jaw cracked. He narrowed his eyes at her. "Did you sabotage this contest?"

"Sabotage," she sputtered. "I thought you were different. I thought you weren't as arrogant as I've believed all these years. But you are proving me wrong."

"Just because I'm good at my job doesn't make me arrogant. Just because I'm more confident in the kitchen than you doesn't make me prideful." Scorn laced his every word. He heard his words and tried to pull them back, but the pain of her betrayal sliced deep. She was taking everything from him again and didn't seem to care.

"I suppose you think I cut my finger on purpose too." She held up her hand, still in its black glove.

"Probably not. That would be a bridge too far. Even for you."

"What in the world is that supposed to mean?" She clenched her hand.

"It's no wonder you're overcompensating all the time, being nice to everyone, complimenting them." Was any part of her real? "Do you mean any of it, or is it just a ploy to make sure people like you?"

"I have integrity. I never do or say anything I don't mean. Look. This was just a silly contest. Sure, it would have been great if we won, but we both have other things going on. And one of those things for me is turning in quality work to my editor." Ava swallowed. "Cooking isn't life or death. Don't make this a bigger thing than it needs to be."

The fire burning in his belly turned white-hot. "It might be nothing to you, but it is everything to me."

He turned and braced his hands on the table. Uh oh. Paul stood across the way, his arms crossed.

"Is this the way you work in a kitchen?" Paul said. "I wanted to give you a chance, even after talking to Louie, but this display and your burnt pasties—" He shook his head as he motioned between them. "I need better than this for my restaurant. I'll be considering someone else for my Chicago position." Paul broke eye contact and walked away.

A giant hand squeezed Zach's stomach.

"Oh, Zach, I'm so sorry." He almost didn't hear Ava's whisper, his blood was so loud in his ears.

He turned back to her and narrowed his eyes. "The only thing I want is to run a restaurant of my own. You took that dream from me six years ago, and you're taking it away now."

"The only thing you want? That wasn't the impression I got last night when you were kissing me."

Acid burned in his gut. "I wish I'd never kissed you."

Ava gasped.

Okay, that was probably a stretch, but if they hadn't kissed, he wouldn't have been so distracted today. However, there was something that was closer to the truth. "I should have never had you as a partner. You don't even know how to cook."

The shock on her face, a stark white against her flushed cheeks, should have felt like the triumphant rise of a perfectly made soufflé, but her betrayal scorched the satisfaction from his heart.

This whole adventure was a big mistake.

Ava stood rooted to the ground as Zach flung incredible accusations at her. Too many of them were landing in the soft places of her heart. In the silence after his last verbal volley, she looked around to see a semicircle of people around them.

"We're destined to fight in front of crowds, I guess." But her attempt at humor didn't land. He still glowered at her. She let the half smile she'd pasted on drop to the ground.

His words *I wish I'd never kissed you* echoed in her ears.

"As far as not knowing how to cook, I trusted you with that information and you practically shouted it to everyone in earshot." She blinked rapidly against the stinging in her eyes. "You said you feel like everyone always betrays you—maybe it's because you treat them like this." She jabbed a finger in his sternum. "I never did any of those things you're accusing me of. At least, not the crazy-talk ones." He leaned away from her, so she moved closer to him. "Yes, I wrote some things in my notebook, yes, I gave that other person some paprika. But I can't believe you'd think I'd actually sabotage everything just for an article." Her breath came in short gasps. "Maybe you really are the person I always thought you were."

Zach wrung out a washcloth and began wiping down the table. "I guess both of our eyes are being opened today."

"Hey, is everything all right here?" Ollie stood on the other side of the table, Eliza beside him. They both wore matching expressions of worry and concern. "Ava, you okay? Zach?"

"We're fine, Oliver." Zach's growl wasn't very convincing.

"Ava, do you need me to take him out for you?" Ollie started coming around the table.

"I'm fine, Ollie." His concern for her was sweet, especially as he was Zach's brother and should, by rights, be on his side.

"She doesn't need you to defend her," Zach said.

Ava straightened. "What I don't need is another person in my life who doesn't know me and doesn't want me." She untied her apron and threw it at the ground near his feet.

Behind her, a crowd ringed around them. Dani pushed her way through until she stood between them.

"What is going on here?" Color was high on Dani's cheeks.

"Ava—" Zach said.

"Are you going to accuse me again?" Something red-hot flared through her chest.

"No. Don't say anything." Dani cut her hand through the air. "This was completely unprofessional, Zach. You're disqualified. Third place now goes to the first runner-up." A murmur rippled through the crowd. Dani shook her head and turned away.

Ava raised her chin. "I guess that's my signal to leave."

Zach's shoulders heaved. He froze. Blinked. Opened his mouth, but nothing came out. He ran a hand through his hair. "Ava. Wait. I—I had some bad news and I'm reacting poorly." He reached out a hand to her. "Let me explain. Please."

Bad news? She'd give him bad news. "Goodbye, Zach."

Weaving her way through the crowd, she beelined for the exit. A few people gave her an "Attagirl" as she passed by.

She broke free of the cooking tent and headed straight for the hotel. If she was lucky, she could make it there before the tears started falling.

She was moving so fast, she almost didn't see Mia. The young woman had Finn by one hand and held Cody's with the other. Cody held Maggie in his arm.

"Ava!" Mia's call stopped Ava in her tracks. "I thought I'd find you here. I know the contest must have just ended."

"We had hoped to be there, but the kids got restless," Cody said. "We ended up finding corn dogs and walking around." Maggie patted Cody on the head.

"I'm sorry we missed it," Mia said. "How did you and Zach do?"

Ava's heart seized. "We took third." And lost everything.

"Oh, I'm sorry. Or congratulations?" Mia's brow furrowed. "Third is good, right? Even if it's not first, at least you placed."

Try telling that to Zach. But Mia didn't need to know the humiliation Ava now felt. "Third is good, but we're disappointed not to have won the money for the Silver Platter." That was an understatement, but again, Mia didn't need someone to rain on her apparently perfect day.

"Mom, can we get cotton candy now?" Finn tugged at his mother's hand. "You promised."

"Just a minute," Mia said. "I have to talk to this lady first. Cody, would you mind taking them to pick out the candy? I can join you in a minute."

"Of course. No problem." Cody gave Mia's cheek a swift kiss, and Ava's heart clenched again.

Mia transferred Finn's hand into Cody's and then dropped a kiss onto each of her children's heads. "Be good, you two." She ran a hand along Cody's arm. "You be good too. They can share a cotton candy. Don't spoil them."

"Who, me?" Cody tried to look offended, but his mischievous smile ruined the look. "They're just so fun to spoil." He kissed Mia again. "Okay, kids. We need to listen to your mom. What kind of cotton candy do you want, pink or blue?" They turned and made their way through the crowd, Finn and Maggie calling out blue and pink simultaneously.

"You really do live a charmed life." Ava crossed her arms over her stomach.

Mia broke into laughter. "Really? Is that what you think? I suppose you don't really know me."

"Um, yeah. Two adorable kids, their dad is handsome, you have life on Jonathon Island all figured out."

"How do you know their dad is handsome?" Mia gave her a strange look.

"I mean." Ava waved her hand at Cody's retreating back. "I'm not like, trying to be creepy or whatever, he's ten years younger than me, but Cody is pretty handsome."

Mia's face cleared, and she began to laugh again. "Cody isn't their dad. At least not until after the adoption papers are signed."

"What? I thought . . ." But no one had actually said that Cody was the father of the kids. She'd just assumed because he was so good with them.

"My first husband died," Mia said. "There is nothing charmed about my life. I got pregnant with Finn in my first year of college and moved home to marry his dad, my high school boyfriend. When I was pregnant with Maggie, Troy died in a boating accident." Mia's eyes grew distant. "Cody helped me a lot during that time, and we fell in love." A half smile formed on her face. "Blessed, yes. Definitely blessed to have known the love of two good men. But charmed? Not at all. That's why that verse from Psalms means so much to me. I had to learn to trust God again after He took my husband."

"I'm so sorry." Now she felt terrible. "I didn't mean to belittle you. I had no idea about any of that."

"How could you? You didn't grow up here, so of course you wouldn't know any of the local gossip." Mia's voice was gentle.

"I'd like to." Ava swallowed hard. "Well, maybe not grow up

here, obviously, I'm already grown. And I don't mean I want to be a gossip. But I'd like to belong to a place where everyone knows everyone. A community to call home." A familiar longing filled her. "Those are some of the things I put in my letter. I'm hoping it swayed them a little, knowing that the person who wants to buy their mom's house wants to make it a home, not just an Airbnb or something." Now she was rambling, but the emotions of the day had her exhausted, and she couldn't seem to turn off the tap that was her words. Her limbs felt like they weighed a thousand pounds each.

"Ava." Mia's face fell. "I'm sorry to deliver bad news, but I wanted to tell you in person." She pulled a letter out of her purse and handed it to Ava. "The sellers went with another offer. I'm so sorry. This is the rejection letter."

Rejection letter. Ava resisted the urge to laugh in her face. It wasn't Mia's fault that the timing was so bad. At least they had the courtesy to reject her in a letter and not in front of a whole crowd.

She wanted to collapse into a heap right there in the middle of the Jonathon Island Flavor Fest grounds.

"Tell me you have another option for me." Ava's lips could barely form the words.

"I'm sorry, I truly am. There aren't any other places in your price range." Mia gave her a pitying look. "There's nothing on Jonathon Island for you right now. I can keep an eye out, though."

The white picket fence. The cute retro bathroom. The tight-knit community. The possibility of belonging someplace, to someone. All gone. Ava dragged herself up to her room in the hotel. She crashed onto the bed.

Her phone dinged with an incoming email. She glanced at the screen. The preview text read "Ava, What were you thinking?" and the sender was Judson.

Now she just wanted to crawl into a hole. But her job was on the line. She swiped open the email.

Ava,

What were you thinking?

These last two articles were trite and full of clichés. Did you lose your talent along the way to the island? I've included some suggested edits for you. Please go down to the beach and find your discarded talent. I know you can do better. I'll be expecting the edits and final few articles next week.

Judson

P.S. It will be hard to sell the others on remote work if this is what we can expect from you.

Cringing, she opened the edits. A horror movie had less red effects.

She read through some of the notes. Okay, Judson had a point. A few of these lacked the attention she usually put in. She'd let Zach and her desires for the new home distract her. Too bad she couldn't bring herself to care about it. Her dream of moving to Jonathon Island was already dead in the water. See? Clichés.

Except, she really loved her job, remote or not.

Somehow she would have to find the strength to write her articles.

Tomorrow she would pull herself up by her bootstraps, stop using clichés like *bootstraps*, and get back on track.

Because she couldn't afford to lose her job too.

Sixteen

VA LAY ON THE COUCH IN HER BEIGE CHI-cago living room, staring at the ceiling. No one had told her that breakups could feel so awful.

When she'd broken up with Elias, it had been different. Maybe because she was still young and full of hope for a different future for herself. She'd had plenty of time to settle down. Breaking up with Zach was totally different. If it could even be called breaking up. They'd only spent time together for a few weeks, only had one date, only kissed once. As a writer, she should probably come up with a more accurate word for the experience.

Except, she knew she'd been falling for him.

And her heart was broken.

Breakup it was.

The room smelled stale after being closed up for the almost two weeks she was away. She'd gotten home late last night, submitted her revamped articles to her editor along with some of the snapshots she'd taken of Jonathon Island, and then collapsed into bed.

This morning, she'd wandered around the small space, given her droopy ficus a drink of water, and tried to summon up the energy to do anything. Anything at all, really. Which was how she found herself lying on the couch, counting the bumps on her popcorn ceiling.

On the floor, her phone buzzed with a text message. She picked it up. Dani.

> **Dani**
>
> Thanks again for coming to Flavor Fest. We couldn't have done it without you. I hope you'll visit Jonathon Island again soon.

Visit.

Not live there.

At least the fight between her and Zach hadn't completely turned his family against her. But maybe Dani was being polite.

Her phone buzzed with another text from Dani.

> **Dani**
>
> Don't let my brother fool you. He's a big marshmallow under all that bluster. I'm sorry you two ended on such a sour note. I'd love to get to know you better.

Okay. Not just being polite.

She keyed in a reply.

> **Ava**
>
> I was glad to see your island in person again. It was everything I'd remembered and hoped for.

She hit send, then hesitated, fingers hovering over the keyboard. Finally, she typed.

Ava
I enjoyed getting to know you and
your family too.

Dani
I hope we didn't overwhelm you.
We can be a bit much.

Ava
No. You were all great.

The ribbing Ollie had given them sprang to mind. Zach's family was amazing.

Dani
If you ever come back here, let me
know. We can grab a coffee.

Ava
Thanks. Will do.

She put her phone back on the floor and laid her arm over her eyes.

Her phone buzzed again. And kept buzzing. A call this time. Her grandma's face popped up. Ava had used a photo of her from her eightieth birthday. A sparkly pink crown on her head as she held up a cake nearly on fire from all the candles.

"Hi, kiddo." Her grandma sounded strong. "Are we still on for lunch today?"

Ava sat up straight. "Lunch?" She put her grandma on speaker and opened her calendar app. "I don't have you in my calendar."

"Hmm, that's weird. Maybe I forgot to ask you. I wanted to be sure to get together to hear all about your trip."

"At least I know where I get my absentmindedness from." Ava smiled. This old joke had run for as long as she'd lived with her grandma.

"I hope you're up for lunch, because I'm downstairs."

Ava laughed. "I guess I don't have much choice. I'll buzz you in."

A few minutes later, she gave her grandma a hug and let her into the apartment.

"Ava, it's a really nice day today. Let's get some of these windows opened. This place needs some fresh air." Her grandma's mauve pantsuit and Vera Wang printed scarf tied at her neck contrasted with the drab furniture she walked past. She opened the drapes and tugged open the window.

"You're not going to get much breeze through there," Ava said. "The building next to mine blocks the wind and sun."

"It's better than nothing." Her grandma dusted her hands together. "Shall we order some lunch to be sent up?"

"Angelino's?" The Italian restaurant on the corner was a favorite of theirs.

"Perfect."

Thirty minutes later, the scent of tomatoes and garlic filled her kitchen. She dished them both a plate of the fragrant tortellini.

"Now, tell me everything." Her grandma pulled her plate closer and took a bite. "I bet nothing on that island compared to Angelino's."

The malfatti she and Zach had made was definitely better. "I had some amazing food over there. No need to be a snob about the island." Her tone was sharper than she meant it.

"I'm sorry," Grandma said. "I'm just loving this tortellini."

"No, I'm sorry. It's just that the whole thing ended so terribly, I'm a little sensitive, that's all." Ava outlined some of the highs and lows for her grandma, including the beginning and awful end of her relationship with Zach.

"Mm-hmm. So, you had some amazing food, found a place you could call home, and fell in love with a boy, is that it?" Her grandma raised an eyebrow. "Sounds like quite a trip."

"It isn't love." Her heart tightened. "It couldn't be."

Her grandma took a drink of water. "I fell in love with your grandfather in one night. He showed up at the dance hall where I was working. Only took one night to convince me he would be the man I would marry."

"Things like that don't happen to me. I'm more of the love-them-and-leave-them type, only it's me that gets left." Ava bit her lip, focusing on the pain.

Her grandma put a hand over hers. "Sweetie. I'm sorry about your ex-fiancé, but he was a terrible person. It had nothing to do with you."

"And Mom and Dad?"

Her grandma sighed. "I should have told you this a long time ago. I think your mom is bipolar. She never had a formal diagnosis, but it fits with everything about her." Her grandma looked away for a moment, then met her eyes again. "That's partly why she said those terrible things about never wanting you. She loved you so much that she didn't want to screw up your life."

"She rejected me because she loved me? That makes no sense." But in a way, it jived with what she knew about her mother. "Okay, fine. I guess I can see that. But Dad?"

Her grandma waved away the question. "Oh, he was always going to follow your mother. He can be quite immature, which is why he won't stand up to her. But he truly loves her, so I forgive him for that."

"They always let me down," Ava said.

"I've got news for you, kiddo. People do that." Her grandma patted her hand. "But if you find the right ones, they will always let you know that they regret it."

"You've never let me down." An idea blossomed in Ava's heart. Her grandma had always been there for her. "Maybe you did in little ways, but never in the ways it counted." Her grandma had been at every one of her school events, she'd made a scrapbook of every article Ava had ever written. She'd shown up. Her grandma had always chosen her, wanted her. Even if her parents were terrible, her grandma made up for it. Sure, she had been lonely, but she'd never had a reason to doubt her grandma's love.

Emily, too, had been there for her. Maybe Ava needed to work on that trusting thing.

"This is probably terrible timing, but I found a place in Arizona," Grandma said. "I'm hoping to move there at the end of summer. I want you to know it has nothing to do with you. But now you can go anywhere."

Gulp. Her heart squeezed. Knowing this day was coming didn't make it any easier. "I know you love me. I'll be sorry to live so far away, though." She took a deep breath to ease the ache in her chest.

"Maybe you can come visit me on one of your newspaper trips."

Ava fidgeted with her fork. "That dream has died. Judson said my stuff wasn't good enough to justify sending me on the road." Her first drafts had been pretty scattered. She'd let everything with Zach distract her. "I buckled down and fully rewrote my articles, but I think I already blew my chance. He hasn't said anything about the revisions."

"I'm so sorry, honey." Her grandma patted her hand again. "I know how much that meant to you."

Ava shrugged. "I didn't get the house I wanted, so staying here in Chicago makes sense, I guess. No need to work remote when I live just a few blocks from my office." But all the truth she tried telling herself didn't erase the bitter taste of loss. She forked another tortellini but then pushed the dish away. "Anyway. I'll be fine. I'll make a new plan."

"Now that we have that settled, tell me more about this young man you're falling in love with." Her grandma popped a tortellini in her mouth.

"I'm not falling in love." Was she?

"Nonsense. I can see it all over your face. You love this boy." Grandma pointed her fork at Ava.

Ava's face felt hot. Fair skin struck again. "He's not a boy. He's a chef. He makes me feel more confident. He's funny, and he's kind. Usually."

"And why are you so sad about it?"

"We left things in a really bad place between us. I don't really even know what we were fighting about. He accused me of some outlandish things, and I fought back."

Grandma folded her hands on the table. "I remember having some doozies with your grandfather. Usually, they weren't about what we were fighting about, if you know what I mean."

"Yeah, there probably was more to it, but our relationship was so new it didn't seem worth it to pursue." Her stomach turned over. That decision held so much regret. But she didn't know how to reverse course.

"Love is always worth it."

"Maybe I wanted to leave him before he left me." As the words left her mouth, they rang true in her heart. She didn't want to be rejected by Zach, so she hadn't even given them a chance to figure it out. She'd just turned tail and run. "He was right too. I put my articles before him—before our team. I should have apologized for that. I just got so defensive." She'd betrayed him, however unintentionally, but the result was the same.

She sat up straighter. "You're right, though. I think I could love him. He's passionate and good to his family. He believes in me."

"Sounds like you two might have something." Her grandma leaned back in her chair and crossed her arms. "Maybe you should give him a chance to stay."

"I should at least make time to hear him out." His last words— *Let me explain. Please.*—rang through her. She owed him that much. She owed herself too.

Because one thing this conversation was making clear: She was falling in love with Zach, and she wanted to give him another chance. She wanted to show up for him in the way that she'd always wanted others to show up for her.

She would never betray him. She just needed to think of a way to let him know.

One more day on Jonathon Island here in the hotel kitchen, and then Zach would have to return to his autopilot life in Chicago. Although what he would do there was anyone's guess. His whole life had changed in the almost two weeks he'd spent here.

Chef Paul's words still burned a hole in his gut. Worse, he knew they were true.

He'd been shot down by Anne as well. Seemed no one wanted a hotheaded chef who couldn't cook three courses without burning something. He couldn't blame them. Maybe he deserved his time at Escargot.

"Thanks again for helping with this added class." Dani handed him a clipboard. "Here's the list of your students." He'd asked her to bring the paperwork a few hours before another class began.

"No problem. I'm glad people were able to wait until after the festival. I can't believe this class got to be so popular."

"Since most of them were local, they were happy to stay on the waiting list. I think they just like the idea of learning from one of the island's own."

Ava's gentle tease of Golden Boy drifted through his mind and stabbed at his gut. He'd been terrible to her. Once he figured out the words to an apology, he would call her.

"I brought the leftover ingredients from the Flavor Fest competitions for you to use." Dani pointed to the dry goods stacked on the counter. "I haven't had anyone put them in the pantry. Of course, the perishables are in the cooler and walk-in freezer. Let me know if you need anything else. I'll have someone pick it up before your class." Dani walked out of the kitchen, already pulling out her cell phone.

Zach ran his hand over the boxes Dani had stacked. Might as well make himself useful. He began unpacking the boxes and placing the supplies on the shelves. Not knowing what else to do, he put them in the order he would want them in if it were his space.

Several half-filled paper bags of flour were in the next box. He hunted around for the square plastic containers the contestants had used, which had been filled with sugar, flour, and other dry goods. There. A few boxes down held the two-gallon clear food storage bins. He started to combine the flour to reduce the number of containers.

Wait a minute.

The flour dumped in the bin marked *Zach & Ava* was not the same shade of white as the flour in the bin marked *Enrique & Lottie*. His hands stilled. No—He turned back to the half-empty bags and began unrolling them.

"Dani!" Three of the bags were standard unbleached, all-purpose flour, but the remaining two were clearly marked as self-rising. He barked a laugh. This answered so many questions. He poked his head out of the kitchen but didn't see Dani anywhere. He gave her a call. Hopefully her other call had already ended.

"Zach! You just caught me."

"Dani, there are two different kinds of flour here."

"Oh. Is that a problem?"

He laughed. "A problem? Yes. It's definitely a problem. If it was self-rising flour in my container last week and the same in Ava's and my bin, that would explain a lot of our problems."

"Janine Dirks—she's one of the locals on the Flavor Fest committee—said they ran out of flour when they were dividing everything up for everyone, so I told her to just grab some from the store. She must not have checked the flour type or known how much it mattered. I'm so sorry, Zach."

He rubbed the back of his neck. "I'm not sure it matters

anymore." He hung up, a terrible feeling scratching the back of his mind.

The question remained. Was the flour they'd used the self-rising kind? Right. Time to Scooby-Doo this thing. He scooped out a small amount of flour from the container marked with his name and placed it directly onto the stainless-steel workbench. Then he repeated the action with some from the all-purpose flour and the self-rising. Three small mounds lined up like the pyramids at Giza. Only slightly less important. Slightly.

The door to the kitchen opened, and his dad walked in. "What's going on here?" His dad's mouth turned up. "Isn't the flour supposed to be in a pan or something?"

Fake it 'til you make it. Uncle Bryan's advice should work for his relationship with his dad too, right? "You're just in time to help me test a theory." Zach stepped back. "Which of these flours seems the most similar to you?"

His dad frowned. "Most similar? They're a pile of white powder."

"Get closer. Tell me if you can see the difference."

"Okaaay." His dad drew the word out but walked across the kitchen to the workstation. "Can I touch them?"

"Be my guest."

His dad ran his fingertips through a little of each pile. "These two feel similar. They also look more similar, lighter in color. But I wouldn't have noticed if you hadn't said to look for something."

"That's what I thought too." Zach walked to the pantry and located a bottle of white vinegar. "Now to confirm my suspicions." He poured a small amount of the vinegar on top of each flour mountain. Two of them began to bubble and boil.

"This reminds me of those volcano projects you kids always had to do for school."

"You remember those?" Zach's chest swelled.

"Of course. Doing those projects was always a highlight for me."

"You were gone a lot." He tried to make it less accusatory but failed.

"I'm sorry for that. Like I told you before, I'm trying to do better. To stick around more, say what I mean. To just be more present in your lives overall." His dad wiped his hands on a towel.

"Dani and Ollie say you're doing that."

"Anyway, what have we got here?" His dad jutted his chin toward the flour piles.

"Confirming a suspicion. These two are self-rising flour." He pointed at the one from his container and the one from the bag, the known commodity.

"And why does that matter?"

"It means that Ava wasn't the one who screwed up. I was. I should have realized it was self-rising flour. I should have known that from the first time I cooked with it."

"C'mon. They're not that different."

"But they are. This one"—he gestured at the one from his container again—"will make a gummy, gross roux. It won't coat a sauerkraut patty very well, and it will make a tart pastry puffy. The only reason it didn't matter in the pastry dough is that you basically want that dough to be a little puffy anyway. But I think that's why the dough cracked and leaked." The self-rising flour made so much sense. It even made sense with his sauerkraut sliders. The added baking powder in a self-rising flour blend would have interacted poorly with the other ingredients, leaving a bitter, metallic taste in the whole dish. It probably was the reason the red cabbage turned blue too. "I should have known right away."

"Don't beat yourself up about it. There's nothing you can do now."

He was wrong. There was something he could do. He could apologize to Ava. He could also address another reason he had lashed out at her, a reason that wasn't even her fault.

"I saw you and Mom holding hands. Is that you trying to be more present too?"

His dad chuckled. "I suppose. I'm learning to appreciate her all over again."

"How can you be reigniting your relationship with her? Don't you resent her? She cheated on you." And then married the man she'd cheated with, who then left her.

"I choose to forgive. Sometimes I choose to forgive multiple times a day. Besides, it wasn't just her that messed up. I was wrong too." His dad leaned back against the counter and crossed his ankles. He stared at the ceiling. "I'm not innocent in any of that. I wasn't there for her."

"That's an understatement." Zach heard the sarcasm and dialed it back. "Sorry. I know you're trying to change. But your being absent doesn't excuse her cheating."

"And her cheating doesn't excuse the horrible way I reacted." His dad finally met his eyes. "Remembering that I'm not perfect helps me not to expect anyone else to be either. I can forgive her because she can forgive me. And she's teaching me that we are all forgiven because of Jesus. I don't really understand it all yet, but I'm getting there."

Zach swallowed. "It all seems so impossible."

"Look around you." His dad stood up straight. "Look at this place. Can you get a more perfect redemption picture?" His dad waved his hand in the general direction of the rest of the hotel. "I nearly burned this whole place to the ground. But your sister and her husband brought it back. They are renewing it day by day. I'm no preacher, but I think you could do worse than learning to forgive. Maybe it's time to put the past behind you and focus on rebuilding."

Zach reached for an answer but came up empty.

His dad clapped him on the shoulder. "I'm glad you figured out your science project. Maybe you should send your cooking partner a text letting her know that you made a volcano out of her ingredients."

As Zach put the rest of the stuff away, he remembered something he'd stuffed down a long time ago. Advice he'd been given by some of the restaurant owners he knew before he'd opened Peach. Things like "Don't try to go too big too fast" and "Track all of your spending," among other nuggets of wisdom. Advice he'd ignored.

Just like the loss of the contest wasn't solely Ava's fault, the loss of the restaurant wasn't either. One bad review wouldn't have tanked the place if he'd listened to their advice. He shared the blame. In some cases, he carried it all alone.

Blaming other people for his problems wasn't very mature. He massaged his forehead. He had a lot of apologizing to do.

His phone pinged with a text. Ollie.

Ollie

Pool and burgers at Kelley's in twenty minutes.

He didn't really feel up to—His phone pinged again.

Ollie

Unless you'd rather mope.

And yeah, he knew the sound of a gauntlet being thrown when he heard it.

Zach

I'll be there.

He flipped off the lights as he left the kitchen.

He walked through the lobby, noting the new flooring. His dad was right. This place was a picture of redemption.

Maybe cracking some pool balls together would make him feel better. Zach walked into Kelley's Bar & Grill, turning left into the bar. The scent of grilled onions and chili fries hit him. He hadn't been back here in years, but the earth-tone walls, wood floor beneath his feet, and the pendant lighting were just how he remembered them. The stares of the patrons who'd turned to look at him as he walked in was also familiar.

After a moment, conversation resumed. He spotted Noah Rampart, part of the ferry crew, navy hat tucked over his sandy hair, sitting with a woman he didn't recognize. He gave the man a wave. They'd had a few classes together in high school, but like so many others, Zach had lost track of him over the years.

Along the bar, Tommy Macintyre, still in his fire chief uniform, warmed a stool next to Simon Manning, also still in uniform, the navy blue of the island EMT unit. Next to them were a pod of women with their backs to him. One looked familiar. From his cooking class earlier in the week, maybe?

Near the back of the room, his brother was racking a set of billiard balls on the mahogany pool table.

He slapped Noah on the back as he went past. "Good to see you, man."

"Hey. You too." Noah raised his glass to Zach. "I heard you were a big hit at the festival. Even if you did get disqualified."

He waited for the barb to hit, but since his afternoon in the kitchen, the pain of not taking first didn't sting as much. "Nah. I coulda showed up better. I let those off-island folks beat me."

"True." Noah crossed his arms. "Someday this town will forgive you for that." Then he winked and grinned. "Just kidding. Everyone seems glad to have you home. Even if you didn't score big for the honor of the island."

"I'm glad to be here." The words rang true. All his angst about coming home had evaporated. He finished making his way to the pool table.

"I racked. You break?" Ollie handed him a cue.

"Works for me. Maybe you should order us a pair of burgers while I line up my shot." He bent over the table as his brother walked over to the bar.

He gave the cue ball a satisfying whack and sent the other balls skittering around the table. The yellow-striped ball dropped into the near corner pocket. Another few striped balls rested in easy positions. He glanced at Ollie, still at the bar chatting with Whitney Kelley, Patrick's wife.

With any luck, he could clean the table before his brother even got back. He lined up his next shot and sank the red-striped ball in the space of two breaths. He pumped his fist, then groaned as the cue ball sailed in after it.

So much for winning. But he was learning to live with that.

He fished the ball out of the pocket and handed it to Ollie as he came back to the table. "You're solids. I already scratched."

Ollie placed the white cue ball near the upper left pocket, lining up his next shot. "Were you able to patch things up with Ava before she left?"

"Is this why you brought me here? To grill me about my love life?"

Ollie shrugged, then sank a ball in the side pocket. "Things got kind of heated, and I know you like her, so I thought I'd check in."

"Did Eliza put you up to this? Or Dani?" His scalp prickled.

"Can't a guy be concerned for his brother and the woman his brother loves?"

Whoa. "Hold on a minute. Who said anything about love? I can't be falling in love with her in only a few weeks. Plus, I'm still working on forgiving her." Except that old burden felt much lighter now, especially since he knew the truth about it—and about her character.

Ollie raised an eyebrow. "Didn't take me that long with Eliza. Ava seems like a good match for you. We can all see it."

That was the problem with a big family: Nothing went unnoticed for long. Except, at the moment, Zach didn't really hate it. It had been a long time since he'd felt like he belonged.

"She certainly challenges me." Always in a good way. She made him want to be better. Do better.

"And she's smart. Probably smart enough not to fall for you." Ollie handed him the cue chalk.

You're growing on me, Golden Boy. Ava's words tripped through his head. He lined up a shot as the memory of their kiss popped into his mind. The cue ball went sailing off the table.

"Wow." Ollie crossed his arms. "You really are a goner."

"Fine. I like Ava." He chased after the ball, which had come to rest at Tommy's foot. Zach shot the fire chief a smile, then took the walk of shame back to the pool table. "She's smart, she's driven, she's super talented. What's not to like?"

"Plus, she's a blonde, which has always been your thing."

Something roared in him. "Watch it."

Ollie held up his hands. "I'm just saying . . ."

Zach sighed. "No. You're right. I'll see her in Chicago, and we can talk through things." Saying the words made his heart pound a little harder. Maybe going back to the city wouldn't be so terrible after all.

"Dude. She's not going to be in Chicago. She's moving here. To Jonathon Island." Ollie put two more balls in the pockets.

"Since when?"

"Since Mia has been showing her properties here. Dani told me."

"What about her job?" She loved her job.

"I dunno what to tell you. Maybe you should call and ask her. But you definitely should figure out how you feel about her first. This push-me, pull-you, back-and-forth of trying to forgive her isn't fair. To her or to you." Ollie tapped the black ball into the farthest pocket. "I'm going to grab our burgers. Loser racks."

Ollie's words echoed in Zach's mind, low and steady, settling into the spaces left behind by the conversation he'd had with his dad earlier in the kitchen—a conversation that had cracked something open deep inside him. His shoulders relaxed. The memories that once stung like fresh wounds, now examined with the light of truth, had lost their power. Zach stared at the floor, his breath catching as if his body was trying to catch up with what his heart already knew.

He takes our bad situations and works them for the good of those who love Him, Uncle Bryan had said. Something inside him unlatched, as if an invisible chain had finally broken loose. His heart whispered a thanks to God for leading him to the truth.

Later, after burgers and another two games of pool, Zach parted with Ollie, who had some bookkeeping to do in the store. He made his way to the silent apartment and sat on the edge of the couch.

"I forgive you," he said to the empty room. He would say it to Ava later too, when he could get his thoughts together, but it felt right to do it out loud now. A wave of peace rolled over him. He had far to go, but Uncle Bryan was right.

Forgiveness could be simple, and so could love.

THIS MUST BE A DREAM.

Ava blinked at her email. She'd ignored her computer the past few days and had planned to continue doing so, but her editor had texted her to answer an urgent message. Her final article on Jonathon Island needed some edits. The series of articles had run for the past few days, but Ava tried to forget all about them.

She groaned. The last thing she wanted was to think about her time on Jonathon Island or anyone from there. She'd already sworn off doing anything in the Chicago Loop where Escargot was located. At least until she found a way to talk to Zach and explain how she felt. The text messages she'd sent him had gone unanswered. Maybe he would never let her explain.

Below the notes from her editor, a message from Mia popped up. Subject line: Who's your favorite Realtor?

She hesitated with her finger over the read button. Did she really want to know about property for sale on Jonathon Island? Was she brave enough to get her hopes up again? She fingered the edge of the couch cushion under her. Her fingertip found a frayed piece, and she worried at it. The beige cushion matched the beige carpet.

A longing for more, for an adventure, for a home she could love swept over her. She needed to move out of this apartment.

Her grandma's words echoed in her mind. *You can go anywhere. I'll be moving to Arizona at the end of the month.* Between her grandma moving and Emily leaving for Los Angeles, there was nothing keeping her here in Chicago. She pictured Zach, his chef's whites rolled to his elbows, showing her how to chop an onion in the kitchen at Escargot. She pushed the thought away. She didn't know where they even stood, or what their relationship would look like after she talked to him.

She tapped the mouse to open Mia's email.

Ava,

A bungalow here on island came up for sale. The owners heard about your letter (I know, small town), and they wanted to offer it to you first. They liked what you had to say about looking for a place with roots to call home.

It doesn't have everything on your wish list, but you can always put up a white picket fence if you still want one.

I've attached pictures. Let me know what you think.

Mia

She clicked on the first thumbnail. A small home with a sloping roofline appeared on-screen. The front of the house boasted a wide porch. The porch was empty but looked perfect for a few rocking chairs, maybe even a porch swing. The next photo showed an open floor plan living and dining room. In the living room were several built-in bookshelves. A few more photos featured the two bedrooms and kitchen area. There was a small patio out back just waiting for a charcoal grill and some lawn furniture.

She loved it.

Not bothering to reply to the email, she called Mia right away. "Sold!"

Mia laughed. "I guess you got my email."

Ava stood and paced. "I did get it. I can't believe there's something available so soon, and in my price range."

"God always takes care of us," Mia said. "I'm learning to trust Him with all my life."

"Same."

"So, what do you think? Do you want to put in an offer?"

Ava looked out her window. The brick wall of the building next to her looked back. "I absolutely do."

"Okay. I'll get the paperwork in motion." Ava could hear papers shuffling on the other end of the line. "What does your editor think about you moving away?"

A pang of fear gripped her. What if she'd come this far only to have it fall through again?

Being on the phone with Mia reminded her of the verse Mia had quoted, the one about delighting in God and Him giving you the desire of your heart. She was working on the delighting part.

She sighed. She'd just have to leave the desires of her heart in God's hands. "I haven't talked to him about it since getting back. He agreed we'd discuss it sometime, but I haven't had the heart to do it since the other house fell through."

"Not to mention everything that happened with Zach," Mia said.

Ava's gut clenched. "Um."

"Sorry. I shouldn't have said that. Small town. We hear all the good news and the bad. I just feel like we could be friends, and I jumped way over the line." Mia's voice brightened. "At least this house is good news. I'll keep you posted on the paperwork."

"I think we could be friends too. If this offer goes through,

you will have earned yourself a commission and a new friend."
Hopefully she heard the tease.

Mia laughed. "It's a deal. I'll try not to stick my foot in my mouth too often."

"As a food critic, I can tell you there are better things to eat out there." Ava's heart lightened with the exchange.

They hung up, and Ava flopped onto the couch. What would she do if Judson wouldn't let her work remotely?

She sat up with a sharp intake of breath, her spine straightening, and squared her shoulders. What if she just left her job altogether? She wouldn't have to rely on Judson's goodwill. Maybe Doug's Market was hiring.

Although, stocking shelves probably wouldn't pay the mortgage. She slumped back against the couch.

Her phone chimed.

Emily
You're famous!

She rolled her eyes. Emily had a flair for the dramatic.

Ava
Famously inept

Emily
Have you checked Twitter?

Ava
I have avoided all social media.
Don't tell me there's a viral video
of me yelling at Zach.

That would be just great. Internet infamy. How embarrassing to have the entire world know that a boy doesn't want you.

Emily
I wish there was—I'd have paid
good money to see that.☺ But
this is something else.

Ava navigated to her social media. She scrolled through a few inane takes before seeing what Emily was talking about.

Several people had quoted-tweeted her articles. One had the subject line:

@jenniBtraveling: Can't wait to revisit this quaint town. Thanks @AvaHarperChowsDown for reminding me of all the fun my family had on Jonathon Island.

The Michigan Tourism Bureau tweeted:

@MITourismBoard: Thanks for the shoutout to a great destination @AvaHarperChowsDown.

The notification number along the side of her profile kept ticking upward.

Ava's fingers felt numb as she typed.

Ava
I can't believe it.

Emily
I'm going to start introducing
myself as Ava Harper's friend.
Might get me some street cred.

Ava
Ha ha.

You do just fine on your own.

Emily
I'm so happy for you, friend. Enjoy
your time in the spotlight.

She knew just how she was going to leverage this. And maybe she could make amends at the same time. She swung a jacket over her shoulders and pointed herself toward the *Chicago Herald*. Better to face the bear than to hide behind a phone line.

A few minutes later she tapped Judson's office door.

Judson looked up, and his face cracked into a smile. His Albert

Einstein hair stood four inches high. "Ava, my new favorite food writer. Everyone is loving your pieces on the food festival. The first ones weren't great. I knew you could rework them into something amazing." He waved her in. "AP called, wondering if they could poach you, but I said you were happy here. Sit."

Stacks of papers teetered precariously on the two chairs in front of Judson's desk. One stack had a banana peel on top. Standing was a good option.

"I wanted to talk to you about those pieces." She laced her hands in front of her. Suddenly her rehearsed words felt hollow. Some of the determination she'd had at home leaked out of her and seeped away.

"I'm way ahead of you." Judson tapped at his computer, and then his printer started spitting out pages. "I'd love to see more proposals on stuff like this." He handed the papers over. Ava flipped through them and found they were all ads for food festivals. The final page was an itinerary. "The higher-ups want you to write about more small-town festivals. They feel you've got the right voice for it." He waved at the papers she held. "They're willing to approve you working remote since they'll have you traveling so much. What do you think about hitting the Desserts in the Desert cooking competition in Albuquerque, New Mexico? You'd have to leave in two weeks."

Her head spun. So much information so fast. Her chest expanded with a feeling of pride so intense it felt like her heart might burst. "Thank you, sir."

"That's all I have for now." Judson bent to his desk again. She was dismissed.

Except she hadn't gotten everything she'd come here for.

She cleared her throat. Judson looked up, a surprised expression on his face. "What?"

"This is great. I appreciate the opportunity. I had an idea for what I could work on before I leave for Albuquerque." Judson glowered at her, so she rushed on. "I'd love a chance to do a feature on Zach Sullivan." Perhaps she could redeem some of the damage she'd done all those years ago.

"That chef you worked with on Jonathon Island?"

"That's the one." If he wouldn't answer her text messages, maybe he would at least read an article written by her.

"Fine. Have a preliminary to me in the morning. You can finish it up and have the copy by next week." He made a shooing motion. "Shut the door on your way out."

"Thank you, sir."

He responded with a grunt.

Ava shut the door, then pumped her fist.

A remote job, a sweet little house, and a chance to show Zach how she felt? The desires of her heart indeed.

Time to make some dreams come true.

Zach cracked the knuckles on his left hand. Ava would be arriving soon. Mia had told Dani that Ava was coming to look at this house, and Dani, with a gleam in her eye, had mentioned it to him.

Over the past few days, he'd examined all the hurts he'd been harboring. Letting them go one by one had left him feeling light and free. Sure, he had a way to go, but he was trusting God to help him through. He'd typed and deleted a baker's dozen text replies to Ava, but couldn't bring himself to send any of them. Looking her in the eye as they talked things through would be so much better.

He looked around the room. Mia had promised to bring Ava to the bungalow and then make an excuse to leave. Everything was set up. The empty front room waited for her.

He heard chatter outside and then the front door opened.

"I'll let you take a look around," Mia said. "I'll be just outside."

Ava stopped in the doorway. "Zach?" She took a half step

forward. Stopped again. She opened her mouth, then shut it again and shook her head. "What are you doing here?"

"I asked Mia if I could show you around," Zach said. "I hope you don't mind."

"No. I mean, what are you doing on island? Shouldn't you be back in Chicago?"

Zach ached to pull her into his arms. But he didn't have that right. Not until he explained. Maybe not even then. "I did go back for a while, but Chef Louie let me go. They're looking for a chef to run the kitchen at the Grand, and I came to interview. I'm thinking about moving back here."

Ava's eyes widened but remained unreadable. "Zach, that's amazing. It's like your dream come true."

"It really is." Zach took a deep breath. "I'm still thinking about it. Praying about it, really. I'm trying to make decisions with God's help these days."

"I get that."

He shoved his hands in his pockets. "I couldn't believe it when I found out you were moving here. All this time, I assumed you were finding a new place in Chicago."

Ava laughed. "I guess I never told you I was looking here. It makes sense you assumed Chicago."

"Is it okay that I'm here?" He held his breath.

"Yes. I've wanted to talk to you, but things got crazy after my articles were published." Ava came into the room.

"I'll just tell Mia that I can lock up." He leaned out the door. Mia stood at the bottom of the porch steps. He gave her a salute.

"I'll take off," she said. "Good luck."

Ava cooed over several details of the house. "Everything looks even better in person than it did in the emails Mia sent me."

"Here's the best part." He led her into the airy kitchen at the back of the house. A long counter ran along the back wall with a large window over the sink facing out to the backyard. The wood flooring warmed the room. White cabinets and gray slate counter-tops lent an air of modern charm to the space. The homeowners had installed an oversized range featuring six burners and a double oven, one of which was a convection oven. "There's a big pantry behind the door over there."

"It smells good in here."

The twin scents of garlic and oregano filled the air. A timer beeped on the stove. He went to it and pulled out a pan of lasagna. He placed it on the stovetop to rest. "I'll just put the garlic bread in. We can eat in a few minutes." He slid the loaf of bread wrapped in tinfoil into the oven. "I thought maybe you'd be hungry after your trip over here."

She put one hand on her hip. "Did you just bake something in someone else's oven?"

"Small town, remember? I grew up with the kid who used to live here. His mom came to my cooking class last week, so I called in a favor." He lifted a shoulder. "I'm learning to embrace that small-town life."

He opened the pantry and took out a basket he'd tucked in there on his arrival. "Plates and silverware."

"Zach. What is going on?" A small crease showed between her eyebrows. "What is all this?"

"I know we got started on the wrong foot. Maybe several wrong feet. Our whole relationship was lumpy." He swallowed against a sudden dryness in his throat. What if she didn't want to forgive him? "I'm so sorry for the way I've acted." He met her gaze. "I should never have accused you. I've been learning a lot about my-self these past few weeks. Like how I blame other people for my problems instead of acknowledging my own faults."

"I've been learning a lot too. I let you down at the competi-tion, something that was important to you. I put my own goals first." She walked over to him. "I'm sorry for reacting instead of listening." She took a deep breath and then released it slowly. "I forgive you. We both messed up, but I wanted to find you and try to start again." Ava put a hand on his chest. She turned her face up to him, a vulnerability shining from her eyes. "To see if there really is a chance for us."

"Can we start over?" He put a hand over hers. "I think we have the right ingredients to make this thing between us work. Maybe we can bake something more."

"A recipe for forever?" She smiled, her face lighting with pleasure. "I'd like that. Even if those were some of the cheesiest lines I've ever heard."

He extended his arms toward her, and she, without hesitation, moved closer into his embrace. Holding Ava felt natural, a comforting warmth spreading through him, a sense of belonging he'd never known before.

"Good thing I like cheese," she murmured into his chest.

He laughed as she nestled closer to him.

She tipped her head up to look at him. His heart rate ramped up several notches.

Rising up on her toes, she pressed her lips to his.

Kissing Ava felt like coming home. It didn't matter where he lived or what he did, he wanted this woman in his life for all of it.

His eyes slid closed.

"Zach." Her lips moved against his.

"Hmm." He slid his hand up to her neck, not willing to break contact.

"I think you're burning my house down."

He pulled abruptly away, heart crashing to his knees. Smoke billowed from the oven.

Ava ran to open a window, and he waved a towel at the oven. He pulled out the smoldering loaf of garlic bread, dashed to the back door, and threw the whole thing on the patio.

The fire alarm began blaring. Ava waved at it until it stopped, then they collapsed into laughter on the floor. Ava tucked her head onto his chest.

"I'm afraid you're going to be bad for my reputation as a chef," he said into her hair. "I seem to burn everything when you're around."

"We still have the lasagna."

"I hope you like floor picnics." Zach stood. "My influence didn't extend to them leaving a kitchen table behind."

"I'll eat lasagna anywhere." Ava stood and took a forkful of lasagna straight from the pan. "This is amazing." She nudged his shoulder with hers. "Too bad there's no garlic bread."

"Watch it, woman." He dug in his pocket and brought out a wrinkled piece of paper. "I wrote something for you."

Ava straightened. "For me?"

"It's a review."

She reached for the paper, but he held it out of her reach.

"I'll read it to you." He cleared his throat. "'Ava Harper is new to the Jonathon Island scene. Some readers may remember her from the cooking fiasco she participated in with Island golden boy, Zachary Sullivan.'"

"I don't think I like where this is going," Ava said.

"Just give it a minute, it gets better." Zach pretended to look for his spot on the page. "Here. 'Turns out, losing that contest was in no way Ava's fault. In fact, none of the things Zach accused her of were true. This reporter spoke to Zach, and he says he regrets his actions from that day and others. In this reporter's opinion, Ava Harper would make an A-plus resident of Jonathon Island. She is smart, funny, kind, and beautiful. Five out of five stars. Completely recommend.'"

Ava laughed. "Thank you for the review. You'll have to expand on what you mean about it not being my fault, but first, I wanted to say that I want to have you in my life."

"I want you too." He pulled her closer.

In that moment, it became clear what he should do. He would

move back home to Jonathon Island. A place where all his dreams could come true.

Eighteen

WAS THERE EVER A TIME HE FELT MORE nervous? Zach looked around the hotel kitchen again. Everything was prepared and waiting. He pushed out to the dining room. Ava was lighting the candles on a long table they'd made out of several smaller tables in the middle of the room.

He'd decided to run the restaurant at the Grand two days after reuniting with Ava. It was a no-brainer, really. Where else could he be so loved and accepted? He could cook anywhere, but only here, on Jonathon Island, could he cook for the people he cared about most.

He'd spent the two weeks since then hiring staff, ordering food, and finalizing the menu for the restaurant.

The hotel dining room hadn't hosted any guests yet, and he felt it was appropriate to christen the space with a family dinner. Full service would start in a few days.

"All set?" he asked.

"All set," she responded. She put her hand to her stomach. "Why do I feel more nervous now than I did for the contest?"

"Relax." He laughed. "It'll be fine. It's not like you're eating with nearly my whole family tonight or anything."

She laughed too. Her laugh stirred something deep within him, a pleasant flutter in his stomach. "I guess I've already met most of them anyway. How are you feeling? It's been a whirlwind these past few weeks."

He came up behind her and put his arms around her waist, pulling her close. Her hair smelled of her shampoo and the rosemary they'd used in the malfatti recipe. "If it makes you feel any better, I'm nervous too."

"What do you have to be nervous about? You already know they love you."

"I doubted that for a long time. I guess it feels weird to find out how wrong I was. Wrong about a lot of things."

She put her hands over his. "And you are forgiven and loved." She turned in his arms and gave him a quick kiss on the cheek. "I'd better go check the garlic bread. We wouldn't want to serve charred loaves."

A few minutes later, his family started filing in. Ollie, Eliza, Kate, and Lincoln arrived together. His dad and mom came in, holding hands. His mom wore a huge smile. Dani and Liam arrived at the same time as Uncle Bryan and Aunt Mary. James came in a moment later. A general hubbub settled over the place as everyone found their places at the table.

His dad stood. He rapped on his glass, the chime silencing the happy chatter around the table. "I'd like to propose a toast. To Zach, who always knows how to rise to the occasion."

Everyone around the table cheered.

Ava stood. "I'd like to make a confession." Zach watched her swallow hard. She'd told him she wanted to do this, even though he'd reassured her it wasn't necessary. "A long time ago, something

I wrote did a lot of damage to Zach's reputation. Most of you know the whole story. But tonight I want to tell you something that might damage my reputation." She gripped her cup, her knuckles white against the glass. The silence lay heavy around them. "I can't cook."

A chuckle from one of the guests, Zach couldn't make out who. Then Dani laughed, Liam going a second later. A wave of laughter rolled across the table. Ava's mouth turned up on one side. Her gaze sought his, and he stood up. He took her hand, and her warm fingers curled around his.

"I'm eating something you cooked right now," Ollie said.

"Yeah, it's amazing. I can barely boil water," Kate put in.

"But Zach made this meal," Ava pointed out.

He squeezed her hand. "We did it together."

Dani got out of her chair. "Ava, for a minute there, I thought you were going to admit to killing someone or something. It's not a crime to not be able to cook."

"It is if you're supposed to know about cooking for your job." Ava crossed her arms over her stomach.

"Nah." Dani tossed the comment aside. "That's no big deal. You obviously know what you're talking about. I've taken your advice many times. I love your column."

"Besides, why would you need to cook when you have Zach right there?" Liam said.

Ava laughed then. Her whole body relaxed. "I guess you're right. I feel better now that my secret has been spilled."

"Hear! Hear!" Uncle Bryan raised his glass. "I'll toast to that."

"Speaking of cooking," Mom said, "Ava was cooking with these words." She fished a newspaper clipping out of her purse. "May I?"

Zach pulled Ava down into her chair and gestured to his mother, curious what she was going to do. Across from them, Dani sat too.

His mother rose. She cleared her throat. "'Zachary Sullivan is not unknown to the cooking community. Some will remember how he wowed the judges at Jonathon Island's cooking competition with his peach tart. And many of my readers will have tasted a dish he prepared at Escargot, even if they didn't know it. Now, Jonathon Island's golden boy—'" The table erupted into hoots and cheers. His mom held up a hand. "Let me finish. ' . . . golden boy will be showing us his best work as he opens a restaurant in the historic Grand Sullivan Hotel. We know many will be eager to try his new creations. If Zach is cooking, you will find me at his table.' Yada yada." She twirled her hand. "I think you get the picture."

Zach stared at her. "What was that?"

"Don't you know?" His mom passed him the clipping. "It's Ava's article about you. There's a very flattering picture of you in your chef's getup. I guess it ran on the front page of the *Chicago Herald* last week."

He turned to look at Ava. She looked like the Cheshire cat. "You did this?" A sense of joy crept over him.

"Yes. I leveraged some of my newfound power with the paper. I hope it was okay." She ducked her head.

He tucked a finger under her chin and lifted her face. "Better than okay. It means the world to me. You mean the world to me. I'm so glad we found each other again." Then he bent and kissed her, tuning out the whistles and laughter of his family.

Take one witty food writer and add one repentant chef, fold in an island full of memories. Mix well and add a dash of love. That was a recipe for forever.

Bonus Epilogue

Thank you for reading *Find Me at the Table*. We hope you loved this story. Find out what happens next for Ava and Zach with a Bonus Epilogue, a special gift, available only to our newsletter subscribers.

This Bonus Epilogue will not be released on any retailer platform, so scan the QR code to get your free gift. You acknowledge you are becoming a Sunrise Publishing and Andrea Christenson subscriber. Unsubscribe from any newsletter at any time.

Thank You

Thank you so much for reading *Find Me at the Table*. We hope you enjoyed the story. If you did, would you be willing to do us a favor and leave a review? It doesn't have to be long—just a few words to help other readers know what they're getting. (But no spoilers! We don't want to wreck the fun!) Thank you again for reading!

We'd love to hear from you—not only about this story, but about any characters or stories you'd like to read in the future.

Contact us at www.sunrisepublishing.com/contact.

Return to Jonathon Island in book 4,
Find Me in the Lyrics
by Christina Miller.

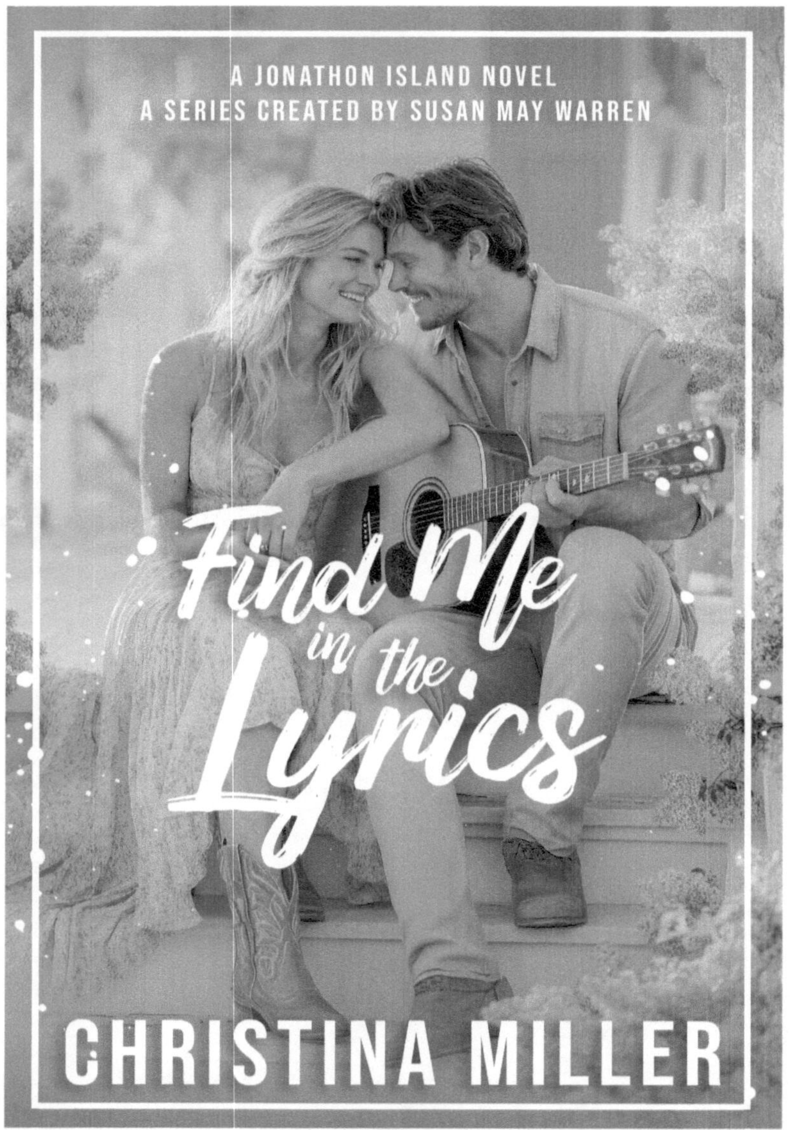

Some songs are meant to be written together.

Ariel Sullivan has performed on the biggest stages in country music—but always as half of "Miss Dahlia and Ariel." When her secret solo album is rejected, she escapes to her hometown island, desperate to find a voice that's finally her own.

Caleb Kennedy was supposed to be touring with his Christian rock band. Instead, he's running his family's crumbling hotel, dodging his grumpy grandfather, and avoiding the locked parlor wing full of memories he can't face. The last thing he needs is a distraction.

But when Ariel offers to help save his inn in exchange for his help reinventing her band, an unexpected harmony forms. Late nights at the piano. Duets that feel like conversations. And a connection neither of them planned.

She came searching for lyrics.

She found home instead.

Because the best songs? They're written by two hearts in perfect harmony.

One

THE TIME HAD COME TO FACE THE FACTS. Caleb was in over his head.

He stood at the top of the old circular staircase of Island House Inn and scanned the early evening crowd below. For the first time in years, the spacious, slightly shabby lobby of Granddad's vintage hotel—make that Caleb's now—felt alive. Felt viable. Felt profitable, with forty or fifty people milling around with various degrees of patience while waiting for their accommodations.

Which would have been great if most of the guests hadn't come here against their will. More accurately, against their preference.

It should have been his moment to shine.

As it was, he sped down the stairs toward the timeworn mahogany reception desk, having delivered a cartload of clean towels and washcloths to each vacant second-floor room.

"We've filled all the first-floor rooms and half of the second, and the lobby's still packed with guests waiting to check in. Plus you have two more carriages coming up the street." Pushing a loaded luggage cart, Caleb's great-uncle Augo Kennedy, in his late sixties with short white hair and an impressive mustache, approached him on the way to the elevator. His little dachshund, Lucy, followed at his heels.

With those powerful forearms and biceps bulging under his green Island House Inn Henley, Uncle Augo could easily have carried the suitcases and tote bags to the third floor if he wanted.

"Where am I supposed to put all these people?"

"You're the boss now." His uncle's basso voice reverberated in the high-ceilinged room. "Better figure it out before the rest of the Grand crowd arrives."

It would've helped if the nearby Grand Sullivan Hotel of Jonathon Island, Michigan, had given them more than thirty minutes' notice to come up with a plan. And if Caleb had more than six employees, not counting the restaurant staff.

However, nobody could have predicted the water break that flooded the sole renovated, occupied section of the Grand—the only other hotel open after the fire that had all but shut down the island eleven years ago.

The lobby's front door creaked open. A gray-haired couple stepped inside, their wooden canes tapping the pine floor, and took in the lackluster lobby. Frowning, the woman shook her head and whispered in the man's ear. He nodded, and they turned and walked out. "In my third week as full-time hotel manager."

"Hospitality industry's fickle," Uncle Augo said over his shoulder as he punched the elevator call button.

Well, his uncle should know.

Any other innkeeper would consider today a win, with more guests pouring into his northern Michigan harbor-view hotel than they had in years. However, those innkeepers would have had training. Filling in for his grandfather for a while last year, back when Granddad had his first stroke, didn't count.

"We can't use the third floor. We haven't aired it out since last fall, let alone spring cleaning." And they couldn't even consider the old parlor wing, the one Granddad had locked twelve years ago and vowed never to reopen.

Caleb raised his voice over the din of a few dozen couples waiting for rooms, soft jazz playing over the sound system, and children running on the wood floors. "There's nowhere else for them to stay, so we have to figure out something. Got any suggestions?"

"Not unless you can fix the Grand's broken water pipes and dry up their guest rooms real quick."

The flooding of the Grand Hotel and the horde of unhappy guests detouring here this evening had confirmed his suspicions. Truth was, Caleb Kennedy had run from Island House Inn—his run-down, six-generation, seventy-eight-room legacy—too long to bring it back from the brink of failure.

At the moment, the hotel didn't look remotely like a legacy. It felt familiar, comfortable, a little worse for wear, and homey—the faded glory of his childhood. But its legacy aspect, its lasting significance for future generations? That part didn't resonate. At all.

And since his boss had given him six weeks to decide whether to come back to work at the job he loved or save this tired, worn-out inn, Caleb seriously needed to turn the fuzziness into clarity. Fast.

For now, duty bound him to Island House Inn—his childhood home, the family relic. And the setting of his deepest grief.

He cast a quick glance out the wide front windows down to the harbor, its waters a deep Caribbean blue in the Jonathon Island summer. He still thought the pink flowers lining the half-circle drive and crowding the front lawn, along with the deep, still waters of the northern Michigan straits and the Port Joseph shoreline in the distance, held the best view on the island.

A view he'd wished never to see again.

A view he wished he didn't have to see now.

"Look over there." Uncle Augo tilted his head, gesturing toward a family of five at the reception desk. "Keep your eye on the guy in the orange shirt."

Caleb shifted toward a thirtyish man leaning against the reservations desk and wearing knee-length denim shorts and flip-flops, his "Great Minds Drink Alike" T-shirt stretched tight across his ample abdomen.

Other than the bad T-shirt slogan, he looked like an ordinary dad. However, knowing Uncle Augo's sense of discernment and his lifestyle prior to his ministry calling, Caleb watched the guy anyway.

The woman with him had a grip on two small, squirming redheaded boys and yelled to another child who ran across the room. Her high-pitched voice bounced off the high ceiling and echoed through the lobby, making Caleb wince.

"If my payment to the Grand was refundable or anyplace else was open," the man bellowed at plump, fortyish reservations manager Sarah Beasley, "we wouldn't stay in this dump." He moved too close to her for Caleb's comfort.

Yep, his uncle had been right as usual. "I need to get in the middle of that. As much as Sarah has done to help Granddad hold this inn together the past fifteen years, I'm not letting him intimidate her."

He left Uncle Augo as the elevator opened, then he quick-walked to the reception desk and eyed the guy. "Sarah, need some help?"

"You could get some cookies for these little cuties." Her uplifting voice and unwavering gaze on him silently spoke of her expertise in dealing with problem guests.

Glancing at the orange-shirt man every few moments anyway, Caleb reached over to the bakery box at the other end of the desk, snatched five chocolate chip cookies, and handed them to him. When the family headed toward the elevator, he leaned toward Sarah and whispered, "I'll bet those kids won't taste a single cookie."

"Then we'll give them more later." She pushed back a strand of her straight blonde hair. "Glad he stopped yelling once you came over."

"He said only what everybody else thought. Each time the lobby door opens, I brace myself for disappointment in the guests' eyes."

The look he'd seen too often today, whenever a would-be Grand Hotel occupant crossed his wide, time-mellowed threshold.

"Not your fault." Sarah spoke in low tones. "Nobody could turn this place around in the two weeks you've been here."

Maybe, but at least none of the guests had recognized him. He ran his fingers through his fresh, short haircut as he scanned the lobby. He'd intended his new, clean-cut image to make him look more respectable. So far, no one had asked why the lead guitar in one of the country's biggest Christian bands spent the summer—or longer—in a stuck-in-the-past hotel. He could always grow back his long hair and beard if he failed at this career and went back to his old one.

Make that *when* he failed.

Caleb grabbed the last four still-warm, napkin-wrapped chocolate chip cookies and a box of fudge, the remnants of his earlier panicked requests to the Fudge Shop on the Corner and Hudson Bakery. He handed the goodies to another mother of two boys as her husband checked in, although his sweets offerings wouldn't make up for the serious downgrade in accommodations.

"A carriage just pulled in with two more families."

He recognized the strong Bostonian accent and light flower perfume before he saw Tara Chamberlain, the fiftysomething, silver-blonde-haired town council member and pastor's wife. And the woman who always seemed to show up when any business in town desperately needed help. Not to mention saving his sanity at the moment.

Tara had apparently slipped in the side door. Wearing a straight, knee-length blue dress and carrying another bakery box, she strode to the reception desk as if on a mission, her low-heeled sandals clicking on the floor. When she opened the box, the aroma of fresh-baked cookies wafted out and somehow made this whole disaster a little more bearable.

"The town is buzzing with bigger news than the flooded Grand," she said. "Annabelle texted me and said Miss Dahlia Denton and Ariel Sullivan's private jet just landed at the airport."

Trust his spinster great-aunt Annabelle Kennedy to know everything that happened on this island. And in this hotel, since she'd lived here all her life except her college years. "Maybe we'll get lucky and they'll fly back to the mainland for a room." Because the one thing Caleb did not want to do tonight was apologize to Nashville's most popular country music stars for his chintzy rooms.

The preacher's wife gave him that big, unconditional-acceptance grin of hers. The one that always reminded him of his mother. Sometimes it made the old guilt rise up in him so strong he could barely breathe.

"No, they'll stay on island as they promised. Miss Dahlia would turn in her wigs and sequins before she'd go back on her word."

True. "We still have a chance. The Grand's assistant manager said he didn't know yet whether the presidential suite had flooded."

Tara glanced at the family of four still waiting near the desk, the boys flopping around on one of the worn sofas, whacking each other with throw pillows. "I'll show them to their room so you can check in the next family."

Caleb reached behind the desk and grabbed two oversized brass keys from the row of hooks. He handed the keys to Tara. "Appreciate the help. Room 203."

The room with the worst view and the ugliest 1980s décor.

She grimaced a little then recovered. "Sure about that?"

"It's my last clean room."

"Then it'll do. By the way, good idea to bless the guests with the cookies and fudge." Tara gave him that too-cheerful smile that always meant she was trying to walk by faith, not by sight. "But you need to decide where to put Miss Dahlia and Ariel."

Tara was right, even if he didn't want to admit it. "Miss Dahlia always demands the Grand's presidential suite."

She grinned. "Better get yours ready. After I get this family upstairs, I'll come back and check in the rest of the mob, and Sarah can go with you to the third floor to get those rooms ready."

"Can you handle our outdated reservations system?"

She waved her pink-fingernailed hand. "It was outdated when I worked here twenty years ago, so yes. I'll put the next family in 301 and go from there."

"Stall them as long as you can." Caleb took off for his office, where he grabbed the heavy ring of extra keys for the third floor and texted Michelle Riley in the laundry room, asking her to bring up fresh linens for the entire floor and start making beds. Running up the employee staircase, he tried to formulate a plan.

When he reached the top of the stairs, the speakers piped out the vintage jazz he'd selected earlier in an attempt to set a calm atmosphere in the chaotic lobby. But while he'd accomplished that objective downstairs, the tunes felt too laid-back for the pace he set for himself now, and he half wished he'd changed it to something peppy. Old ragtime, maybe.

Starting with room 301, Caleb propped open doors and raised the windows. The sweet scent of lilacs wafted in with the breeze and soon filtered into the hallway like a natural air freshener. Then he grabbed a fully stocked cleaning cart and a commercial vacuum from the storage room.

When fast footsteps fell on the stairs, he called out, "Want the cart or the sweeper?"

"Cart," Sarah puffed out, stopping to draw a few deep breaths, a sheen on her face.

Caleb pushed the cart into 301 for her, plugged the extension cord into the wall, and turned on the vacuum.

Before he'd finished sweeping eight months' worth of dust from the wide hallway's dark-green carpet, Michelle's linen cart came flying around the nearest corner, swaying as if it could topple over at any moment. "Mr. Caleb! Where you at?" she yelled in her heavy Deep South accent from behind the giant cart.

He flipped off the switch and waited for the next disaster.

"Josh called from the Grand." Michelle's long, dark ponytail swayed as she steered that flying linen cart toward him like a NASCAR driver. Young, slender, and toned, she managed to skid to a stop, dangerously close to Caleb's vacuum, her tennis-shoe heels digging into the carpet.

"That gossipy old Miss Annabelle was right. The presidential suite flooded too." Michelle's eyes grew wide, and she clapped her hand over her mouth. "I'm sorry, Mr. Caleb. I shouldn't have said that about your aunt."

He somehow held in the groan that wanted to escape. "You said only what everyone in town knows."

"Josh called and left a message at the airport, asking them to tell Miss Dahlia Denton and Ariel Sullivan to come here instead." Michelle grabbed a giant stack of sheets and ran toward 301's door. "I gotta make all these beds. That'll take eighteen minutes. Then I'll go back downstairs to the suite and get it ready. Send Sarah to help me as soon as she's done here."

Caleb nodded, then flipped the vacuum switch and again attacked the carpet. Accommodating all these people would have presented enough of a challenge, even if he didn't face humiliation in front of two country music greats. One of whom was Ariel Sullivan—the near stranger he'd never managed to get out of his mind.

He'd been in over his head before he knew Ariel would soon walk into his inn. Now he was full-out drowning.

Where could a girl go to return a legacy that didn't fit?

Ariel was no closer to an answer than she'd been a few months ago, when she and Great-aunt Dahlia had walked away from the Country Music Awards with six Italian crystal trophies. Or today, during a two-hour pep talk from her aunt as they flew from Nashville to Jonathon Island.

Or maybe the legacy did fit but Ariel didn't yet know how to wear it.

"A legacy is a gift—and I'm giving it to you." Her little blonde aunt had sat in her leather recliner with her high-heeled feet up, her East Tennessee accent as twangy as ever, when her jet lifted off from Nashville International Airport. Ariel had heard it all before. But since their record-setting CMA haul, Aunt Dahlia seemed more determined than ever to make Ariel Sullivan one of country music's all-time greats.

Smart, business-savvy, and the most brilliant soprano on the music scene, Aunt Dahlia knew Nashville and she knew music. But since her sixtieth birthday on New Year's Day of this year, her aunt seemed to care more about setting up Ariel as her musical heir than she did about the music itself.

Aunt Dahlia never did acknowledge that eternal blind spot of hers where Ariel was concerned.

"We'll have a great month," Aunt Dahlia said, her blue eyes wide and her smile big. "We'll relax at the Grand, get inspiration, and choose some new songs. By the time we play at the Jonathon Island Beachside Music Festival in four weeks, we'll have a whole new, reimagined band."

Which seemed like an impossibly short window of time.

"Hitting a big low isn't the only time to make changes." Aunt Dahlia lifted the lid from a little wooden bowl of pumpkin seeds and took a bite from a sterling silver spoon. "Whenever a band has a huge success, like breaking the record for CMA awards, they should mix things up a little. Or, in this case, mix them up a lot."

"The audience needs to hear us improving and growing with each song." Ariel parroted her aunt's famous line, even though it brought a wave of panic to her middle every time Aunt Dahlia spoke about this new change in the band. In their lives.

Ariel gazed out the window, watching for the familiar sight of giant Saginaw Bay from her champagne-colored cashmere sofa. Having a superstar aunt might mean the niece could someday succeed on her own. But in Ariel's case, probably not.

The thought scared her more than her first appearance at the Grand Ole Opry.

She reached into her hot-pink tote and picked up her hardback idea book with a picture of a rocky beach on the cover and turned to her current page. She uncapped her vintage fountain pen and wrote in lavender ink.

> By the end of our month on Jonathon Island, I intend to find out whether or not I can make it on my own in the music world.

She slid the idea book and pen back into her tote bag—the one that said *I don't always sing. Oh, wait . . . yes I do.* Jonathon Island would provide the perfect atmosphere for Ariel to form a plan for her own new music, her own new style.

Of all the luxury hotels and resorts Ariel and Aunt Dahlia had enjoyed through the years, none inspired her like the Grand Sullivan. Although she hadn't stayed there since the Grand's fire years ago, she remembered the presidential suite with its pictures of past and current presidents and first ladies, her big pink bedroom, and the wide balcony overlooking Lake Huron. Mostly, she recalled the room's effect on her. Creativity flowed there like the clear-water spring running through her father's Jonathan Island pumpkin farm.

If any location could inspire a new vision for the future and give her direction and a path, the Grand Hotel was that place.

"They loved you at the Country Music Awards," Aunt Dahlia said.

Honestly, did she always know exactly what Ariel was thinking?

"I heard Molly criticizing you that night. You still stew about it." Her aunt swiveled her recliner and leaned forward, took Ariel's hand. "I know from experience that a bad word from a peer feels worse than a bad review from a stranger. But Molly did not take home an award. You're still the best alto in the biz."

"Seems like every time I get on a stage, she's there to throw me off." Molly Banks. One of Ariel and Aunt Dahlia's competitors for the coveted Single of the Year award. Ariel had let the insult slide at the time. But the woman's voice, smooth as milk gravy on a biscuit, came back and haunted her at all the worst times, just as it had the first time she'd said it, back when they were both child stars. *You're good, but you'd never win anything if Dahlia Denton didn't prop you up.*

Three years ago, when Molly had slammed her in public, another musician defended Ariel and had impacted her so much, she'd all but forgotten the insult. Until her latest failure, which she'd kept from even dear Aunt Dahlia. Ariel had selected new music, recorded a solo album, and sworn their manager to secrecy as he sent it to their record label's producer last month.

He'd rejected it quicker than an eighth note.

It's good, but it doesn't offer anything you and Miss Dahlia don't already give me.

The producer's words never drifted far from her thoughts.

"Molly has a great voice, but she doesn't have your heart." Aunt Dahlia's tone turned silky with affection. "You touch people with your music. Molly just sings and prances around on the stage, treating the audience like a commodity to hoard and manipulate. Just keep lovin' your fans, and don't pay any attention to her."

Having worked in the fickle music industry since childhood, Aunt Dahlia should know. However, the producer's rejection had told Ariel otherwise.

By the time the jet landed at tiny Jonathon Island Airport an hour before sundown, Ariel's thoughts turned to her childhood home. A month ago, when she'd landed here, she had only one day to spend on island—the day of her cousin Dani Sullivan Stone's wedding—since their spring touring season had begun. Her time with her family hadn't amounted to much more than sitting together at the wedding supper. She hadn't even seen their old white farmhouse.

But soon she'd find her parents, her brother, and her nephew waiting for her at the other side of the terminal.

In Nashville, June had arrived with the heat of midsummer. But here in northern Michigan, the waning sun and cool breeze as she disembarked felt like a welcome change. She slipped her arms into the denim jacket she'd shed in the plane.

"I can't wait to see all the town's businesses reopened. Last year, some of them looked as if they'd lost hope and knew they were dying but couldn't quite give in." Ariel finally set foot on island soil—or rather, its runway pavement—with her Martin N-20 guitar, her pink crossbody bag and tote, and a giant Barry the Bear gift bag containing three stuffed bears for her nephew, Sam. "Whenever Mama talked about all the loss the island suffered the past eleven years, I almost wished I wouldn't have to come back until someone—probably Dani—restored it to its former glory."

Aunt Dahlia reached the ground, carrying her handbag, guitar, and rolling briefcase, and gave Ariel that big, toothy smile that always made her believe everything would eventually work out. Well, almost always.

"But we get to help bring back the island's tourism through the music festival next month. Between the proceeds from our concert and my cash donation, they'll have no problem renovating a couple more abandoned shops on Main. We'll draw big crowds to the island. And we're spending a month in the Grand Hotel's most expensive suite." Aunt Dahlia's voice turned businesslike, her Southern-country accent deepening as they crossed the tarmac. "The songwriters start rollin' in tomorrow, the production team later, and the band bus left Nashville this morning. That's a total of twenty more people staying here, and we're all spending money on hotels, restaurants, souvenirs—and clothing stores."

"Plus the six big-name bands who agreed to perform after you contacted them. Aunt Dahlia, you've given so much to Jonathon Island through the years. You're the most generous person in show business."

"I know I am, darlin'." Her big soprano laugh rolled out from deep inside. "I have a street named after me in this little ole town to prove it."

They rounded the pretty little white terminal building with its copper-roofed breezeway and saw only a green dray wagon, pulled by a pair of brown Percherons, on the road ahead.

Aunt Dahlia squinted against the low-hanging sun, then took her Jep Horn sunglasses from her hot-pink Lady Dior handbag and slipped them on, looked around. "Where is everybody? I thought your family and Dani would meet us."

Ariel pulled out her phone to check messages. Sure enough, she'd missed a text from Dani twenty minutes ago. She skimmed it, then dropped her phone back into her handbag. "Ethan and Sam stayed home, but Mom, Dad, and Dani should get here anytime now."

Aunt Dahlia set her hands on her hips, looking cute in her silver-studded flare jeans and matching long-sleeved shirt, and glanced around the deserted grounds. She cocked her head toward a bench facing a wooded area bordered with lilacs in full bloom. "Well, I guess we're gonna wait."

As Ariel followed her aunt to the bench, the fresh, fragrant air brought back early memories of flower-picking excursions all over the island with four-years-older Dani. Town would smell even better, with hundreds of purple bushes blooming and perfuming the harborside streets.

The scent of lilacs still wafted through her dreams when least expected, a memorial to her earliest years, their fragrance strong and powerful to evoke a sense of home that had begun to drift away when she first moved to Nashville at age ten. The details of life on the little pumpkin farm of her childhood had also faded.

Her few trips back to the island since hadn't strengthened those memories. It seemed her time at home on the farm always flew by in a rush, and she hadn't come home during the years her parents lived with Ethan and Sam off island. If only she could reenact those quiet evenings at home around the big farm table with her parents, her brother, Ethan, and her sister, Charlotte.

Especially Sam, Ethan's eight-year-old son with Down syndrome.

Maybe this time, things would turn out different.

The big wagon drew nearer, the only vehicle on the narrow road, two dark Percherons pulling and a tawny-haired youth driving. The man sitting next to him held a corncob pipe between his teeth and wore a gray vintage workingman's costume that matched the boy's. Stroking his long, white beard, he kept his eye on both the driver and the road.

The boy stopped the wagon a few feet from Ariel and Aunt Dahlia, looking about thirteen and quite cheeky, and jumped down from his perch. With a broad grin and mischief in his eyes, he handed Ariel an old *Miss Dahlia for President, Ariel for VP* T-shirt and a Sharpie. "Me and my grandpa will take your stuff to the hotel. But would you autograph this before I give you the bad news? You too, Miss Dahlia. Because you won't stay after you hear."

"Bad news?" Ariel bent over and scrawled her name on the shirt the best she could while draping it over her knee.

When she'd finished, Aunt Dahlia reached for the shirt. "Now, what could be so bad that we'd up and go home no sooner than we got here? And what's your name, child?"

"Harry Campbell. That's my grandpa, Finley Campbell, in the wagon. But would you please give me my tip first too?"

Ariel slipped over to the wagon, drew a twenty from her bag, and dropped the bill into the can marked *Tips*.

Aunt Dahlia gave him a theatrical wink, then scribbled his name and hers on the shirt. "You're smart enough to make it in show biz, Harry. Now give me the news."

"The Grand Hotel sprang a leak. There's water everywhere, even in your suite. They're sending the guests to Island House Inn. But a lot of them went in, looked around, walked right back out, and called us for a ride to the ferry." He puffed out his chest. "I got a tip for bringing them in and another tip for taking them away."

"I remember Island House as homey and comfortable." Years ago, of course. Surely they'd refreshed it since then.

"The inn looks like it always does—not quite ready to fall down. And they didn't have enough rooms ready."

Aunt Dahlia sighed, casting a glance at Ariel, then back at Harry. "How do you know so much about the hotels?"

He gave her a squinty look. "Haven't you ever lived in a small town?"

"Well, yes, and I guess that explains it," her aunt said. "Since you know everything that goes on around here, Harry, tell us about the other hotels or bed-and-breakfasts."

"There's the Grand, and there's Island House Inn, and that's it. Or you could take the ferry to the mainland."

He sounded earnest enough, but should they take travel advice from a precocious boy? She glanced at the older man, who'd eased himself down from the wagon and now carried the rest of their luggage to the dray.

"My grandson's telling the truth," the man called in the same distinctive, somewhat Nordic island accent her dad had. "The Grand Hotel redirected all their guests to Island House Inn."

Then it hit her.

She'd soon land at Island House. Not the Grand—the atmosphere she'd counted on to stoke her creativity. Help her find her path.

Save her pride.

"Do you want to go to the ferry?" Harry asked.

"No, we want to help the local economy." Aunt Dahlia made up her mind in a flash as usual. "Besides, we gave our word that we'd stay on this island and help with publicity for the music festival."

This could be a bad idea, but . . . "We could go to my family's pumpkin farm."

"Honey, that little bit of a house could never hold us, your family, the writers, and the band."

Yes, compared to Aunt Dahlia and Ariel's Nashville-area home, the two-story farmhouse would seem small.

Suddenly, a long-ago memory crossed her mind—one of kindness, warmth, generosity she'd once experienced at the centuries-old inn. "Then let's go to Island House and rough it. We don't need a five-star hotel every time."

"Let's consult our junior travel agent." Aunt Dahlia gave her that look that said Ariel should go along with whatever she said. "Harry, would we like Island House?"

He nodded. "At first, I didn't think so. But now I know you will."

"Give us your number, Harry, and you can be our driver during our stay." Her aunt eyed the wagon. "If your fleet of horse-drawn vehicles includes carriages and not just wagons."

"Me and Grandpa work for the Quinn livery, and they have two dozen new white carriages. We can come back and pick you up in a carriage."

Ariel couldn't help grinning at the junior businessman. "Thanks, but our family is coming for us."

Harry rummaged under the driver's seat, produced a handmade business card on heavy paper, and passed it to Ariel, who checked it out, showed it to her aunt, then pocketed it. "Here's a card. I could have made them on my Chromebook, but Grandpa thinks people like this better."

"He's right." Aunt Dahlia turned to Ariel, brows raised. "It's settled then? We'll spend the month at Island House?"

Island House Inn. For a split second, Ariel could smell logs burning in the parlor fireplace and fresh pine wreaths and trees, hear Christmas carols piping from antiquated speakers. Feel warmth seeping through her soaked ski pants and heavy coat. Taste sweetened hot milk Mrs. Cara Kennedy had given her after the children's traditional tromp in the state forest during the season's first snow.

Ariel's family home had held similar scents and aromas, and they'd sung the same old carols there too. But that one evening at Island House, those little comforts had felt different. To this day, she believed Mrs. Kennedy—and her kind, older son, Caleb—understood her more than her family or her classmates had. Classmates who considered Ariel an oddity, since she'd spent two months traveling and singing at Aunt Dahlia's Christmas concert tour the previous year. And because she'd soon become a country music star herself.

Mrs. Kennedy might also have paid extra attention to Ariel because she knew the Sullivans had expected Aunt Dahlia to arrive later that night.

Arrive to take her away.

Away to Nashville. To stardom.

Leaving her family and their farm far behind.

She took in the quiet little airport, the tangle of trees beyond. Could an old historic inn on a tiny island hold more than just lodging? Give her back that sense of home she missed, fill the emptiness of life on the road six months every year?

Maybe even inspire her to prove herself in the crazy industry she hadn't chosen?

Ariel lifted her gaze to the bright blue, seemingly endless sky. "Yes. Harry, please take our things to Island House Inn."

Acknowledgments

Whenever I write acknowledgements, I always panic. Will I forget to give a shoutout to someone integral to the process of putting this book together? Will I write something witty enough that everyone is glad they read this part? Will I misspell gnudi (the inspiration for Ava's favorite dish, malfatti) and inadvertently shock my readers? Hopefully, I've been able to pull off a flawless acknowledgements page this time. Maybe they will even want to hang a copy of it in the Louvre because it is so beautiful.

More likely, I've forgotten someone. Consider yourself thanked, because I am truly grateful for each person reading this.

Firstly, I want to give a round of applause to the team at Sunrise Publishing. They are tireless and amazing. Thanks for all your work in polishing this manuscript. Love you guys.

Next, I have to give a shoutout to a bunch of ladies who helped me brainstorm some of the dishes in this book. Kim Beebe, Alicia Baird, Val Anderson, Allean Christenson: You are all fantastic.

Dave Campbell, your advice regarding newspapers helped shape many pieces of the book. I appreciated you taking the time for me.

Thank you to Brennans in New Orleans, whose eggplant gnudi changed my life forever.

A big hug and an overdue gourmet dinner to my family, who helped me come up with names and plot points and just generally put up with me during all of my writing shenanigans. Love you, Eric, Macy, and Anna.

Lastly, all my gratitude to the One who created good food, good friends, and a path for forgiveness.

Andrea Christenson lives just outside of Minneapolis, MN with her husband and two daughters. She is a lifelong lover of books, and at an early age, she realized reading great stories wasn't enough; Andrea wanted to create them. She began to write fairytales, and as she matured into her teenage years, her stories did too. No longer did her pages only include princes and princesses, but mirrored real-life situations featuring her friends and their love interests. Today, Andrea writes contemporary Christian romance that is meaningful, engaging, and wholesome. She writes clean, faith-filled, family-honoring stories that can be trusted to entertain the heart, engage the mind, and edify the soul. If you encounter Andrea in the wild she will most likely ask you if you want to grab a cup of coffee and talk about books, your favorite authors, family lore she can mine for a story, or whatever is on your heart. When she isn't writing you can find her reading anything that strikes her fancy, taking long walks in beautiful places with her family, checking out a new coffee shop, or bingeing a TV show five years after it's popular.

WELCOME BACK TO
Jonathon Island

where you'll find the magic of small town happily ever afters.

"Cozy, heartfelt, and irresistibly romantic—Jonathon Island is my new happy place."

—SUSAN MAY WARREN
USA Today bestselling author

We solve the problem of what to read next.

YOU MAY ALSO LIKE...

When Noah Hebert inherits the struggling Blue Pirogue Inn, he must solve a puzzle left by his grandfather to save it from his family's nemesis, Isaac Bergeron. Teaming up with Elisa Bergeron, the café manager and his rival, they must navigate family feuds—and unexpected sparks—while racing against time.

Where I Found You **by Besty St. Amant**

Grace Howell leaves her life as a ballerina and returns to Heritage, Michigan, to heal. Teaching dance is just a temporary gig, until she finds herself unexpectedly charmed by small-town life and her growing attachment to Seth Warner, a man from her past with a troubled history of his own.

You're the Reason **by Tari Faris**

Dani Sullivan is determined to revive Jonathon Island's fading charm and reunite her fractured family. Her plan? Reopen the Grand Sullivan Hotel. But without the funds to restore the hotel, Dani's forced to accept help from Liam Stone—a big-city hotel developer whose sleek, modern vision is everything she's trying to avoid.

Meet Me at the Grand **by Lindsay Harrel**

We solve the problem of what to read next.

WHERE EVERY STORY IS A FRIEND,
AND EVERY CHAPTER IS A NEW JOURNEY...

Subscribe to our newsletter for the latest news, weekly giveaways, exclusive author interviews, and more!

---

follow us on social media!

 @sunrisemediagroup

 @sunrisepublish

 @sunrisepublishing

Shop paperbacks, ebooks, audiobooks, and more at
SUNRISEPUBLISHING.MYSHOPIFY.COM